André Caroff's
MADAME ATOMOS

The Spheres of
Madame Atomos

also by André Caroff:
1. The Terror of Madame Atomos
(translated by Brian Stableford)
2. Miss Atomos
(translated by Michael Shreve)
3. The Return of Madame Atomos
(translated by Michael Shreve)
4. The Mistake of Madame Atomos
(translated by Michael Shreve)
5. The Monsters of Madame Atomos
(translated by Michael Shreve)
6. The Revenge of Madame Atomos
(translated by Michael Shreve)
7. The Resurrection of Madame Atomos
(translated by Michael Shreve)
8. The Mark of Madame Atomos
(translated by Michael Shreve)

also translated by Michael Shreve:
Charles de Fieux, Chevalier de Mouhy: *Lamekis*
André Laurie: *Spiridon*
John-Antoine Nau: *Enemy Force*
Pierre Pelot: *The Child Who Walked On The Sky*

André Caroff's
MADAME ATOMOS

The Spheres of
Madame Atomos

Translated by
Michael Shreve

A Black Coat Press Book

Acknowledgements: Thanks to Françoise Carpouzis & Catherine Losserand.

Madame Atomos Cherche la Petite Bête and *Les Sphères Attaquent* Copyright © 1970 and 1979 by The Estate of André Caroff; English adaptation Copyright © 2014 by Michael Shreve.
Introduction, Copyright © 2014 by Jean-Marc Lofficier.
Madame Atomos' Holidays Copyright © 2008 by Jean-Marc Lofficier and The Estate of André Caroff.
With the Compliments of Nestor Burma Copyright © 2011 by Michel Stéphan and The Estate of André Caroff; English adaptation Copyright © 2011 by Jean-Marc & Randy Lofficier.
A Day in the Life of Madame Atomos Copyright © 2009 by Xavier Mauméjean and The Estate of André Caroff; English adaptation Copyright © 2009 by Jean-Marc & Randy Lofficier.
Timeline Copyright © 2014 by Jean-Marc Lofficier.
Cover illustration Copyright © 2014 by Jean-Michel Ponzio.

Visit our website at www.blackcoatpress.com

Table of Contents

Introduction

This volume collects the seventeenth and eighteenth installments of the saga of Madame Atomos, a series of 18 novels published between 1964 and 1970 in the *Angoisse* horror imprint of French publisher Fleuve Noir. Our introduction to Volume 1 contains a biography of its author, André Carpouzis, a.k.a. André Caroff (1924-2009). More information about Fleuve Noir and its popular brands of science fiction and horror can be found in the introductions to the other volumes translated from their imprints and published by Black Coat Press: Richard Bessière's *The Gardens of the Apocalypse*, Gérard Klein's *The More in Time's Eye* and Kurt Steiner's *Ortog*.

The saga of Madame Atomos (her real name is Kanoto Yoshimuta) is about a brilliant but twisted middle-aged female Japanese scientist who is out for revenge against the United States for the bombings of Hiroshima and Nagasaki—where she was born, and where her family died in the nuclear holocaust.

Madame Atomos seeks to repay the United States by unleashing deadly new threats, such as radioactive zombies, giant spiders, a madness-inducing ray, flaming tornadoes, etc. The heroes opposing her are Smith Beffort of the FBI and Yosho Akamatsu of the Japanese Secret Police.

Volume 2 introduced the character of Mie Azusa, a.k.a. Miss Atomos, a younger version of Madame

Atomos, groomed to continue the fight in the event of her death.

In Volume 3, after Mie fell in love with Smith Beffort, she joined the fight against the deadly Madame Atomos who, in the meantime, had returned from the dead. In Volume 4, Madame Atomos overreaches and the US Army finally destroys her powerful flying fortress. With her organization in shambles, she is forced to regroup, while increasingly devoting all her energies to achieve revenge on Smith Beffort and Mie.

In Volume 5 Madame Atomos continues waging war on the United States, first by turning the hapless residents of Baltimore into blood-thirsty monsters, then by unleashing uncontrollable wild fires over Nevada. In Volume 6, Madame Atomos exacts a terrible revenge upon her enemies by killing both Dr. Soblen and Bob Beffort, the baby son of Smith Beffort and Mie Azusa. The latter swears revenge upon her once-mistress, while the deadly Japanese mastermind attempts to rebuild her evil empire.

In Volume 7, Madame Atomos discovers that her frequent use of teleportation has rejuvenated her body, and she now looks like a very attractive young woman, Not only does this help her evade the FBI, but she uses her charms to seduce Yosho Akamatsu who is, of course, unaware that the beautiful Miss Icho Fuji is, in reality, her deadliest enemy. In Volume 8, Madame Atomos, fully rejuvenated, is back, deadlier than ever, exacting a terrible toll on her enemies, plotting to release deadly bacteria in Oakland and spreading terror with her new freeze ray

Now read on…

Jean-Marc Lofficier

André Caroff

Mme ATOMOS
CHERCHE la PETITE BÊTE

ANGOISSE

FLEUVE NOIR

THE SLAVES OF MADAME ATOMOS

Chapter I

Mrs. Doubrough did not look her age. At 72 she was obviously not a young girl, not even a young lady, but she knew "old ladies" at 65 who were not half the woman she was. It was true that Mrs. Doubrough took great care of her health and her life was calm, with no conflicts, under the watchful authority of a career military man who had passed away a few years earlier. A widow now, Mrs. Doubrough, even though she was deeply saddened, had practically not changed her way of life or her habits. The death of her husband had given her a respectable pension and when the material needs are provided for, everything is a lot easier.

Mrs. Doubrough had simply sublet the second floor of her house to an engineer who was married with three charming kids, and then, feeling a little lonely, she had adopted a cat. A fat, tawny Siamese, majestically calm and as dignified as a bishop. She had fallen completely in love with him. She named him Royal. So, when Royal ran away and could not be found for a whole month, Mrs. Doubrough could not sleep or eat. She spent a small fortune on signs and had given up hope when one Monday night Royal showed up calmly at the door of the house.

Mrs. Doubrough scolded him, picked him up and hugged him. Royal meowed and glanced at the kitchen where his dish used to be. He was fat, looked in good shape and his fur shined rather nicely. She gave him something to eat and went upstairs to tell her tenants the good news. They all fawned over Royal, who let himself be fondled and petted while making faces and then, since it was late, everyone went to bed.

On his cushion Royal looked like a big, fat, happy cat and Mrs. Doubrough fell asleep with a smile on her face.

On Tuesday morning at 7 a.m. the milkman left three bottles of milk at the Doubrough house: one bottle for the widow and her cat and two bottles for the Reynolds and their three children. At 7:15 a deliveryman tossed a newspaper over the gate without getting out of his car. He had had training and the paper fell exactly between two bottles. At 8 a.m. the school bus stopped at the crosswalk and honked its horn. Five children left their houses and ran to the bus. The driver checked his list, noted that the Reynolds were absent, then left.

In our day everyone lives selfishly, so no one worried too much about the curtains drawn over the windows of the Doubrough house. However, this was terribly abnormal. Mrs. Doubrough usually got up early to go jogging and do her stretching exercises in the nearby park before trotting merrily home. It was precisely for this and her attractiveness that people still called her Mrs. instead of Widow Doubrough...

At 9:35 Reynolds' boss called the house to know why he was not at work. Nobody answered his calls. He put on his angry face, swore to bawl out his subordinate and buried himself in work.

There it is: Mrs. Doubrough had not gone jogging, the children had missed their bus and their father had not shown up at work for the first time in ten years and no one gave a damn!

At 6 p.m. the curtains were still drawn, the three bottles of milk and the newspaper were still on the porch and life went on as if it was nothing. Over the course of the day the postman had slipped the mail into the mailbox, a vacuum cleaner salesman had leaned on the doorbell and in the afternoon a classmate of Bob Reynolds had come over at his teacher's request and also tried ringing the bell, but nothing happened until officer Edwards passed by.

He had already walked past the Doubrough house two times in the course of his daily rounds of the neighborhood. The third time, around 7 p.m., it seemed weird to him that the curtains were still closed and that the bottles and newspaper were still not picked up by the widow and her tenants. He went through the gate, past the lawn and rang the doorbell. He could clearly hear the ringing, so he kept pushing, but in vain. Then he walked around the house while mopping his forehead because the evening was hot and muggy. In the backyard was a small vegetable garden, some gardening tools, a swing and a window that was cracked open. Edwards approached and called out before sneaking a peak through the open slit. The kitchen looked like any other but a strange smell leaked out. Edwards sniffed and thought it smelled like rotting meat or wet cabbage. A second later he changed his mind and would have laid his money on old fish.

Whatever it was, meat, cabbage or fish, Edwards' duty was to investigate because of the open window. If no one was there a prowler could easily enter the house and make off with some of their money or jewelry. He was thinking about exactly what to do when the odor, obviously riding on some unseen draft, gusted into his face. This time Edwards shuddered. After 15 years on the force he could recognize the distinct stench of a corpse.

He turned around, left the yard and hurried to the phone box on the corner.

Twenty minutes later two detectives provided with a warrant crawled into kitchen. On the ground floor they found the widow Doubrough dead in her blood-spattered bed. At first sight it looked like her throat had been cut with some strange weapon which did not so much cut as mangle, like a saw or a cheese grater for example.

On the first floor the policemen discovered the Reynolds family, likewise corpses with gaping throats, but there were bloody paw prints on their beds, on the beige carpet and on the stairway landing.

The detectives called headquarters. First the photographs, then the coroner. The investigation would only start after that.

That very night at 8 p.m. the police knew for a fact that the widow Doubrough and her tenants had been attacked by a wild animal with strong fangs and claws. It might be a small puma or a panther or some other carnivorous wild cat. They also thought that it could be a regular cat because of the bloody prints, but this seemed so unlikely that the hypothesis was quickly set aside.

Moreover, they had to admit that the affair was shrouded in mystery. The animal, if animal it really was, undoubtedly possessed superior intelligence. To kill six people, even while sleeping, with such precision was practically a magic trick. There was no struggle, which was amazing given the fact that the wild cat in question was not powerful enough to kill them with one swipe of its claw or one bite of its fang but rather "gnawed" on the throat of its victims. The word made them shiver, but it was nonetheless true.

Therefore?

While the police asked themselves questions, Margaret Anderson was peeling potatoes in front of the kitchen window. Under the stormy skies you could sweat even while standing still. In their yard Robert Anderson was working hard to mow the lawn. Since his bungalow was the smallest in the neighborhood, the young engineer made it a point of honor to keep it the best maintained. The lawnmower purred merrily along as the grass flew off emitting a heady odor. Robert finished the corner by the fence, turned around and found himself face to face with a fat cat sitting calmly on the lawn. It was a Siamese with huge green eyes that seemed to have materialized out of nowhere in the Anderson's yard.

Robert cut the lawnmower's power, dried his sweaty forehead and said, "What are you doing here, big boy?"

Of course he was not expecting the Siamese to answer. The cat just sat there, but from the kitchen Margaret asked, "Who are you talking to, Robert?"

"We have a visitor. Come and see."

Margaret left her potatoes, went into the yard through the French door in the living room and saw the cat which turned to look at her. Right away she knew that it did not belong to any of the neighbors. Margaret knew all the cats and dogs in the area, but obviously had not the slightest chance of meeting Royal anywhere since he came from far away.

"He doesn't look like an alley cat," Robert noted. Margaret leaned over and petted Royal who stretched and started licking his paws. Margaret picked him up and thought he was very heavy but still carried him into the kitchen where she gave him a bowl of milk.

"At least," Robert said following after them, "he doesn't look like he's dying of hunger. He's as fat as a pig!"

Since the day was waning, he turned on the four lights in the kitchen and scratched Royal's back before going back outside to put the lawnmower in the shed. Margaret went back to peeling potatoes while keeping a lazy eye on the Siamese. The window was still open so the cat could leave anytime he wanted. Before getting married the young lady had had a cat. She knew that you could not rush a touchy cat or hold one back if it wanted to go out hunting. Royal lapped the milk, then jumped onto a chair, curling up on the cushion before closing his eyes.

Robert came in a minute later and washed his hands. "Your protégé looks like he's comfortable," he frowned. "You figure on adopting him?"

"Don't start grumbling," Margaret enjoined as she set the table. "You can' adopt a cat, it adopts you. And if it wants to leave…"

"Okay! But I think we're going to have a boarder. He looks like he's making himself at home, anybody can see that. I hope he'll earn his keep by getting rid of the rats in the shed…"

They did not talk about Royal during dinner and he did not move an inch. He gave the impression that he was exhausted and, in fact, he was. After leaving the Doubrough house, he had crossed the city from north to south, which was a mighty long stroll. In a train parked on a side track he had relieved himself and cleaned off his bloody paws, whiskers and belly, then after a short nap had gotten back on the road. To all appearances his arrival at the Andersons had nothing deliberate about it.

Margaret did the dishes before joining her husband who was watching a variety show on the television. A minute later Royal crept into the living room, looked around, then finally jumped into Robert's lap.

Purring little, plaintive meows, etc. Royal was a pro at seduction.

The next morning Robert went to work. Margaret did the cleaning and Royal disappeared for exactly five and a half hours. Margaret was thinking that she would never see him again when the animal leaped over the fence and dashed into the kitchen. The young lady tried to pet him but for some unknown reason the cat would not let her near him. He ended up hiding on top of the armoire in the bedroom where Margaret could not reach him and he sulked there until Robert came home at 7:15 when he acquiesced, came down from his perch and acted normally.

At dinnertime Mrs. Hubsher, the Andersons' next-door neighbor, showed up to ask Margaret for some vinegar. Mrs. Hubsher noticed the big Siamese but carefully kept her distance. She hated cats, saying with a sour face that "they're bad luck and my dog will gladly snap this one's neck if he catches it on the other side of the fence."

To which Margaret snapped back that her dog kept the whole neighborhood up with its crazy barking and that if he broke her cat's neck she, Margaret Anderson, would not hesitate to shoot it in the rear-end. In a huff, Mrs. Hubsher stomped out leaving the vinegar on the table and swearing that she would never set foot in this house again.

Margaret was upset, but Robert doubled over laughing. He could not stand the sight of "old Hubsher" and figured that it would be a good thing if he never saw her again in his house.

The Andersons had dinner in the kitchen as the storm, which had been threatening for two days, broke out. It cleared the air and calmed the nerves of the inhabitants of Casper, Wyoming, but the Siamese's fur bristled eerily and had a strange metallic hue. He hid under the table for a few seconds, scurried into the living room whipping his tail in the air, then came back to snuggle against Robert's leg while meowing absolutely deliriously.

"Calm down, pal," Robert said as he petted him. "It's just an old thundercloud letting loose."

"Let him be," Margaret advised. "If you bother him, he's going to scratch you."

"Him? You think? He's as gentle as a lamb... Even if he smells awfully funny. Look, it's like his fur is secreting some kind of powder."

Margaret leaned over and clearly saw that the cat's fur was emitting a kind of fine dust as her husband petted it. And it had a peculiar odor that the young lady could not identify. She sniffed hard.

"D.D.T.?" Robert asked.

"No, it's more like a mix of ether and chloroform."

Robert had a good laugh. "The lab assistant has returned," he joked, referring to his wife's occupation. "Poor cat, he keeps this up he'll sleep like a log!"

They left it at that and like every night they sat in front of the television after Margaret did the dishes. This Wednesday night had a local news show and a good fifteen minutes was devoted to *The Mystery of the Doubrough House*. It was very good, as far as news, but concerning the actual police investigation the viewers understood right away that it had not made any headway. Then the reporter resorted to melodrama by speaking about a strange, bloody-thirsty creature that fed on the gore of its victims... It was as if they were back in the times of vampires! It was stupid but fascinating and it took the Andersons quite a while before they surrendered to the overwhelming need to sleep.

Robert turned off the television and followed Margaret to their bedroom on the first floor. With his green eyes Royal watched them undress. Then he stuck our his pink tongue, extended his claws and stretched out on the couch. Margaret glanced down into the living room, slipped on a see-through nightie and started closing the door.

"Oh, no," her husband protested in a sleepy voice. "If you close the door, we're going to suffocate in here." He buried his head in the pillow and fell asleep.

Margaret hesitated, but finally left the door wide open and went to bed. She turned off the bedside lamp, settled in and dropped off to sleep right away.

Time passed.

The televisions and lights were turned off throughout the neighborhood and silence fell over the sleepy town.

Around one in the morning, Royal awoke, stretched, stood up and jumped to the ground. Slowly he headed for the Andersons' bedroom where he crouched and then leaped onto the bed.

Chapter II

Mrs. Hubsher was a good woman and immediately regretted her argument with Margaret Anderson. She spent her Thursday morning waiting for her neighbor to appear, but when she had not seen Robert Anderson leave for work she started to worry at 10 am.

At 10:30, seeing that the house remained desperately quiet, Mrs. Hubsher made up her mind. She went through the fence, marched down the walkway and knocked hard on the Andersons' front door. At this very moment, her dog started barking. Mrs. Hubsher had put him in the shed to avoid an altercation between him and her neighbor's cat and now he showed up, the stubborn beast, right when his master was about to make things right.

Mrs. Hubsher grumbled to show her disapproval of the barking in case Margaret was listening behind the door and she knocked again. After four tries without an answer, she went over to the kitchen window, which was cracked open, and was startled to find traces of blood on the sill. A jumble of ideas rushed into her mind associating these traces with the news the night before about *The Mystery of the Doubrough House*. No blood was visible on the lawn, but inside the house on the kitchen tile and in the living room she could see a lot more. With a knot in her throat, ready to flee, she cried out, "Mrs. Anderson!"

No one answered, but her dog's barking got louder. Under the circumstances Mrs. Hubsher knew for a fact that her dog was howling bloody murder. She backed away and ran straight into her house to the telephone…

They found Margaret and Robert Anderson slaughtered in their bed, exactly like the widow Doubrough and the Reynolds family had been. The preliminary investigation almost got sidetracked because Robert Anderson and John Reynolds had the same job, but they concluded that this was a minor coincidence. The two men were both engineers, but they worked for different companies and held no State secrets. Consequently, there remained the bloody tracks…

When questioned Mrs. Hubsher responded, "Yes, my neighbors had a cat for just a little while. A big, mean-looking Siamese that came from who knows where."

Well, one of the policemen remembered that the widow Doubrough had lost a cat answering to Mrs. Hubsher's description, except that the old lady's neighbors said the cat had never returned home. Nevertheless, the tracks found at the Andersons looked a lot like those at the Doubrough house and even if it sounded insane, they had to start suspecting Royal!

At the late widow Doubrough's house they found a picture of Royal and that very evening the inhabitants of Casper were surprised to find a photograph of the cat on the front page of the local paper with the headline: His name's Royal. He's already killed 8 people. Kill him on sight!

They were banging their heads against the wall.

Because of the rain that had fallen Wednesday night, the police dogs could not pick up the scent of Royal beyond the fence. The men from the pound went out in the field and through the press and all the news outlets the authorities in Casper mobilized the population.

Someone offered a reward for the cat's hide so that Royal very quickly became the prey of a mad hunt. In different parts of the city they killed a dozen Siamese cats that were rushed to police headquarters to get the reward, but none of them turned out to be Royal. The SPCA spoke out alongside the owners of the cats who were unjustly killed and all of them got together to release a statement saying that a house cat could not be the perpetrator of such atrocious crimes. In their view the police had invented this despicable excuse to cover up their incompetence. The murderer of the widow Doubrough, the Reynolds and the Andersons had to be a man!

Meanwhile, Royal proved to be decidedly intelligent and avoided all the traps set in his way until he arrived quietly in the yard of a run-down workshop near Children's Home. Only a year ago a certain David Millay, a manufacturer of plastic containers, had up and fired his staff and for reasons of health shut the shop down temporarily. Since then it had been deserted, covered with dust and cobwebs, surrounded by high walls and a gate that was starting to rust.

Royal slid through a hole, crossed the yard, snuck between two loose boards and strolled into David Millay's old office where a small, yellow man, hideously ugly, was toying with a device which had six telescopic antennas sticking out of it. On seeing Royal the little man cracked a smile but did not utter a word. He simply turned a knob and Royal walked softly to his place between a huge boxer and a beautifully feathered parrot.

All around the room, under the table and on the old file cabinets, were other sleeping animals. Rats, monkeys, cats, dogs and birds all tagged with the names and addresses of their owners. Being tame these small creatures were naturally not dangerous and yet every species still possessed its offensive and defensive weapons: a strong beak, powerful jaws, sharp claws, etc.

The little man obviously had no problems with his roommates. All the animals got along just fine in startling silence. The rats here were surprising, but less so since they belonged to the family *ondratras*, native to North America, relatives of the beaver, intelligent and easily tamable.

The little man lay down on a mat on the ground and dozed off until 8 pm. Then he went up to the boxer, took off the tag and buckled a collar around his neck. Sleepily the dog put up no resistance. And he did not budge when the Japanese man sprayed him with a gray powder that smelled of ether, but when the man flipped a switch on his device, the dog stood up.

The Japanese adjusted the screen of his transmitter and led the dog outside. He opened the front gate a crack so the dog could slip through and he watched it trot down the sidewalk into the growing darkness.

The Hoppers had given up all hope. Gib had been missing for three weeks without a trace in spite of his collar with the name and address of his owners on McKinley Street, not far from Washington Park. Gib was three months old when the Hoppers had adopted him. He was almost eight now. When a dog lives that long in a house, he is part of the family and his disappearance had created a great void. Like the widow Doubrough had done for Royal, the Hoppers had spread missing posters around but to no avail. It was an opportunity, however, to realize how many animals had been disappearing in Casper for a while.

Tonight around 9 pm the Hoppers and their three older children were studying a map for the itinerary of their next vacation. In the next room Mary, three years old, and Joan, five, had already been sleeping for an hour.

Ray Hopper drew a red line, made two crosses and said, "We leave Tuesday at daybreak. By evening we'll be in Sinks camp where I've reserved a spot for our trailer."

"Well," Gary said, "I'd rather go to Fox camp." Being the oldest he never agreed and felt it was his duty to challenge his father's decisions. Moreover, the family vacations were starting to be a drag for him. He had friends who were going together to a "bad" camp over by Provo. Boys and girls in two neighboring camps for fifteen days! And he was going to miss out!

"You," his father snapped back, "can go wherever you want when you're 18. Until then you go with the family. So, first Sinks and then…"

A short bark interrupted him. His pencil hung in mid-air. His wife and children were stunned.

"Dang," Gary said, "that sounded like Gib!"

"Don't be an idiot," his sister argued. "A dog doesn't just come home by itself after three weeks. Besides, I'm sure Gib was run over by a truck."

Gary shrugged his shoulders and went to open the door. Immediately Gib ran into the living room yapping and wagging his tail.

May Hopper started crying with joy and Ray Hopper, to hide his emotions, said, "Well, you big stupid mutt, where have you been running around?"

The children started screaming with joy so loud that they woke their little sisters who came in to see what was happening. Gib was cuddled, petted, spoiled and given enough food to stuff a tiger. For more than an hour they talked on and on about what Gib might have been doing over the past three weeks. Since he was fat and apparently in good health they figured that he must have been picked up by an animal lover whom he finally managed to slip away from to return home.

Then Gib went to lie down in his favorite spot. Mr. Hopper, whose eyes were getting heavy, sent everyone off to bed, put on his pajamas and ordered lights out. As he was falling asleep he wondered if dogs were allowed at Sinks camp.

It was May Hopper's mother who found the seven corpses on Friday morning at 10 am. The poor woman lost her mind and the news exploded like a bomb in Casper before spreading through the rest of the United States.

This time the matter was serious because Ray Hopper was also an engineer, and this was not the least of surprises because it was clear from the start that the Hoppers had not been mangled by a cat but by a dog with particularly powerful jaws.

Right away the investigators found out about Gib the boxer and were obviously struck by the fact that, just like Royal, the dog had disappeared a few weeks earlier not to be seen again. They learned that Gib had a collar and tag so it was strange that the animal had eluded both the dogcatchers and all the inhabitants of Casper. If he were lost, a dog like this would certainly have been picked up and thereafter returned to its rightful owners. Nevertheless, even though they knew that the Hoppers had been the victims of a dog's powerful jaws, nothing proved with certainty that it was their dog. To make matters worse there was the undeniable fact that Reynolds,

Anderson and Hopper were all engineers and at this point they could no longer consider it a coincidence.

"It just doesn't add up," Burt Wyatt, the local police chief whose common sense was well known, declared. "I can believe that a cat and dog get rabid, but not that they can tell the difference between an engineer and a newsboy. Someone's mixed up in this and they're trying to pull the wool over our eyes."

Strangely, even though it was obvious, nobody thought of Madame Atomos! The sinister woman had evaporated a little over four months before in Mexico, in Sonora to be exact, and she had given no sign of life since then. The optimists lost no time in imagining her dead. Chief Wyatt had no opinion on the matter. Anyway, Casper was far from Mexico and why would Madame Atomos decide to attack this small city in Wyoming?

In short Chief Wyatt missed the truth in spite of his common sense, or maybe because of it, and concentrated on determining the relationship that existed between Hopper, Anderson and Reynolds.

The investigation quickly proved that the three men, even though they had the same profession, did not know each other and had never met and the wives and children were not acquainted, even superficially. Moreover, Royal did not belong to the Reynolds but to the widow Doubrough. And the Andersons did not have a pet before the Siamese showed up (who was maybe not the cat they thought he was) and the Hoppers, even though slain by a dog and having lost one, had certainly not been killed by the same one.

It was all so twisted and complicated!

But exactly Madame Atomos' style…

"Get me the names of all the engineers in Casper," Chief Wyatt ordered, trying above all to stay level-headed, "and see if they have pets."

Without realizing it he had just hit the bull's eye.

That Friday, around 6 pm, Wyatt's men came back to headquarters with a complete list of the engineers working and living in Casper. There were 22, all married with children. Besides this family status and their profession they also had one remarkable point in common: all of them without exception had lost a pet in the last month! Dogs, cats, monkeys, birds, muskrats. 22 animals lost under mysterious circumstances, searched for but never found!

Chief Wyatt suddenly felt that the situation was getting too big for him.

Chronologically speaking Royal had disappeared first so Wyatt assigned him number one. Gib was given number two because the Hoppers had lost him a week later. After that things sped up to the point that an animal disappeared every day. Number three was a monkey belonging to Arthur Chapin. Number four the parrot of Jim Freemont, etc.

"Logically," Chief Wyatt's deputy said, "the Chapin family is going to be the next family to die."

"Not necessarily," Wyatt grumbled. "The process hasn't been proven."

"You mean the Andersons, chief?"

"Yes."

"They're the exception that proves the rule," the deputy assured. "They didn't have kids or a pet so they sent Royal to them."

Chief Wyatt looked at him blankly and asked, "Are you feeling okay, Walter? You said 'They sent Royal to them' as if there were someone behind this. Did you know that the cat is the only animal that can't be taught tricks?"

"On T.V. I saw…"

"Yeah, on T.V., right?" Wyatt exploded, getting irritated by the whole matter. "You saw a cat walk across a plank of wood on *Mission Impossible*. You saw a cat in a Disney film! But have you ever seen or heard of a cat slaughtering eight people practically on command? Come on, Walter, be realistic!"

"Okay! Let's be realistic," the deputy replied, "and let's say that the Chapins' monkey comes back home tonight, that it goes bananas and strangles or mangles the whole family…"

Wyatt shrugged. "Ridiculous! I don't believe that the widow Doubrough, the Reynolds, Andersons and Hoppers were really victims of a cat or dog. It's obvious what they're trying to make us believe that and you're biting. You're the kind of guy who swallows everything. Look, Walter, if you want my opinion, I'll tell you that we're obviously dealing with a madman here. He's lashing out at engineers, but only by chance. It could just as easily be you or me. Maybe it's a maniac who hates animals and people who take care of them… Maybe…"

Wyatt could imagine anything but he would never get near the truth unless Madame Atomos had him tied and gagged to convince him.

Chapter III

Wyatt was tied and gagged on Saturday morning when he learned that the Chapin family had just been found murdered. According to the evidence a monkey had been there and its fangs had made a real carnage. Blood from floor to ceiling, on the walls and one of the balconies. Thus they could follow the animal tracks for a short distance down the sidewalk until they abruptly disappeared for no apparent reason.

"The mystery grows darker," Walter stated.

"Not at all," Chief Wyatt barked. "A guy took the monkey in his car that was parked here and for obvious reasons. If a patrol car saw the animal walking around Casper in the middle of the night, it would have to react. Unbelievable! How can animals…"

He cut himself short on suddenly seeing the enigmatic face of Madame Atomos on the other side of the street. The poster had been stuck on a fence. It was partly torn and one of the corners was flapping in the wind, but the sinister woman was still pointing her dark eyes at the Chapin house. Hundreds of thousands of these posters had been put up around the United States and like everyone Chief Wyatt was used to them. This morning, however, the face of Madame Atomos took on a new meaning in his eyes.

Walter saw his chief's expression, followed his eyes and turned pale. "Damn, chief, you don't think that…?" The rest of his question got stuck in his throat.

Wyatt turned to him and in a distant voice said, "I don't know, Walter, but before alerting the FBI boys we need some proof. We'll look just great if a veterinarian comes out and says rabies has been reported in the Casper area."

"Proof? How do you figure on getting it?"

Wyatt held up his hands. "By capturing the widow Doubrough's cat, the Hoppers' dog or the Chopins' monkey we'll know what we're dealing with, but I think that's impossible, don't you?"

Walter nodded. "It's impossible for them so I see only one way."

"How's that?"

"After the Chapins, if we stick to the chronological order, the Freemonts are next. Theoretically, their parrot should show up Saturday night or Sunday. Tonight. Let's set up a quiet stakeout of their house and we'll see if the parrot comes back alone or if someone drops it off in a car."

Wyatt accepted his deputy's suggestion without a second thought, but to give the plan a personal touch he also made arrangements to protect all the engineers living in Casper.

On Saturday night, starting at 7 pm, plainclothes police officers were wandering all over the city and particularly around the hot spots or the spots that might become hot at a moment's notice, while Wyatt and his deputy took care of the Freemonts' house where the chief wasted no time. Leaving Walter outside he introduced himself to Jim Freemont and his wife.

"I'm the chief of the Capser police. Here's my identification. I'm here tonight because I think your parrot is coming back."

It was a strange introduction, but the Freemonts did not smile. Like everyone in Casper they knew all about the inexplicable tragedies that had happened over the past week. Besides, they had already been questioned by the police about their parrot and were starting to feel like they were on death row.

"Come in and sit down," Jim Freemont said. "Spend the night here with us if you want. Have you eaten?"

"No, but that's not why I'm here," Wyatt said dryly.

"Excuse me, I thought…"

"Think first of all about your own safety," Wyatt interrupted. "I'm sure you don't really believe that your parrot might be dangerous. You know the bird, you've had it for years and you can't imagine for a second that its beak could suddenly transform into some kind of murderous hook that'll pluck out your eyes while you're sleeping!"

"Oh!" Mrs. Freemont exclaimed. "What a horrible thing to say!"

Wyatt stared at her coldly. "Keep in mind how your husband's colleagues were found dead and you'll face the facts, Madame. I'm sure they and their families didn't feel the least bit afraid when their pets came back. And yet facts are facts, isn't that right?"

From that moment on the atmosphere became heavy. The Freemonts and their two children remained quiet. A threat hovered over them and its unlikelihood spawned a fear bordering on panic. If their parrot had suddenly turned up in the room, Wyatt was sure that Mrs. Freemont and her children would have screamed.

Time passed. Night fell.

From his car Walter watched the street, noted the license plates of all the vehicles that stopped near the Freemont house. Still, his notebook did not fill up fast. The neighborhood was calm and traffic, which had been heavy for an instant because of people leaving for the weekend, became lighter and lighter as the hours ticked by.

At 10 pm Jim Freemont was lighting the last cigarette in his pack when the parrot flew out of the shadows and alit on the back of a chair. It was so swift, so surprising, in spite of Wyatt's warning, that no one moved. The bird leaned forward and let loose a kind of cackle. Then it flew to its perch and immediately tucked itself into a ball.

Mrs. Freemont wanted to stand up, but Wyatt said, "Stay seated, please. Mr. Freemont, could you hook it up please?"

Jim Freemont approached the perch. It was fitted with a light chain and an adjustable bracelet to hold the bird so that it would not leave its droppings all over the house. Jim reached out and hooked the bracelet around the leg of the parrot, which showed no resistance. Then he looked at Wyatt and said, "If that's what you call a wild animal…"

The children murmured and Mrs. Freemont said, "He's as normal as ever and you'll never convince me that he could pluck out our eyes."

"Give him a good looksee," Wyatt said to Jim Freemont, "and make sure that nothing's changed."

Jim inspected the bird very closely for a while before saying, "He's missing a few feathers on his head and he doesn't smell very nice but otherwise I don't notice anything different."

"What does he smell like?" Wyatt pressed.

Jim leaned over, sniffed, and frowned. "Well, it's weird but I think he smells like chloroform. His feathers look like they're covered in dust, too."

Chief Wyatt walked up but kept a distance from the perch, asking, "Is it normal to find dust on bird who has just made a long flight?"

"Of course not. But how do you know that he's just made a long flight?"

"I don't. I'm guessing. I imagine that you scoured the neighborhood when you lost him, so if he wasn't in the area we can suppose that he's coming from farther away. Except with this dust on him wouldn't it be reasonable to assume that someone let him free just outside your window? And this smell of chloroform, is that normal?"

The Freemonts looked at one another, trying to reassure themselves, but Wyatt had raised doubts in their minds for the second time.

The policeman continued, "And you said your parrot is missing a few feathers on his head. How could that happen?"

"My Lord," Jim responded, "I really don't know! Don't you think you're going a little overboard?"

Wyatt sneered. "The widow Doubrough, the Reynolds, the Andersons and the Hoppers were all murdered in their sleep! Your bird stinks of chloroform! Do you finally get it?" He was getting nasty because he himself was just starting to understand.

Jim Freemont shrugged his shoulders. "Absolutely insane!" he said, but he could not help yawning. "Stay here all night long if you want, but I'm going to bed."

Wyatt grabbed his arm. And said in a smarmy voice, "Sleepy, Freemont?"

"Yeah!"

"And before sniffing your damned bird you felt fine. What time do you usually go to bed?"

"Around midnight," Jim said while his eyelids drooped.

"Okay! Sit down. We're gong to see if you can hold out. Come on, Freemont, make an effort! No, don't fall asleep! Freemont!"

The man did not answer and he made no reaction when Chief Wyatt shook him rudely.

His wife was worried. "What's wrong with him?"

"Don't get worked up," Wyatt said. "Your husband is just drugged from breathing too close to the parrot. Give me a second, please." He opened the front door and waved to Walter. The deputy hurried into the house and jumped when he saw the parrot on its perch.

"How did he get in here?"

"Through the window," Wyatt informed him. "But—and this is the most interesting part—Jim Freemont sniffed its feathers and you can see for yourself what's happened to him. Now what if the whole family did the same and the bird was free?"

Understanding how the process worked made him a bit lyrical and gave him an unpleasant tendency to imagine a probable outcome which had not yet happened.

Walter spoke to him diplomatically. "The parrot looks calm enough, doesn't it?"

"Aha!" Mrs. Freemont gloated. "What did I tell you!"

Now more confident than ever Wyatt would gladly have slapped the two of them. But he knew all too well that nothing would convince the woman. He sat down comfortably and said, "Perfect! We're going to wait for the beast to awaken. Get ready for a long night, Mrs. Freemont. According to the coroner's reports your husband's colleagues and their families were killed between midnight and four in the morning. If I were you, I would put the children to bed."

Mrs. Freemont knew that there was no way she was going to get rid of the stubborn officer. Besides, she was curious now and she was sure that she would not be able to sleep until this astounding story was resolved. She went to put her children to bed, then put Jim's feet up on a chair and wedged a pillow behind his head. Being a good sport in spite of everything she offered Wyatt and Walter a beer, which they accepted.

At one in the morning the parrot was still asleep. Wyatt called headquarters and then his wife to tell her he would be home late. Walter did the same and Mrs. Freemont opened the bottles of beer. With the parrot sleeping and Jim snoring like a freight train, the scene was a little ridiculous and Wyatt was aware of this. To tell the truth he was starting to wonder if he was wrong. From time to time he caught Walter and Mrs. Freemont sneaking a peek at each other. Both of them were against him, obviously.

At 2 am the parrot said "Rouaaa," softly and opened its eyes. It shook itself, beat its wings and unleashed a violent blow with its beak on the perch. Then its eyes got bigger and bigger as it examined the room.

"Stay calm," Wyatt whispered. "He has to think we're sleeping."

Walter and Mrs. Freemont sat still and Wyatt gripped the butt of his .38 that was hidden from view by the edge of the table. The parrot geared up and tried to fly off, but the chain stopped it. As it stood on the perch again it squawked loudly. Feathers bristling, eyes agoggle, wings flapping—it suddenly looked like a bird of prey.

Nervous in her chair Mrs. Freemont turned pale. "He's going crazy! I've never seen him like this."

The parrot turned toward her, gave a ghastly screech and lurched forward with a force that seemed absolutely disproportionate to its size and weight. The perch toppled over giving enough slack to the chain that the bird landed on the Mrs. Freemont's lap. The woman screamed while the bird pecked at her and Wyatt barely had time to kick back the perch. The bird lurched and bobbed, squawking furiously, but the chain and the weight of the perch kept it from attacking now.

In the doorway the children, agape, witnessed the astounding spectacle and they saw Chief Wyatt with his .38 in hand keeping careful watch over the parrot's savage dance. This lasted five long minutes, then the bird stopped beating its wings, let out a piteous cry and fell to the ground. It tried to stand up, almost managed, but collapsed in a heap.

Wyatt approached with caution and turned the bird over with the tip of his shoe, saying, "Okay, Walter, you can call headquarters. Ask for a vet. This animal is dead and I want to know what it's got in its belly!"

On the close examination of the parrot they took samples of the powder it carried. After being sent to the lab, the powder was found to be a new composition, extremely volatile, with an ether base mixed with unidentified products. It was a particularly powerful and effective sleeping drug.

Once this was established, the veterinarian first looked for the reason why the bird had died so quickly and he found just as quickly that its death was due to some kind of brain trauma.

Wyatt laughed and shrugged his shoulders casually. Then he roared, "Some kind of brain trauma? What does that mean, exactly?"

The veterinarian had seen too much to take offense, especially since they had dragged him out of bed at three in the morning to perform an autopsy on a parrot!

"That means that this bird got hit on the head and it died from it. See for yourself."

Wyatt leaned over but saw only a bloody mess. He straightened up and said, "I was there when it fell and I can guarantee you that no one hit the bird."

"Well, that doesn't matter. It could have hit something when it fell and…"

"No," Wyatt cut in, "nothing like that happened."

He explained in great detail the incredible scene he had witnessed at the Freemonts, but even though the veterinarian was intrigued by the bird's strange behavior, he did not change his mind.

"Look," he said, "and you'll see that this bird's skull literally exploded from some violent and terrible blow. Its brain is mush so it's no surprise that it dropped dead."

"Then tell me," Wyatt objected, "why is there no trace of a blow on its feathers?"

"Sorry, but you can see here that it's missing a few feathers."

"That happened before it came back to the house," Wyatt said. "Jim Freemont pointed that out to me right after the bird returned."

The vet said nothing for a while and then finally, "Well, we have to believe that the bird must have hit something outside and the effect of the impact wasn't felt until later. All things considered I like this explanation better because it would explain the madness that the bird appears to have suffered. I've seen such cases before in my career. To make myself clearer let's look at it on a human level. After a car accident a man can get up and refuse help because he feels okay, but then he dies all of a sudden a few hours or a few days later. It happens often and..."

Wyatt let him talk. Deep down inside he was convinced that the parrot died because he could not kill the Freemonts.

Chapter IV

On Sunday morning Wyatt woke up late. He had gone to bed at 5 am and kicked his wife during his sleep, tossing and turning and talking incessantly like a candidate for president.

Haggard and gloomy he listened to the radio and read the newspaper. They were talking only about the events in Casper, but the journalists were one step behind because they did not know about the Freemonts and their parrot. Wyatt holed up in silence and focused.

Tomorrow or Tuesday at the latest he would have to hand it over to the FBI if he could not solve the mystery beforehand. That animals were murdering humans was certainly not a federal crime and no regulation obliged Wyatt to step aside for the G-men, but knowing what he knew and suspecting, rightly or wrongly, that Madame Atomos was involved, he felt morally compelled. In the afternoon he let his wife and kids take the car and once alone he dove into his file of newspaper clippings about most of Madame Atomos' attacks against the USA.

Meanwhile a black car was cruising slowly through the nearly deserted streets of Casper. A small, yellow man, hideously ugly, was driving it. He was probably an inexperienced tourist looking at the sights because he stopped often and pointed a big camera at some object, took a picture and left to drive at random through the streets and avenues.

No one paid any special attention to him, but if an observer had noted his actions, it would have been interesting to see that the little Japanese man was only taking pictures of people walking their dogs. Moreover, the camera that he was using was a rather old model, pretty beat up, and anyway very far from the famous Japanese miniature devices.

The man "worked" from 1 pm until nightfall, "photographed" thirty or so dogs, then finally put his camera away and continued driving without any specific destination across Casper. In the dark of night he turned his car toward Children's Home, glided down a dark alley with no houses and stopped in front of a gate that was starting to rust. Five minutes later, after parking his car in a hangar, he entered the old office of David Millay and saw Royal, Gib and all the other animals in a deep, artificial sleep.

Of course the parrot was missing, but this was just a minor detail. With the help of his transmitter with the six antennas the little Japanese had done what was needed for the grand project of Madame Atomos to stay top secret.

Brush was a six year old shepherd weighing around 75 pounds and a champion show dog before his owner got tired of taking him all over Wyoming for little compensation. Medals and certificates are pretty but the trips were expensive, especially if you worked for the city and had a sick wife who needed constant and costly care. Therefore Louis Donahue was satisfied now with walking Brush down the street when he was not working. That is what he did on Sunday afternoon and it would have had no adverse consequences if Brush had not been the very first dog photographed by the little Japanese.

From the second that the Japanese man had clicked a picture with his big camera, Brush, without either him of the Donahues knowing it, was carrying a tiny piece of metal, no bigger than the head of a pin, in his brain.

The device was the result of five years of labor by Dr. Miwa whom Madame Atomos had brought to her laboratory on San Esteban Island in the middle of the Gulf of California. With infinite patience the old doctor had succeeded in recreating the famous motor-brain of the early Atomos years, but he also made some fantastic improvements on the technical level as well as its size. With all the qualities of the old motor-brain, this super-minibrain had the advantage of being able to self-destruct if the subject did not respond to the signal. With it the subject would obviously drop dead and leave no evidence behind.

In the old days they had to open the skull to give the subject a motor-brain. Today the super-minibrain was implanted by an air gun. The injecting weapon looked like a camera and was extremely precise. Still, this precision was only relatively important because no matter where in the body of the chosen victim the super-minibrain entered, it automatically coursed through the blood up to the brain and stopped. Once it found the sensory and motor zones the microscopic device worked like a computer so that every neuron obeyed its stimulations.

After several trials in the laboratory, Madame Atomos entered the second phase of "field tests" so that her operators could get the knack of it as well as to test the efficacy of the device under any circumstance and in any weather.

Brush, therefore, was the first subject of a series of *Sunday* experiments, code name *Fresh Air*, which would allow the super-minibrain a wider range of use. Brush, along with 29 other dogs "photographed" by Madame Atomos' little worker, stayed calm until 9 pm. Then the Japanese turned on his six antennaed transmitter. The radio waves soared off to the receiver of every super-minibrain, which in turn emitted a series of irresistible stimulations.

At the Donahues, Brush suddenly jumped up, bared his teeth, growled and attacked his owners with incredible savagery. Louis Donahue was gripped by his throat before he even had time to know that his dog had gone rabid and by the time he could defend himself he was already on his last breath, which the powerful jaws snuffed out with a single snap.

As for Esther Donahue, stuck in her wheelchair and whimpering feebly, she was a simple formality, a treat for the animal who was suddenly imbued with superior strength and an unquenchable thirst for blood. After that Brush jumped through the window, smashing it to bits, and since the Donahues' apartment was on the fourth floor, he crashed into the sidewalk, stone dead. Instantly perceiving that the animal was not responding to the stimulations, the super-minibrain literally blew him up by causing an internal hemorrhage in the dog's brain and destroying forever all traces of the deadly device.

Elsewhere, things went smoothly with a few minor variations so that operation Fresh Air was a total success for Dr. Miwa, the condemned soul of Madame Atomos. 20 people lost their lives, 12 dogs killed themselves or were killed by the super-minibrains or by men, but the survivors spread out in Casper and attacked passers-by. There again were a dozen victims before the police came in with their pistols and machine guns, shooting on sight all the dogs who rather than trying to run away kept attacking with astonishing aggressiveness.

Casper finally calmed down. All the "rabid" animals had been killed and their remains were brought to the police laboratory on the orders of Chief Wyatt who was starting to get some ideas about the problem and straightaway called FBI headquarters in Cheyenne. They in turn contacted Washington.

Meanwhile, the little Japanese man snickered and gleefully restarted operation *Engineers*!

Stiff, glum and planted behind his glasses like a revolutionary behind a black flag, James Edward Evans was looking suspiciously at the report filed by Chief Wyatt, which the Cheyenne office had just sent him. At first sight J.E.E. was against it.

After four months of quiet and wanting to believe in the total, definitive disappearance of Madame Atomos, the FBI chief seriously frowned upon a second-rank policeman sticking his nose where it did not belong and sounding the alarm. This guy, this Wyatt, was plainly claiming that the Atomos Organization had been reborn from the ashes and that Casper was under an insidious attack by animals that were certainly radio-controlled!

Wyatt talked about Royal, Gib, the Chapins' monkey, the Freemonts' parrot and drew a startling picture of the previous night when 30 or so dogs had turned into killers. But—and this was the cause of J.E.E.'s suspicions—Chief Wyatt was unable to furnish any proof of his hare-brained hypotheses.

In the final count, J.E.E. shrugged his shoulders and dropped the report in a bottom drawer, then he lit his daily cigar.

To be perfectly fair, it must said that James Edward Evans was not being sloppy or negligent because periodically the Atomos psychosis took hold of Americans and a bunch of very sincere people claimed to have seen the sinister woman in a taxi, on a train, at the movies or in a corner drugstore. If a fire broke out, if an old house collapsed, if a ship ran aground, if a plane crashed, there was always someone who swore that Madame Atomos was there just a few seconds before.

J.E.E. took care of day-to-day business until 10 am and at 10:05 the telephone rang. He picked up, barked his name, but calmed down on recognizing the voice of Smith Beffort. "Hello. How are you, Smith?" he asked.

"Good," Beffort answered. "Say, Evans, have you listened to the radio or seen the papers this morning?"

"No, I never do. When by chance I have five minutes free I put my feet up on my desk and smoke a cigar thinking about my next vacation. My responsibilities are…"

"If what I suspect is true," Beffort jumped in, "you won't be having vacation this year. Funny things are happening in Casper, Wyoming."

"What? You too?"

"How's that? Don't tell me you knew all about it and didn't do anything! Since Madame Atomos got away from us in Mexico, nothing important has happened. Did you know that animals are becoming rabid in Casper?"

Evans took a deep breath. "I've known since I got in this morning. I was handed a report by a cop name Wyatt."

"What did he say?"

"Well, he went whole hog! According to him the animals in question are being radio-controlled by members of the Atomos Organization. Are you surprised?"

"No, I've been following the affair from the start, I mean from the death of Mrs. Doubrough and her tenants and Wyatt's conclusions seem pretty logical to me."

"Logical!" Evans exploded. "I'll be damned! Wyatt claims that the animals are radio-controlled but he also swears that no device has been found in the bodies. Now, I know the story as well as you, Smith! Unless Madame Atomos has supernatural powers, she would have to be using her famous motor-brain to control the animals as she wants. Right?"

"Right," Beffort admitted sullenly, "but didn't you bring up supernatural powers?"

"It was just a figure of speech."

Beffort laughed hollowly and said, "You're a chronic skeptic, Evans. I'd bet my right eye that Madame Atomos discovered a way, supernatural or not, to control the animals in Casper. And it's only the beginning. What works on animals can, with a few tweaks, work on man in 80 % of the cases. I'd like to see your face when you find out that all the inhabitants of Casper have turned into robots."

J.E.E. made a sound like he had swallowed his cigar. Just thinking about it gave him goose bumps. A minute earlier he was a quiet civil servant, well paid, smoking a good cigar and dreaming of trout and pike. Now his belly was rumbling, his heart beating and beads of sweat were trickling down his spine.

"You're not serious, Smith?" his voice cracked.

"If you really think so, change the conversation. Either way I'm catching a plane to Casper in one hour with Mie and Yosho."

Evans was speechless. Beffort, guessing he was devastated, said, "Lack of energy, Evans?"

"Not at all. Why?"

"The vague impression that you lost your grit during the long break that Madame Atomos took. Am I wrong?"

"Absolutely!" J.E.E. argued, with some outrage in his voice.

"Good, good," Beffort approved. "You'll have to have all your wits about you for the upcoming battle. The longer Madame Atomos rests, the more lethal are her attacks. I can tell you now that it's going to be a bloodletting in Casper."

Evans felt himself become weak. Good God! What was wrong with him? He would not have admitted it for anything, but over the past few days he had fallen into a strange state of depression, jumping at the slightest noise and having a devil of a time controlling his nerves.

On the other end of the line Smith was surprised by his chief's silence. Evans usually talked a lot and loudly. At the start of this conversation he had very conveniently protected his reputation and then on hearing about robots was clearly crushed. Smith had not seen him for a month so it could be that since then Evans had aged overnight.

"How long have you been stuck behind a desk, Evans?" he asked.

"Uh... two or three years, I don't know..."

"Four years. Since the death of the Boss," Smith informed him from his remarkable memory. "So, in four years you haven't taken a single day of vacation. Sometimes you even sleep in your office eating only sandwiches and drinking coffee. Do you think you can hold out like that for long?"

"I'm going on vacation and..."

"Keep your head screwed on. If Madame Atomos is behind this, no one's going on vacation and you least of all! Have you seen a doctor?"

J.E.E. paused and with a sudden burst of energy said, "Listen, Smith, I'm big enough to know what I have to do and don't be adding your advice to my wife's who's been nagging me constantly! If I listened to her

I'd be locked up in a rest home for five or six months! Go to Casper, see what's going on and call me right away, okay?"

Beffort hung up at the same time as Evans. Then Evans leaned back in his chair and did not move for a long time. His cigar went out, but he no longer wanted it. All of a sudden he had the extraordinary feeling that he was a complete stranger to the FBI.

Madame Atomos alone was all he could think about since Beffort's phone call. For the rest, all the rest, he felt nothing but apathy. It was not normal. Evans knew this for sure, but by some strange phenomenon he could not muster up enough concentration to analyze it. In fact, he was troubled by a swarm of contradictory feelings and vague ideas, all of which flew through his head at supersonic speed. To think intelligently, it would have been necessary to stop the movement. Except Evans had no desire to do so.

He felt good, that was all.

Chapter V

The special FBI plane flew over Wyoming after passing over Van Tassel. Yosho Akamatsu leaned over, saw a kind of high plateau sheared off from the high peaks of the Rocky Mountains and asked Beffort, "Why would Madame Atomos have chosen this particular state for her reappearance?"

They asked this question every time and the sequence of events showed that the terrible woman's choice corresponded to the demands of her almost mathematical rigidity.

"I don't know," Smith answered. "Wyoming is far from Mexico. Madame Atomos never set foot here so if she came here it's no doubt because she knew that we wouldn't be expecting her so far north in the country."

Mie Azusa-Beffort took the little blue book, New Horizons USA, published by Pan American Airways, opened to page 224 and read aloud, "Wyoming is has the second smallest population (290,000 inhabitants) even though it has the eighth largest area."

"And?" Smith said.

Mie smiled kindly and said, "Wyoming is the smallest state after Rhode Island. Madame Atomos attacked Rhode Island in January 1967 and won an unprecedented victory. However, that state is only 37 miles wide and 48 miles long and Madame Atomos ran out of room to move at will. Here in Wyoming she'll have a field day."

Smith frowned. "What you're telling us is not very reassuring, Mie. Until now, after losing her super powers, Madame Atomos has been forced to lose herself in the crowd. In case of an emergency this allowed her to escape more easily. Showing up out in the open marks a change in her method that doesn't look good to me."

Akamatsu turned to him and said simply, "Motor-brain?"

"No. Wyatt was sure that no suspicious device had been found in the dead animals' remains. Now, we all know that a motor-brain is stuck in the subject's skull and can't escape a serious examination. There's something else, but what?"

The plane started its descent, flew over Casper and landed in the airport to the west of the city. When the Befforts and Akamatsu stepped off the plane, they were immediately led to a police car that brought them to the headquarters in Casper where Wyatt was waiting for them. Even though he had never seen them, he recognized the Befforts and Akamatsu right away since they looked exactly like he thought they would, not at all like the really bad pictures in the newspapers. This was not surprising because in order to fool any would-be observers from the Atomos Organization, J.E.E. had never given the papers photographs of the three crack agents.

After the usual introductions, Smith asked, "Have you made any progress since last night's alarm?"

Wyatt shook his head. "Not an inch. Some veterinarians are still examining the animals killed by the police patrols, but so far the results are all negative."

His face looked like papier-mâché for want of sleep and discouragement was written all over his drawn and pale features. He added, "On reading over my Atomos file, I became certain that the animals are being controlled by a motor-brain and the report I sent to Washington via Cheyenne is of value only if we can confirm it. But now I'm sure of anything anymore."

Beffort offered him a cigarette and said, "I didn't read your report. You want to tell us everything from the start?"

Wyatt did so, narrating the events since officer Edwards discovered the open window in the back of the Doubrough house. Beffort listened without interrupting him. He knew the facts from the radio and the newspapers, but while listening to Wyatt tell them, he realized that the press had embellished freely.

When Wyatt finished, there was a moment of silence, which Akamatsu broke by declaring, "In my opinion we are definitely in the middle of a new Atomos offensive. The parrot's behavior is significant."

"And the absence of motor-brains, Yosho?" Mie questioned.

"That's a problem," the Japanese admitted. He turned to Chief Wyatt, "Has anyone thought of using a Geiger counter?"

Wyatt straightened up. Smith and Mie stared at Yosho with a touch of astonishment.

Akamatsu explained, "If Madame Atomos isn't controlling the animals with her famous motor-brain, it's logical to conclude that she's using a different system. Now, considering what we know about her, we should be considering the worst possible outcome. I mean that she's found a way to domesticate atoms!"

"Good God!" Wyatt swore. "I hope you're wrong!"

"I hope so, too," Akamatsu said sincerely, "and nothing could be simpler than to check it out. Let's get a Geiger counter and head over to train it on the dead dogs killed last night. Even if the radiation has weakened in the meantime, there will still be enough for us to get some idea about it."

Two minutes later they left Wyatt's office, not a single one of them smiling. In Madame Atomos' arsenal nothing was more terrifying than domesticated atoms!

Just as the group was leaving police headquarters, the little Japanese man working for Madame Atomos had just finished setting up the final phase of Operation Engineers. Because of the measures taken by the police following the night's events, the hideous little man was forced to drop almost all the animals off near their homes.

It was forbidden for anyone to let dogs and cats wander around freely in Casper. Every animal caught "rambling" would be killed on sight.

Therefore, the Japanese man had to turn into a delivery man, taking risks that Madame Atomos would certainly have refused if she had known about it. Unfortunately Madame Atomos did not have the ability to be in all places at once so she could not oversee her Casper agent and at the same time make sure everything went smoothly with her action in Washington...

In his big black car the Japanese man cruised around Casper from east to west and north to south, making several trips because all the animals could not fit in his car without attracting attention. He finally managed to drop off the last animal around his owners' house without being spotted. At least so he thought.

Afterward he went back to Children's Home, parked his car, entered the office and started working his transmitter with six antennas. Of all the pets he had only Royal, Gib and the Chapins' monkey who were unusable for the moment after already completely their missions. Soon, in less than ten minutes, the other engineers in

Casper would give up the ghost, except for Jim Freemont whose parrot was dead.

The problem was that when you have a boss like Madame Atomos and the slightest bit of success, you think the rest of humanity are a bunch of idiots. The little Japanese thought he only had to push a button to cause a catastrophe, but just as he was thinking this, all the animals he had dropped off were already in the hands of the police.

The gasman was telling Chief Wyatt, "I don't know if he was Japanese or Chinese, but I'm sure he was yellow. He stopped his car here, opened the door and the dog jumped out. Since I knew the mutt had disappeared 15 days ago, I was surprised and never thought of noting down the license plate. All I can tell you is that it was a big black Chevrolet..."

"Can you describe the Asian?" Smith Beffort asked.

The man squinted in concentration. "You know, he was sitting behind the wheel and I only glimpsed his face. Then he sped off."

"Was he older?"

"No, I think he must have been around 30."

"Wearing glasses?"

"No, no glasses... but yeah, he had a hat and was not very pretty."

"Who? The guy or the hat?" Wyatt asked.

"The guy."

That was all. The gasman had not been working. When the car stopped he was mowing his lawn and given the circumstances he had just given a remarkable eyewitness account. Wyatt got the description of the mysterious Asian circulating in all the police stations in Casper and the environs, then he took the Befforts and

Akamatsu to the pound. They had an unpleasant surprise awaiting them.

A few minutes after being captured the animals went into a mad rage and died. "A kind of epileptic fit," one the veterinarians explained. "The amazing thing is that all the animals died at the same second!"

"Have you determined the cause of death?" Smith Beffort asked.

"A team is on it as we speak. If you want to wait, I can tell you in a little while."

As he left Wyatt said, "Exactly like the parrot at the Freemonts! You don't find it astounding?"

Beffort calmly lit a cigarette. "Since I found out about the Japanese in the black Chevy, nothing can surprise me anymore. It's obvious that this guy is working for Madame Atomos. Apparently he brought all the animals home. The operation took him around 45 minutes and if we'd known what he was doing, he'd probably have been caught during his last delivery. All we needed to do was to stake out the houses with engineers."

Wyatt felt personally targeted and defended himself, "If it weren't for last night's events, the we would have done it. I thought the attacks against the engineers had stopped."

"No need to apologize," Beffort advised, "because anybody could have been taken in. You know that Madame Atomos would have been incapacitated a long time ago if we could have anticipated her actions. Just now we thought that she was using domesticated atoms and thanks to a Geiger counter we know that this is not the case. With domesticated atoms and motor-brains eliminated, what's left? We have no idea so we have to wait for Madame Atomos to show her hand. Look, Wyatt, fighting this woman is the worst thing in the world!"

He knew what he was talking about, having brushed death 100 times in his battle against Madame Atomos and her different, always dangerous, organizations. The worried faces of his wife and Akamatsu were sure proof of the gravity of the situation. Wyatt felt discouraged. So far he had not really comprehended the terrible threat that loomed over Casper. Reducing everything down to the animals, his vision had, in a way, been distorted, grotesquely minimizing the risks by envisaging them as claws and fangs. Now he understood that Madame Atomos was controlling these claws and fangs and the danger took on a whole other dimension.

The door of the laboratory opened and broke off his reveries. The veterinarian appeared, stepped toward the group and said, "Cerebral hemorrhage!"

"In all the animals?" Smith Beffort asked.

The veterinarian nodded gravely. "All of them. I don't have to tell you that none of us understands it, right?"

"Exactly like the Freemonts' parrot," Chief Wyatt repeated, obsessed by the idea.

Akamatsu had a wicked little laugh, then shouted, "I want to see these animals. I'm no veterinarian, but I'd take a step back if I were you. Cerebral hemorrhage! You say it like it's normal and you tell us you can't understand it even before you start trying to! How could such an attack strike 26 animals, apparently in good health, all at the same time? If they were men, your reaction would be far different, wouldn't it? Well, I…"

"Calm down, Yosho!" Beffort cut him off.

Akamatsu bit his lip, but stayed quiet. Since he had held Madame Atomos in his arms—aka Icho Fuji at the time and for the occasion—and since she had tried to atomize him, he thought of nothing but strangling her, slowly, for a long time, over and over again because a single death, short and quick, seemed too kind for such a criminal.

One death for Bob Beffort, one death for Dr. Soblen, thousands of deaths for the thousands of Americans struck down or atomized or disintegrated...

Yosho Akamatsu hated Madame Atomos with a passion because he had loved her passionately in her new skin disguised as a Japanese journalist called Icho Fuji. He killed her every night, in his nightmares, and cried afterwards over her corpse.

It terrified Yosho. He was sure of his hatred, but not of his love.

"We don't need to supervise your examinations," Smith Beffort told the veterinarian who was traumatized by Akamatsu's unjustified reproach. "Let's sit down and have a talk."

Forcing himself to stay friendly and diffuse the situation, he invited rather than ordered. The veterinarian sat down. Mie smiled at him and since Akamatsu stayed in the background, the doctor instantly loosened up.

"What is a cerebral hemorrhage?" Beffort asked.

"First of all, of course, it's an internal hemorrhage where the blood spreads through a natural cavity. There are three types. An arterial hemorrhage that presents itself as red blood, gushing forth in spurts. The venous hemorrhage is black blood that leaks out continually. And the capillary hemorrhage, often circular, meaning it covers the whole surface by seeping out. Am I clear?"

"Like crystal," Smith said. "Continue."

"In these 26 animals our inability to understand comes from the fact that it's impossible for us to determine what kind of hemorrhage killed them. To be fair, I have to tell you that each animal's brain has been turned to mush. Ach! You see?"

Smith saw nothing at all and said so. The veterinarian leaned forward, like he was trying to convince him, and specified, "In simple language, the animals look like their brains were suddenly smashed in. A blow that the skull could have survived if…"

"Let's not digress," Beffort interrupted. "Regardless of how you feel, we can't lose touch with reality. Knowing that every animal was captured at home after the owner called to tell us they had returned and that every animal was brought here with utmost care, we know that there were no blows or shocks."

The vet nodded.

"But," Smith continued, "in spite of all this, appearances betray us and the organs really do seem to have experienced a trauma. How can you turn the brain of an animal to mush without touching it directly?"

The vet said nothing and no one tried to answer for him.

Smith stood up. "That's the problem we have to solve before everything else." He let a moment of silence drift by and added, "But we're going to waste a lot of time trying to find the solution and I think it'd be useless to sit around thinking about it when no one knows anything about it. Wyatt, get your men on the move. Yosho, call Owen Bernitz and tell him to mobilize the members of the Green Dragon Force. Me, I'll call Evans to get in touch with Witter, Hyde, Stone, and the rest. Our goal: nab the little, "not very pretty" Japanese who's driving a big black Chevrolet!"

Chapter VI

Shibuki knew very quickly that he had been thwarted because the 26 control lights on his transmitter went out when he sent the signal for action. There was only one possible explanation, but for some reason that Shibuki did not know, the 26 animals with super-minibrains had been put out of service from answering the transmissions from the device invented by Dr. Miwa.

Since he had started working for Madame Atomos this was the first time that Shibuki faced such a situation. Until now, except for the incident with the Freemonts' parrot, everything had gone according to plan.

Sorrow! Shibuki was like a driver with a broken car and knowing nothing about engines. For a good fifteen minutes, he kept pushing buttons on his device. Even though he knew that each super-minibrain was self-destructing, he kept trying, just to see…

He saw nothing. The transmitter stayed dark, silent, inert, without a single light blinking and Shibuki gave up. Operation Engineers had failed.

A different man would certainly have thought about his own safety because it was obvious that Madame Atomos' little beasties had been stopped by a superior force, most likely by the police or one of its sections. But Shibuki, even though small and hideously ugly, had been conditioned to have no fear. Under the leadership of Isadori, the giant servant-lover of Madame Atomos, Shibuki had gone through months of grueling training like a kamikaze, a samurai, following the old Japanese traditions. He was prepared to risk his life, to perform harakiri, to swallow his tongue or cut his wrists…

In brief, Shibuki was not a little joke because what he could do to himself, he was, of course, ready to do to others without batting an eyelid.

However, for the moment, he was in Casper with a specific goal and it was no time for showing off his judo or karate. In fact, Shibuki's mission was to attract the attention of the Americans to this part of Wyoming while performing the final trials of the super-minibrain before using it on humans. To execute this remarkable and interesting experiment, Shibuki had received a certain number of devices that he needed to use.

He turned off the transmitter with six antennas, put it in his jacket, donned his hat and loaded his false camera with 50 super-minibrains. After that he turned off the office light, close the door on Royal, Gib and the Chapins' monkey, then crossed the yard. For a few seconds he debated whether to drive his car and finally decided to take a taxi. It was not out of caution but a question of convenience. While the cabbie was driving Shibuki could concentrate on targeting his subjects and shooting them. Serial work...

A shadow among shadows, clownish but extremely dangerous, Shibuki snuck along the wall of the factory, snuck into the street and reached the busiest intersection of Children's Home. He politely hailed a taxi and politely asked the driver to cruise around Casper, as he wanted to visit it at night. The cab took off and for more than just appearances Shibuki screwed a flash onto his camera. Being a good sport, the cabbie played tour guide, choosing the most interesting route and recounting the history of Casper. Hideously ugly, but smiling, Shibuki nodded, squinting his already squinty eyes between his high chin and low forehead, which gave his face the look of a deflated ball.

Though his eyelids were almost closed, his eye remained very sharp, taking everything in, but it saw not a single dog on the deserted sidewalks. Right away this nocturnal expedition was proving particularly fruitless. Then the darkness was pierced by a garland of lights. Shibuki saw a circus tent, heard music and applause.

"What's that?" he wheezed.

"The Pangani Circus," the cabbie answered.

Circus equals animals!

"Stop," Shibuki smiled. "I'm going to the circus."

He paid the fare, got out and went to buy a ticket. An usher led him to a seat on the edge of the ring. He sat next to a kid who was chewing his gum excitedly, his wide eyes trained on the trapeze artists. Shibuki adjusted his camera and laid it in his knock-kneed lap.

Over the course of the evening Shibuki "photographed" 12 horses, six elephants, 10 Bengal tigers, four brown and five white bears, all during the show. During the intermission the Japanese visited the cages and photographed four gorillas, three black panthers, two lions and their lionesses, a python and by mistake an old, toothless puma who could, even when driven mad, do nothing but gum oats in its gummy jaws.

Shibuki had graduated from little pets to big game and was thereby overstepping the framework laid out by Madame Atomos, he knew, but he told himself it was excusable because done in good faith. Then out of novice curiosity, he was eager to know what effect the super-minibrains would have on the elephants. He left the circus and took another taxi back to Children's Home. He had noted when the tigers would be in the ring: 10:30 to 11:30 pm...

On the same night, while Shibuki was watching the Pangani circus, the police and the FBI were slowly checking on the male Asians who lived permanently or temporarily in Casper. As always at the start of a hunt, the job of the trackers was far more complicated than that of the prey. One cannot think of everything or have eyes everywhere. They were searching for a big black Chevrolet being driven by a Japanese man who was not very pretty and wore a hat, which meant that Shibuki ran into no trouble on his way home.

Moreover, on Smith Beffort's orders, the search was carried out discreetly, without using the police, in order not to alert the Japanese or his fearsome boss. To move ahead, Smith was waiting for the Green Dragon Force, a veritable mobile army, with its 300 men, its radio cars, its paralyzing rifles, a mobile dispatch for instant contact and, above all, Beffort's private car: an armored Chevrolet Malibu with bullet-proof windows, four machine guns and two paralyzing cannons, all controlled by an electronic trigger. Puncture-proof tires, an unsinkable chassis, etc. The Malibu was like a combat tank able to reach almost 200 miles an hour, easy to handle and practically indestructible.

Therefore, while waiting for his armada to land, Smith preferred to walk on tiptoes. Casper went on like it was nothing at all. There were no roadblocks, no roundups and cops in uniform went on their beats without looking unusually suspicious or aggressive.

At the same time, in silence, teams of two or three plainclothes officers visited the hotels, boarding houses and apartment buildings. The city was quickly combed and on Tuesday at 9 am Chief Wyatt gave Beffort a negative report.

"It's to be expected," Beffort said. "The members of the Atomos Organization are generally not choirboys but they know how to lay low. Our man has obviously chosen to stay in a place where the police have no reason to look."

"There's not many," Wyatt objected, knowing his city well. "Outside of the hotels, boarding houses and apartments, there's only the campgrounds."

Beffort stared at him with sudden interest. "You may have something there, Wyatt! Our man keeping his HQ in a camper wouldn't surprise me!"

Wyatt shook his head. "Nothing doing. Before coming here I personally checked the registrar of the campground's manager. He hasn't had an Asian there for months and there's no black Chevy. But I have another idea to suggest."

"Go on," Beffort offered.

Wyatt cleared his throat, stalling. He himself found his idea far-fetched and wondered how Beffort would take it.

"Speak up, pal," Beffort said, "and keep in mind that I wouldn't keel over if you told me that Madame Atomos was hiding in your house disguised as your maid. When it dealing with her, the most ludicrous speculation becomes reasonable. So?"

Wyatt sat down and said, "Maybe it has nothing to do with the Japanese guy we're looking for, but when I was doing my checks I noted that the register called *Foreign Visitors* in Casper had 653 extra names grouped under the title *Pangani Circus*."

A little light flashed in Beffort's eyes, encouraging Wyatt to continue.

"There's nothing weird about that," he said. "The Pangani Circus plants its tent in Casper every year at the same time and I wouldn't have paid it any attention if the date of its arrival hadn't been just 48 hours before the death of Mrs. Doubrough and her tenants. What's more, when I looked at the names of the artists, musicians and personnel, I noticed four that were typically Japanese. They're four men on the flying trapeze whom the posters call *Omona*, which is only a stage name since the four of them are not related. There you go."

"Damn!" Smith shouted, "why didn't you tell me this n earlier?"

Wyatt shrugged. "Just because Royal, Mrs. Doubrough's cat, had been taken by our Japanese around a month before the circus got to town. Then the dog Gib followed. Then there was the Chapins' monkey. In fact, all the animals disappeared before the circus arrived. If they hadn't shown up again after the circus came, it wouldn't have been important at all."

Wyatt's reasoning was off base, but of course Beffort could not know it. Madame Atomos had more than one ace up her sleeve. To slip in a commando team of the new Atomos Organization as an act in the Pangani Circus was right up her alley.

"The idea deserves to be investigated," Beffort said. "Royal, Gib and the other animals were certainly nabbed before the circus set up tent in Casper, but Madame Atomos could have seen to this easily. I imagine that the itinerary of a circus is determined beforehand, at the start of the season, and the trips are all planned out to the slightest detail... Come on, Wyatt, let's go get a closer look at the mugs of these Omonas!"

It was a waste of time, in the end, or almost since from then on the police and the FBI had their eye on the Pangani Circus.

Stubborn as a mule and tenacious as a grappling hook, Yosho Akamatsu entered the pound's laboratory right when Wyatt and Beffort were heading out to the Omonas and maybe to the "not very pretty" Japanese.

Yosho had everything he needed in mind. For him, Madame Atomos had simply made a new kind of motor-brain and the fact that the animals had died of a cerebral hemorrhage was due to chance. Akamatsu followed his nose, which was itching to do something, got in to see the veterinarian whom he had pushed around a little the day before and immediately held out his hand to clear the air. He said, "Doctor, I'm bothered by these brains reduced to mush."

"Don't worry, you're not the only one. I didn't get any shuteye last night and my colleagues have sworn not to sleep tonight. To be frank, I'm pretty glad to see you here. You were hard on me, but it only forced me to think more about it. Now I'm sure that these animals did not die of a natural hemorrhage."

Akamatsu breathed deeply. He had been afraid of hitting a brick wall when he met the civil servant and was more than pleased to find that he had beat him to the sensational deductions that he had mind.

The veterinarian continued, "Yesterday I told Smith Beffort that the hemorrhage had certainly been caused by a shock. I talked about hitting a wall. Today, my opinion has changed. I've given up the wall. I hold to the shock but with a twist: it was triggered internally, simultaneously causing the three kinds of hemorrhaging that I mentioned yesterday."

Akamatsu sat on the edge of a desk. "An internal shock… is that common?"

"Yes, although the word isn't appropriate in this circumstance. When there's a hemorrhage, we talk about a ruptured artery or vein or capillary tissue. Here we have all three hemorrhages together at the same time, but I still think we can use 'shock' to describe it."

Akamatsu furrowed his brow and offered, "Would 'eruption' fit better?"

The vet smiled. "If you'd like, but doesn't an eruption always follow a shock?"

"Okay. How about an explosion?"

"I'm sorry, but medically speaking it doesn't exist."

Akamatsu understood that he was not out of the woods yet for two simple reasons. Firstly, he himself did not know what he was looking for. Secondly, the doctor, even though recognizing that these were not natural hemorrhages, was not informed enough about the Atomos methods to start taking wild guesses.

Then, against all expectations the veterinarian asked, "Why did you mention an explosion?"

Strangely this had bothered him. He must have thought of it vaguely, without really believing it, since it was outside of his medical field, and Akamatsu's proposition came just in time to raise a doubt.

"Do you know what a motor-brain is?" Yosho asked.

"How could I not? The papers talked enough about the destruction they wrought during the first attacks of Madame Atomos against our country."

Akamatsu nodded. "Let's go see the animal remains. I'll tell you what I have in mind when we're both on the same wavelength."

Slowly but surely Akamatsu was heading in the right direction.

Around 10:30 a Cadillac entered Casper and drove toward the residential area of Yellowstone where the black driver stopped before a property protected by high, thick hedges and flashed his headlights. Ten seconds later the gate opened and then closed automatically after the Cadillac went through. The car followed a winding driveway into a yard where an imposing structure was built, unseen from the road and stopped at the foot of a double spiral stairway. The black driver got out, opened the back door and a woman in mourning appeared, her face covered by a veil.

The woman walked up the stairway without waiting for the other man climbing out of the back seat, but she stopped before the front door. The man, an Asian giant, also dressed in mourning, stepped in front of her and opened the door. The woman entered. The man followed and closed the door at the same time as the Cadillac drove around the building and disappeared.

The scene transpired very quickly, without a wrong move, and even an observer in the know could not have recognized Madame Atomos as the woman in black. Madame Atomos who had taken care of business in Washington and come back to personally direct the operations in Casper. Shibuki was stepping down. Madame Atomos and Isadori were taking over, but a little late because a big mistake had been made by their predecessor.

Carried away by his zeal, Shibuki had not thought about the mess an elephant makes...

Chapter VII

Smith Beffort and Wyatt did not need much time to be absolutely certain that the Omonas could not be working for Madame Atomos. In fact, their work was so hard and so dangerous that they had to devote every minute of their lives to it.

"When you're on the flying trapeze," Holburn, the circus manager concluded, "everything else takes a back seat. No alcohol, to tobacco, no women. Practice and rest. Besides, the Omonas have been with us for five years and nobody has anything to complain about. By the way, what exactly are you looking for?"

Smith smiled. "Nothing special, I assure you. It's just a routine check."

As soon as he saw the Omonas he knew that none of them was the "not very pretty" Japanese described by the gasman. Once he was certain, there was no need to investigate further unless he wanted to do the same for every Japanese living in or around Casper, then all over Wyoming and the rest of the United States.

Intrigued, Holburn asked, "This routine check is only done on the colored folk in my troupe?"

"Not the colored fold," Beffort corrected, "just the Japanese. Truthfully, we're looking for an ugly little Japanese man wearing a hat and driving a big black Chevrolet. Don't tell me you have such a character here..."

"No," the manager smiled, "but unless it's a coincidence, a guy like that was at the show last night. We noticed him for three reasons. One: he was really, really ugly. Two: he was sitting in the front row. And three: he wouldn't stop taking pictures of the acts, especially the animals. Weird, isn't it?"

Beffort and Wyatt glanced at each other.

"If that was him," Wyatt sighed, "it would be truly miraculous. But why not? Say, Mr. Holburn, was he really so remarkable?"

"You know, when a guy clicks his flash 50 times over the course of an evening, he doesn't blend into the crowd so easily. To tell you the truth, we all thought he was a reporter from the local rag."

"At *The Star*," Wyatt informed him, "there are no Japanese. And you know perfectly well that a reporter doesn't spend all night taking pictures. Besides, he would have arranged to get in without paying."

Beffort, who looked anxious for a moment, spoke up, "Don't you find it strange that this guy was taking pictures mainly of the animals? If he was an amateur photographer of animals, the choice at the Casper zoo would have been a lot better, right?"

"At the zoo," Holburn answered, "you don't see an elephant balancing on a ball or a tiger walking over two men. This guy didn't do anything out of the ordinary, really. But why are you looking for him?"

Beffort was expecting this question. "We suspect him of being responsible for the events that have happened here in Casper over the past week. By the way, Mr. Holburn, are you animals always in such good health, always so calm?"

The manager's face turned a little gray. "What are you insinuating?"

"I'm not insinuating anything. Chief Wyatt and I came to check on the Omonas. By chance you told us that a Japanese man fitting our description was at the show last night. Moreover, you said that he took 50 pictures of your animals. Knowing what we know, there's good reason to be a little worried, don't you think?"

Holburn wiped his forehead. Normally he was a man of action, but at the moment he obviously did not know what to do.

"In your place," Beffort advised, "I'd give my animals a check up."

Holburn nodded, hefted his bulk and walked to the door of his office wagon. "Sam!" he yelled. "Get over here!" Without waiting for an answer, he sat back down in front of his visitors, pushed a box of cigars toward them and said, "Even if the Japanese was the one you're hunting, I don't see what he could do to our animals with a simple camera. He didn't leave his seat except during the intermission and besides he couldn't get any closer than 10 feet to an animal. With that in mind…"

"I'm not going to repeat myself," Beffort cut in. "We're not sure of anything but we think you should check it out, so that's what we're telling you. Who's Sam?"

"My assistant. Look, here he is."

A solidly built man climbed the steps to the wagon, knocked on the door and entered at Holburn's word. The latter immediately asked, "How are the animals this morning, Sam?"

"Like always, boss. Why?"

Holburn pointed at Beffort and Wyatt. "These gentlemen belong to the Casper Veterinarian Department and think the sickness that affected the dogs on Sunday night is contagious. The big cats aren't nervous?"

Sam shook his head. "No. I think they're even calmer than usual."

"Nothing special to report?"

"Nothing."

"Okay, you can get back to work." Sam left and Holburn said with relief, "There you go. A false alarm."

Beffort and Wyatt stood up. Wyatt held out a card and offered, "Keep a careful watch, Mr. Holburn, and if anything happens, call this number."

"Will do."

"By the way," Beffort asked, "what time does your show start?"

"8:45."

"Last night you noticed this Japanese guy. I guess it was exceptional but if you could tell me what time he arrived, you'll get a standing ovation. Think about it. It's important and I'll tell you why. Last night, starting at 8:30 the police were all over the streets of Casper looking for this black Chevy that our suspect drove. It was a failure, which makes sense if the guy came on foot or drove here before 8:30. But unbelievable and inexcusable if this Chevy was driving around under our noses without being stopped. Plus, if we know what time he got to your show, we'll have precise questions for the taxis. Do you think you can tell us?"

"Not me personally," Holburn said straight off, "but the ushers or cashier should remember. The guy was in section 3…" He tried to remember and finally said, "If I'm not mistaken it was Jenny, the horse rider, who took care of that section. Let' see."

This time he pushed a button on the interphone, got someone on the other end and asked for Jenny to come to his office. After the other assured him that she would be there in a few minutes, Holburn relit his cigar.

Wyatt took the opportunity to ask, "Are all the artists also ushers for you?"

"I didn't start it," Holburn answered. "It's like that with all the traveling circuses. It cuts down on personnel and therefore the number of beds and wagons. And the tips make up a pretty good chunk of the show's income. The cashier sells the tickets, takes care of the accounting and sometimes even helps out in the kitchen. We work as a team here, Mr. Wyatt. Come tonight and you'll see me as ringmaster or selling tickets if we need it. The big circus family is not an empty word!"

He loved his work, his traveling companions and his animals. Without all this, his life would no doubt be meaningless. In the meantime Jenny showed up behind the door. Holburn opened it for her, purposefully neglected to announce the profession of his visitors and asked right away, "Do you remember that Japanese photographer, Jenny?"

The young lady nodded. "Sure. He didn't stop snapping pictures during my entire act and the horses got nervous. You know, I'm sure he got close-ups of all dozen of my horses."

"Besides that," Holburn said, "could you say if he got here before the show started?"

"No, he didn't. He came later, during the Omonas number. I remember perfectly because he got the last ringside seat and that's all I was waiting for so I get backstage. I know the Japanese like taking pictures, but this guy was something else!"

Holburn thanked her and the young lady left.

"What time do the Omonas come on?" Smith asked.

"9:15 sharp."

Beffort and Wyatt left Holburn to his work. They had learned enough to start looking for the Japanese photographer. They just had to see if this man was the same one driving the Chevrolet.

In the middle of the afternoon, Wyatt and Beffort had questioned 16 cabbies to no avail. The 17th lived on Boxelder Street. His name was Camden and according the cab company's records he worked at night. When they found him at home, in pajamas, unshaven and eating, they immediately asked him the question.

Camden answered without hesitation. "Come on, of course I remember him! We went on a big tourist ride before I dropped him at the edge of town to go to the circus. Yeah, he had some mug on him! Sure, he was lugging around a big camera with a flash, but he didn't use it even once during our trip. All he did was look at the sidewalks!"

"Where did you pick him up?" Wyatt asked.

"On a corner in Children's Home. If you want my opinion, the guy was at the circus because he couldn't find any girls walking the streets."

Camden had the right to think so and neither Wyatt nor Beffort tried to stop him. All the more so since without proof to the contrary he might just be right.

Outside, Wyatt said, "I feel like we're getting closer and closer."

"This thing with the sidewalks, eh?"

"Of course! The tourist trip was only an excuse to use his big camera and I'm sure our Japanese was searching for a few animals to 'work on'!"

Beffort laughed. "Nice phrase, but I wonder how close to reality it is."

"Yeah, unless that camera wasn't made to take photos. Actually, the only big camera I know of is a Polaroid, but you can't take 50 pictures with it. Every picture develops automatically in the minute after…"

"Enough! I agree with you. Our ugly little Japanese is not in Casper to take photos, we know that. His camera is used for some very specific purpose, seeing that he's always carrying it around, but what? Radio wave emissions that paralyze the will? Don't smile, Wyatt, because just such a device—I mean a wave transmitter—was indeed part of the Atomos arsenal."

"I'm smiling because the range of weapons we could think of is too vast. From a motor-brain to waves paralyzing the will, from hypnotism to lethal injections, not to speak of what Madame Atomos might have created lately. We have an assortment…"

"Hold on!" Beffort cut in. "Didn't you tell me that the Freemonts' parrot was missing a few feathers on its head?"

"Exactly. Except it was so unnoticeable that you could only see it up close."

"Really up close?"

"Yes. Without Jim Freemont, I never would have noticed."

"In your opinion, Wyatt, could it have been the result of an injection? Stay calm because you put the idea in my head. In fact, Madame Atomos has already tried all kinds of things except this lethal injection that you just invented out of the blue. Not bad!"

I'm flattered," Wyatt joked. "But how could a shot make a bird's feathers fall out?"

"Okay. Find whatever plucked the parrot's skull and I'll bite! What time is it?"

He had changed the subject in a flash because he was starting to worry about not hearing from Owen Bernitz or anyone else from the Green Dragon Force. Usually a very short time passed between a call to James Edward Evans and the arrival of one of Owen's men.

"Almost 4:30," Wyatt said. "My car's here. Where do you want to go?"

"Back to headquarters. We have to start combing Children's Home where our ugly Japanese hailed a cab. He must be stowed away there with his phony camera. I'd love to catch him in his hideout."

Wyatt climbed into his car, started the engine and took off after Beffort was in the passenger seat. Everyone at headquarters was bustling around, but no one had anything to say about the "not very pretty" Japanese who was still the object of a very active search. Wyatt got the wheels rolling by giving the extra details about the man and directing the search parties to the corner in Children's Home.

In the meantime Beffort found Mie and Akamatsu in Chief Wyatt's office. Mie was in charge of coordinating the movements of the Green Dragon Force and was therefore sitting by the telephone all morning, but when Smith asked her about them, she answered, "No, Owen Bernitz hasn't called. Neither has Ralph Stutton, Eddie Witter or Charlie Hyde. In desperation I called Evans. I could only get his secretary who said she knew nothing about it. I don't know what J.E.E. is cooking up, Smith, but it all smells fishy to me."

Beffort turned thoughtful. "Have you tried to contact Owen?"

"No! You know very well that Evans takes care of that. Just because he's not in his office, I'm not going to go over his head and call the Green Dragon HQ directly."

"It's almost five o'clock," Beffort looked at his watch. "The Green Dragon commando teams should have been in Casper at 9 am! To hell with hurting Evans' feelings, Mie! Call Washington back immediately! If Evans doesn't answer, skip the middleman and call St. Louis directly. Go!"

While she dialed Evans' number Mie told Beffort, "You're going to upset him, Smith."

"Could be, but I'm pressed for time. The Japanese guy we're looking for was spotted in the Children's Home area and we might just get our hands on him very soon. As soon as Madame Atomos finds out that one of her acolytes has been collared, she's going to attack full force and I'll need all the men of the Green Dragon. And don't forget that I listen to Evans out of politeness, Mie! I have more authority than he does, more than the field supervisors of New York, Chicago and Los Angeles put together!"

Mie nodded and turned around. Akamatsu smirked.

When Smith Beffort flew off the handle for no good reason, it meant that he was on edge and that the Atomos Organization, if not Madame Atomos herself, better watch their step.

Chapter VIII

The secretary of J.E.E. said that her boss had not come back and she did not know when he would—she knew nothing at all. Like hitting a wall of silence there was nothing more to do. Smith grabbed the phone and shouted, "Listen, Ms. Scott, you can tell his wife these stories, but not me! I talked to Evans last night. He was supposed to call St. Louis! Did he do it, yes or no?"

"I don't know, Mr. Beffort..."

"Damn! You're his secretary! Where's Evans right now?"

"I think he's at a conference at the Justice Department."

"You think! Don't you know?"

"Uh..."

Smith suddenly calmed down. He felt like something was screwy in Washington and Ms. Scott seemed caught between a rock and a hard place. Evans must have given her specific instructions not to be disturbed, which was so unusual for this poor girl that she did not know how to react. Smith decided not to panic her by pushing her into a corner.

"Okay," he spoke in a soothing voice. "Let's forget about it. If Evans is in a conference, he'll be back before long. In fact, Ms. Scott, what's your impression of him lately."

"Excuse me?"

"Does he seem all right? Don't be shy, we're not talking business anymore. The last time I spoke to Evans he seemed tired to me, worn out, run down. Don't you think?"

"To tell you the truth, Mr. Beffort, the boss seems to me to have aged suddenly. I wouldn't dare say such a thing if you hadn't asked, but the fact is that J.E.E. is out of sorts."

The floodgates had opened and Smith listened without interrupting.

"... he arrives late, shuts himself in his office, walks around in a daze. For four days he's made me cancel the meetings that he called himself and urgent documents are sitting in his wastebasket. Are you listening to me?"

"Go on, Ms. Scott. I'm listening."

"To be perfectly frank, I think he's on the verge of a nervous breakdown. This morning he just drifted by. His tie was crooked, one of his laces was undone and his shoes were scuffed! When you know how meticulous and careful he always is to be impeccably dressed, it was shocking!"

Beffort was not sorry for the time lost on the telephone. Only a secretary who had worked for a long time for the same boss could have noticed such minute details of dress. A crooked tie, an undone lace, scuffed shoes... it was nothing, but for James Edward Evans, director of the Federal Bureau of Investigation and always dressed to the nines, it took on tremendous significance.

"Thanks for confiding in me, Ms. Scott. Tell Evans, if he comes back to the office, that I'll call back tonight."

"Got it. What I just told you..."

"Stays between us," Smith assured her. "Don't worry."

He hung up and turned to face Mie and Yosho who had heard everything through the speaker phone. "What do you think about that?" he asked.

Akamatsu did not give his opinion, but Mie said, "J.E.E. is tired, that's all. When he sees a doctor, he'll prescribe a tranquilizer and a couple of weeks of rest. I'll call St. Louis?"

"Go on. We're going to find out just how out of whack Evans really is."

Mie dialed a number, got a priority line and was talking to Owen Bernitz in less than three minutes. "Hold the line, Owen, I'll pass you to my husband."

Smith took the phone. "Hello, Owen! What's new?" he opened with.

"Nothing, boss. Everything's okay here. Why?"

"No news from J.E.E.?"

"No... Say, is there trouble brewing?"

Smith felt a nerve cause him to blink as a warning signal. Owen was dumbfounded, Evans had dropped the ball so completely that the Green Dragon Force had still not even taken off from its secret base in St. Louis, Missouri. In the history of the anti-Atomos fight, this was the first time that such a serious incident of this kind had happened.

Smith kept his pessimistic thoughts and vague fears to himself and asked, "How long will it take for you to get all your men, weapons and baggage to Casper, Wyoming?"

Bernitz whistled softly. There was the sound of paper rustling, probably a roadmap unfolding, then Owen said, "If it's an emergency, Ben Brady and his team can be in Casper in two hours, but the better part of the Green Dragons won't make it before two or three in the morning."

"Okay! Get Brady and men out here. Paralyzing pistols, regular clothes, immediate contact with the police headquarters directed by Chief Wyatt. My wife will be at the phones."

"Mama what's-her face?" Owen was hopeful.

"Not yet sighted," Smith responded, "but since there's a guy from her organization in the area, it won't be long before she pops up. Tell Brady to keep his men from grouping up. For now, until I give the word, we have to go easy. Okay, Owen?"

"We're on it, boss. That it?"

"That's it."

Bernitz hung up at the same time as Beffort who noticed Akamatsu's silence. He asked, "Problems, Yosho?"

"No, I'm just waiting for you to finish up the urgent business. Now if you have five minutes, I'm ready to give you some relatively important updates concerning the sudden death of the animals…"

"Cerebral hemorrhage," Smith threw out. "I know that already."

"Yes, but you don't know yet that the hemorrhage was caused by an internal explosion. Tiny metallic fragments, visible only under the microscope, were just discovered in each animal's brains and after very close examination we found marks from an injection on every animal. All of it was on a microscopic level, which explains why the vets at the pound couldn't see it in their initial exams. We still don't know why the animals were injected, but we know for a fact that they were carrying around some metal object in their brains. Does that remind you of anything, Smith?"

For a second Beffort was stiff as a board. "A motor-brain!"

"Undoubtedly a possibility, Smith. But the real problem is that Madame Atomos can now "load" a subject without needing brain surgery. Within the bounds of reason, given the undeniable fact that every animal had a shot mark, we can suppose and not be going off the deep end that the motor-brains are injectable."

"Huh?" Beffort was stunned. "Injectable. Do you realize what that means?"

Akamatsu grinned and chuckled. "Microscopic, injectable, self-destructing," he hammered out. "If Madame Atomos has any kind of projecting weapon—and I think we can trust that she does—it's possible for her to "load" an animal or a man from a distance. That means that if you barely feel the injection that shoots the motor-brain into the body, any of us could be a carrier at this very moment…"

"Be quiet!" Mie shouted, standing up. "It's monstrous!" Being the ex-Miss Atomos whose body and soul were at the service of Madame Atomos' Great Brain, she knew what she was talking about.

Akamatsu waved an apology and said, "Sorry to call up bad memories, Mie, but the situation is too serious for us not to look things in the face. Whether you like it or not, Madame Atomos can reduced us to slaves with ridiculous ease. For example, J.E.E.'s case intrigues me. He might be starting a nervous breakdown, sure, but willingly or not he started this new battle against Madame Atomos with a sabotage disguised as negligence. Thanks to him the Green Dragon Force will be in Casper two hours late."

Akamatsu stopped talking and the room fell silent. All of them were thinking of Evans and Madame Atomos' terrifying new weapon.

Finally, Beffort said, "When Madame Atomos turns her victims into robots, they turn pale and move like robots so that we can almost always spot them. Maybe she's perfected a new kind of motor-brain, but she can't keep the subject's brain from trying to reject it, causing a certain imbalance. So if James Evans really was "loaded", it's clear that his change in behavior is due to the motor-brain. Therefore, if one of us ever shows the same problems, we'll have good cause to worry. Meanwhile, to be extra sure, I propose we all get x-rays as soon as possible."

Akamatsu and Mie agreed. Of all the urgent measures that needed to be taken, this, without a shadow of a doubt, was of utmost priority.

In the Children's Home area Chief Wyatt had the sinking feeling that his men were looking for a raspberry in a strawberry patch. Certainly everything seemed to indicate that the hideous—this was progress because before they thought he was just ugly—little Japanese lived near the intersection, but if they had to go through every building with a fine-toothed comb, it would take more than a week.

In spite of this, the plainclothes detectives and small team of G-men had just launched the search with confidence. They hoped to find the car before the man. One group took the garages, another the cars parked on the street and paid lots. Wyatt and his deputy took the rest of the team to hit the closest houses.

An initial, simple method, but effective: ask the older residents if a Japanese man fitting this description is among the newer tenants... It went quick and easy but ended in utter failure.

Wyatt looked like he got up on the wrong side of the bed and his face darkened when he found out that the black Chevrolet was nowhere to be seen. "Don't tell me there's not a single black Chevy in Children's Home!" he shouted.

"There's a bunch, chief, but none of them has an Asian owner, small or ugly…"

Wyatt suppressed his disappointment and formed two-man patrols to stakeout strategic points. Even if he's hiding in a cellar, the damned Japanese would have to come out eventually!

When night fell he still had not shown and the patrols who were sweeping Casper reported nothing new. Wyatt was patient and determined, but he decided to restart everything from scratch with the interrogation of the people in the neighborhood.

It was 9 pm when a woman living on the second floor of a nearby apartment building said, "An ugly, little Japanese man? Of course I know him. For more than a month now he's been coming into the corner drugstore."

Wyatt could have slapped himself. He had thought of everything except for the usual questioning of the neighborhood stores!

At the drugstore they also remembered the Japanese very well, but they could tell him nothing more. Nevertheless, this proved that the guy lived very close to this corner in Children's Home and he probably lived alone since he did his own shopping. Therefore, his car must be parked in the area.

"Logically," Wyatt's deputy surmised, "if none of the people in these apartments have seen him on the stairs, he must live alone in a house."

Wyatt threw him a menacing look. "All the houses have been checked and the people questioned."

"So our man might be living in some abandoned dump. He does his own shopping so he must do his own cooking, which leads us to assume he's set up somewhere."

"He could eat sandwiches!" someone shouted.

"No," Wyatt denied him. "At the corner store they told us he bought a lot of rice and a fair amount of meat. Anything can be eaten raw except that. Let's get back in the saddle, boys! Objective: all the buildings that look empty, deserted, abandoned, falling down or being built! Keep an eye out for lights, smoke from chimneys, the smell of cooking, etc. You haven't eaten dinner yet, right? Well, keep your noses open! At home they always told me that an empty stomach heads straight for the taters! Go!"

In Washington James Edward Evans was acting more and more strangely. There was nothing threatening in his attitude and he was not mean, he just gave the impression of being a little drunk, sad and terribly mysterious. Around 7 pm he came back to his office. Ms. Scott had noticed that even though his lace was retied and his tie was straightened out, his shoes looked like they had just come out of a bathtub full of dust.

Evans closed the door with unusual gentleness, cast an empty look at his secretary and snuck off to his office like a man up to no good. Under other circumstances Ms. Scott would have probably found this funny, but at this moment she felt only pity mixed with a touch of fear.

"Good evening, Mr. Evans," she rattled off. "Smith Beffort called from Casper. He said he'll call back tonight."

Evans froze, lifted a hand, glanced around the room as if to make sure that no one was spying on him and said, "Very good, Ms. Scott, very good. Don't tell anyone else. We're in a tight spot here and the walls might have ears. You understand? Ah, now that I think of it, would you be kind enough to call my wife and say that I'll be coming home late tonight? I have a lot of work to do in my office, don't I?"

Ms. Scott relaxed a little. Evans was out of sorts, but his mind was still working reasonably well. "You have a lot of work," she confirmed, "and with all the meetings you missed, you're not going to see the end of it anytime soon. I can stay late if you want."

Evans thought long and hard about that, puffing up his cheeks, before he finally said, "Thanks."

He tossed that word out like he was throwing a rock in the water and Ms. Scott did not understand if it was a "thanks" yes or a "thanks" no.

"So, I'll stay?"

"No need," Evans mumbled. "You'll be alone because I'm only stopping g by. Don't ask. We're in a tight spot and the walls might have ears…" He repeated himself and looked around suspiciously.

All of sudden Ms. Scott got goose bumps, but she forced herself to ask, "What should I tell Smith Beffort if he calls?"

Evans raised both hands and slinked away. A man snowed under with responsibilities who wanted to hear nothing more! "Come on, Ms. Scott, leave Smith out of this! You know very well that I'm still at that conference at the Justice Department."

"But…"

"Don't try to understand, okay! I've got a top secret document in my briefcase and for once I have to take care of it myself. No more questions! In this old federal bureau a file marked top secret is sacred! Shush, Ms. Scott, shush!"

He left her sitting there and disappeared into his office. Ms. Scott heard drawers opening and slamming shut while Evans started humming. After a few minutes of this flurry he came out carrying a briefcase and from the bulge in his coat his secretary knew that he was armed.

Evans smiled, "Good night. See you tomorrow."

He left and foolishly Ms. Scott started crying.

Chapter IX

Naked in front of the big mirror in her room Madame Atomos licked her lips, stood on her tiptoes, arched her back and pushed out her chest. Standing in a corner Isadori admired her. A magnificent girl. A sweetie.

"When we've finished with Casper," Madame Atomos murmured softly, "I want Beffort and Akamatsu lying in the morgue... Do you think I put on a little weight in San Esteban?"

Isadori shook his head. Madame Atomos saw him through the mirror and knew from his avid eyes that she had lost none of her beauty. She turned around, swaggered up to the giant and leaned against him like leaning against a wall.

"Fondle me. It helps me think..."

He put his big hands on her ivory skin and caressed her. Madame Atomos closed her eyes and a little smile crossed her sensual lips.

"Tomorrow," she said in a luscious voice, "you'll tell the Rising Sun to go into action. They'll start with the traffic cops and security guards... Then they'll hit the civil servants, the mailmen, bus drivers, the gas and electric and phone companies... Tomorrow night Casper must be buried in darkness with no water or gas and all the public transportation paralyzed. And then we..."

She paused when Isadori stroked a sweet spot and she clenched her teeth as his hand became more insistent. She knew that he was playing her like a violin, that this was his way of dominating her, but even using all her willpower, she could never overcome her body's violent erotic needs.

Then Isadori's desire became concrete, flagrant, and Madame Atomos felt the heat, waiting for it, her flesh quivering. She swung around and embraced him. He wrapped his arms around her and bent down toward her parted lips.

"Take me!" Madame Atomos gasped, flaring her nostrils.

Isadori was a good servant. He did what his mistress asked, coldly, like a technician, suppressing his own desires to better satisfy those of his partner. Usually ferocious and authoritarian, Madame Atomos became extraordinarily submissive in the arms of a man. Isadori knew her well enough to sense the moments when the terrible woman needed domination and violence. Tonight was one of those nights and the Japanese used his strength to conquer the mock resistance of Madame Atomos who enjoyed playing the raped virgin.

All this was purely animal, but it was perfectly suited to Madame Atomos' temperament. Beaten and pawed, enslaved and treated like a whore, she finally pushed Isadori away, telling him with the cold glare in her eyes that playtime was over and he had to get out.

Another man, less familiarized, would have left. Isadori, aware of his power of persuasion, crushed her under his weight and decreed the needs of man with unfulfilled desires. Madame Atomos struggled, bit, scratched and threatened, then in a fit of rage sank into her sea of lust once again. In fact—and both of them knew it—the game had just begun…

But while Madame Atomos reveled in her debauchery, things were moving forward without her and not necessarily to her advantage. You can't be everywhere at the same time. Madame Atomos should have known this and instead of surrendering herself to bedroom acrobatics, she should have been worrying about Shibuki. But her newfound sensuality had pushed into the background everything that did not satisfy her immediate desires.

For, it was true that Shibuki was running into bad luck. The stars must have been against him because Chief Wyatt's men had zeroed in on the old factory where David Millay used to make plastic containers.

Wyatt wrinkled his nose and narrowed his eyes to get a better look at the thin strip of light that escaped from some unseen door. To have seen it from the street the deputy must have had an eagle's eye.

Wyatt strained his sight, unbelieving. "Good God! If he's really there, boys, the drinks are on me at Bully's!"

Someone let out a kind of fart with his mouth, but no one moved. They looked like statues grouped behind the gate. Wyatt stood up slowly; his face was a grey blotch in the shadows.

"Okay," he whispered. "Let's surround the shop. Careful, right? If this guy escapes, I'm sticking you all on traffic control tomorrow."

The statues came to life, sliding along the wall whose top was lined with shards of glass. In the dimly lit, deserted street, the movements only looked like furtive shadows shifting, then a quiet whistle blew, indicating that the building was surrounded. Wyatt turned his watch light on and saw the hands pointing to 10:30.

At the same time Shibuki was fiddling with the knobs and buttons on a transmitter with ten antennas. At the Pangani Circus it was time for the tigers to enter their cages... Shibuki did not want to miss it. He put on his hat, turned off the lamp and opened the door leading to the yard at the very second that Wyatt had chosen to push open the gate.

Shibuki heard the hinges creak and saw four figures step into the entrance. He knew instantly that trouble had come. He scurried along the wall and stopped behind a metal drum, glancing back into the yard. Now the grill was wide open. The four figures were in the yard, walking slowly toward the office, but there were other men outside, armed with rifles.

Shibuki backed up. A few seconds earlier and he would have been cornered in a room with only one exit and with no weapons except his hands to defend himself. But now, if he could reach the Chevrolet and the Colt Cobra in the glove compartment, he would go down fighting. Staying in the shadows, he reached the hangar where the Chevy was parked, knowing full well that they could not see it from the street. In fact, the entrance to the hangar opened parallel to the shop front so the men sitting behind the gate saw only the side.

Like a snake the Japanese slithered into the car through an open window and grabbed the Colt Cobra. He checked that it was loaded, then he waited. He did not have the jump on them, but he did have some quiet time to analyze the situation. If he did not act, they would end of finding him. He would fight it out and after fending them off for as long as his ammunition held out, he would be arrested or killed.

Shibuki had no special attachment to life. He often thought about the paradise of his ancestors, but like everyone else he still preferred to be alive and healthy than dead and buried in a cold, wet hole. He also thought of the mission ending in a kind of disaster. The transmitter, the "photo" camera and three animals carrying the super-minibrain would fall into the hands of the police. And finally Madame Atomos would know nothing about the latest developments, which might lead her to commit some grave, perhaps fatal, mistake.

After this supersonic reasoning, an idea flashed like lightning in his head: before dying, he had to warn Madame Atomos, who might be in the Yellowstone property.

Shibuki slid over to the driver's seat and reached for the key, but froze. In the midst of this total silence, an engine starting would explode like a bomb and the alerted police would open fire on the Chevrolet at first sight. 50 yards to cover before the gate. Enough to be shot 100 times!

Attentive but strangely calm Shibuki stayed frozen, but he shivered when he heard a distant rumbling. The last Oak Crest-Evansville bus going along 12th Street was stopping at the Children's Home intersection where it always left with a great deal of noise because of the hill after the turn onto Conwell Street. The Japanese's thumb hovered over the start button. The bus was his last chance.

In the yard Wyatt and his colleagues were playing Indians on the warpath. The ray of light from under the door had gone out shortly before, which was great if it meant Madame Atomos' agent was sleeping, but big trouble if he had heard the creaking gate and was waiting to ambush them, his finger itchy on the trigger of a machine gun.

Here, too, they preferred life over death…

Wyatt raised his hand and the team snuck along the wall of the workshop, stopping near their goal. Wyatt watched the door. As far as he could see in the dark, it looked like the door was shut tight, with no opening but the keyhole, so he saw no way that the Japanese could have really kept a watch on the premises. This observation made up his mind. He signaled to his three men to advance before running the last few yards to the door to meet them. Nothing moved inside the shop, but a rumbling engine could be heard from the nearby intersection. Chief Wyatt figured that this noise would drown out his own when he turned the knob. He waited a few seconds because the engine had just quieted down.

His deputy whispered, "It's the bus at the corner stop."

"Got it," Wyatt whispered back. "When it takes off, we'll go in. If the door's locked, you bust it down, Mac. And watch out! Remember that I want this guy alive."

Outside, the bus grinded into first and started rumbling off. It shifted into second as it turned onto the hill and the engine howled as it sped up to shift into third. Wyatt quickly turned the knob, pushed open the door and rushed into the dark, musty room. Someone turned on a flashlight and Wyatt saw the empty crates, a table, a gas lamp, a cook stove and a cot. In one corner were a cat, dog and monkey sleeping soundly. Against the wall stood a small, metal box, a kind of computer humming softly with all its lights blinking…

"The camera," the deputy exclaimed.

Outside, tires screeched ominously. Then shots were fired, two crashes of metal and shouting. Wyatt and his team ran out and reached the gate, which was splattered and dripping with fresh blood. Three G-men were crumpled on the sidewalk, gutted, with their brains bashed in. A squad car was already taking off down the street, its siren wailing, its light swirling through the night.

One agitated cop hollered, "The Japanese! He took off in the Chevy!"

Another car sped off. Policemen were running, gun in hand. The air smelled of gunsmoke as they walked over the spent shells.

Wyatt grabbed a man by the arm. "How could this happen?"

"His car came from the back of the yard with the lights off just when that damned bus hit the hill! The Chevy was on us before we knew it. It crashed through the gate running over the men and smacking into cars. It caught us by surprise and sped off. In the dark here the guns didn't have much chance to stop it!"

Wyatt jumped into his car and got the radio working. "Calling all cars! Stop a black Chevy sedan at all costs. It's being driven by a Japanese man and is probably banged up. I repeat: At all costs, stop that car!"

Hunched over the wheel and with a bullet in his shoulder Shibuki sped down the nearly deserted streets of Casper. To reach the Yellowstone neighborhood he had to cross almost the entire city from east to west and when he saw the headlights topped by a flashing red light he knew that his rear-view mirror was showing him a picture of his impossible mission. In a rage and bleeding Shibuki floored the gas pedal, ran a red light and turned like a shot onto 5th Street.

Behind him were two police cars now, flashing and wailing, driving side by side less than 500 yards away. With his shoulder in flames, his shirt and coat sticky with blood, Shibuki blinked his eyes in the glare of the advertisements. His arm weighed a ton being slapped by the air rushing in from the shattered windshield. Yellostone... Yellowstone... At the intersection of Railroad Street, a team of policemen armed with rifles and sub-machine guns lined up and took aim. A rain of bullets hit the Chevrolet. Shibuki heard the impacts like in a dream before feeling a red-hot burn sear his left thigh. He watched all the windows disintegrate and his hat flew off with a .45 bullet. The Chevrolet jumped onto the sidewalk and scraped over the front of a building, swerving this way and that, shattering a window and then plopping back onto the road, its hood miraculously pointing to Yellowstone and its tires and engine intact.

Shibuki sped up and zigzagged through the maelstrom, but saw the two police cars still in his rear-view mirror, dangerously closer. The sirens burst his eardrums and his blood beat hard against his temples while waves of pain washed over his body, which was leaning forward toward Yellowstone and the huge Athletic Field at the entrance.

Yellowstone... Yellowstone...

From afar a machine gun started spitting, then another staccato could be heard. The whistling, pain-ridden universe of Shibuki was filled with terrifying wails. In the rear-view mirror the police cars were topped with orange lights, but the speed threw off their shooting and most of the bullets went astray. Driving with one hand, slumped over in pain, transformed into a kamikaze nose-diving into an aircraft carrier, Shibuki turned wildly onto Walnut Road, knocked over a parking meter and continued on his way, the right fender smashed in and slicing the tire into thin, smoking strips.

His speed dropped. The Chevrolet started swerving badly from one side of the narrow street to the other, scraping against the sidewalks and the trees. Then the right fender just snapped off and flew away, falling with a bang and a shower of sparks under the chassis of the first police car. Spinning round with the noise of a freight train screeching to a halt, it blocked the way of the second car right behind it because the street was so narrow...

Freed of the broken fender the Chevrolet resumed its pace and Shibuki sped into the maze of little residential streets, as sure of his direction as a pigeon homing in on its base, in spite of his semi-consciousness and fatigue. He drove for centuries in an unimaginable nightmare, a kind of free-fall with gales of wind that tore his eyes from his sockets. Lights, shadows, screaming sirens, explosions, the banging of hammered sheet metal and lethal bullets whizzing by... Dazed and traumatized Shibuki did not even realize that no car was following him anymore. Moreover, if he reached his goal, he would also be finished driving and would bleed out, inevitably, through the gaping wound in his left thigh that was as big as the nozzle of an old garden hose.

Through a thick fog Shibuki finally recognized the tree-lined street and the high hedges that he was dying to see since he escaped Children's Home. He made a last ditch effort to raise his head, then jerked back under the inhuman glare from a handheld spotlight. He slammed on the accelerator stupidly and uselessly to rush headlong toward an armored truck that was blocking the end of the street.

Right away the automatic weapons started firing, all centered on the speeding Chevrolet. The car was riddled with bullets, but still being driven, unbelievably, by this apparently invulnerable Asian. Shibuki jerked again, let go of the wheel and died, nailed to the back of his seat by the deluge of lead piercing his already bloodless corpse. His body sat there for an instant before suddenly falling backward with the seat and disappearing while the Chevrolet crashed into a tree. A frightening racket followed by total silence.

The smell of gun smoke. Gas flowed down the gutters. Hot engine oil leaked out of a thousand cracks...

The armored truck drove up and stopped. Its spotlight was still aimed at the metal heap from which a bloody arm dangled as the police surrounded the wreck. Far off but coming closer, the cars alerted by radio were speeding along with their sirens wailing. Ten minutes later Chief Wyatt showed up, pale, stunned, a little ashamed of the methods used to stop the diabolical Japanese.

"Dead?" he asked, just to say something.

"Mincemeat," a lieutenant brayed. "No more blood left in him than a rifle barrel! No joke, chief, nobody understands how he could have gotten this far."

Behind a hedge, less than 20 feet away, Isadori understood. He stepped away and went back into the house where Madame Atomos was waiting for him. At least Shibuki's sacrifice would not be in vain...

Chapter X

The tigers were still in the aisle when Shibuki worked the transmitter. At first, nothing very remarkable happened. Hermann, the German tamer, spun around majestically and bowed slightly to make the audience understand that he appreciated the sudden silence under the big top.

He nodded his chin at the ring workers and the last gate was lifted, opening up the aisle. The tigers sauntered in, very quickly, and Hermann instantly knew that something was wrong with his animals. Not a single growl as their tails whipped their flanks.

"Here," Hermann barked. "Sultan!"

The big cat hesitated, but finally jumped off his stand and his fellow tigers followed in surprising unity. Hermann exchanged glances with Holborn and Sam, who were standing behind the cage. Usually when the animals came out of the aisle they were nervous, undisciplined and tried to run around a little before being brought to order, like a house dog suddenly let free in the country. Holborn gave his thumbs up and the audience applauded.

When Hermann turned his back to Sultan in order to check the tension of the cables, without any warning the old tiger pounced and gave him a horrible swipe with its paw. A shriek of fear escaped the public, then the cry died down because nothing was moving in the cage.

Sultan was moving away from the tamer lying dead with a broken neck. It stood still, just like the nine other tigers, so that if it were not for the body on the ground you would have thought the whole drama unreal. Sam grabbed a pitchfork while firing off two blanks and headed for the small emergency exit that Holborn was standing by. This was not the first time that a tamer bit the dust in the Pangani Circus and as long as the public did not panic, no disaster would result.

At just the right time the voice of the emcee announced, "Don't move! Stay calm! Maestro, music please!"

Sam was hanging onto Hermann and backing away to the door, dragging his weight before the cold eyes of the still frozen tigers. Holborn unfastened the hitch and leaned over to help Sam, but he was swept away by Sultan and rolled into the side of the ring, lay motionless, conscious, but unable to move.

He heard the crowd screaming, saw the other tigers rushing among the spectators, heard their death cries and their bones breaking. Then he was standing, stricken with a white panic, running, catching glimpses of mangled bodies in a bloody human mass, and the quiet, hard-working tigers killed methodically. Shots rang out, barely audible in all the din, then Holborn came out behind the tent and barely escaped the charge of a raging horse who was trampling lifeless bodies under its hooves. Bears, gorillas, panthers and lions were making an infernal racket behind the bars of their cages, which were fortunately shut tight. A clown passed by, holding his maimed arm, and Holborn recognized Jenny, the horse rider, but only by her costume because her face had been smashed by a furious hoof.

Horrified, covered in someone else's blood, Holborn gave plenty of room going around the elephants, who were rather calm, then he ran, got knocked over by a terrified group, and got up. He reached his wagon in a dream, climbed the steps, pushed open the door and stumbled toward the telephone. Outside the crowd was in turmoil, howling, and, as if to increase the panic, the elephants started trumpeting woefully.

Holborn bit his lip until it bled, but managed to control his trembling hand so he could call the police. A voice answered and Holborn shouted, "Help! Here at the Pangani Circus! The animals have escaped. There are dozens dead and…"

His wagon shook, turned over and he was tossed like a ball. Before losing consciousness he knew that the elephants had gone mad, broken their chains and were stomping through the crowd…

At two in the morning Smith Beffort and his team had a headcount: 200 dead, 400 wounded, 50 cases of madness and 80 missing. The tigers and horses had been shot down, but all the other animals died in their cages. Only the elephants were safe and sound. One of the tamers had rounded them up in Casper. Now in front of the tragic circus they were swaying in their chains, nervous and agitated. The super-minibrains had been found in their skulls after painstaking examination. The size of a pinhead that fortunately sparkled in the surgical lights…

People were wandering around Casper talking to themselves. They had escaped the massacre, but their minds were reeling and with distressing resolve they kept looking for a relative whose shredded corpse, however, they had seen in the stands of the Pangani Circus.

In spite of the late hour, the city was no longer asleep. The news had spread like wildfire and the dreaded name of Madame Atomos was on everyone's lips. In the darkened streets ambulances and police cars were speeding around, lights flashing, sirens wailing, and a troop from the National Guard was trying to calm the population through loudspeakers.

All this was a little like the sinking of the Titanic, but when Madame Atomos attacked a city, this was generally the kind of reaction she produced.

At 3 am, after an extraordinary meeting with Beffort, Wyatt and Akamatsu, the Mayor of Casper decreed a state of emergency and called for the full mobilization of the National Guard, the closure of most of the shops and of all the factories, workshops and offices. Moreover, leaflets were printed in record time and handed out just as swiftly so that the inhabitants of Casper knew exactly what they would risk if they left their houses. Super-minibrains the size of a pinhead shot by a camera or some other device changed into an air gun would penetrate their skin, rush up to their brain with the circulating blood, etc.

Enough to make your teeth chatter!

Lost in the crowd, an old lady was leading a blind man, a big, bearded guy with black glasses and a cane. The old lady pulled him into a alcove and whispered, "If we let them keep going, Isadori, the Rising Sun will find nothing but a deserted city! How can we keep these people from locking themselves inside?"

The "blind" man did not answer. He just lit a match. Madame Atomos giggled. "Fire! Of course! But if the roads are closed down, our agents won't be able to start the fires."

Isadori leaned forward. "We have to start right away, mistress," (Madame Atomos loved being called this double-meaning name.) "We have to scatter some time bombs pretty much everywhere. Like that the Rising Sun can act."

Madame Atomos hugged him as a sign of appreciation and then led him back to the Cadillac that was parked nearby. Only Isadori and the chauffeur were needed to make the time bombs.

Beffort, Mie and Akamatsu were listening to Chief Wyatt describe Shibuki's escape, the chase across the city and the final run-in with the armored truck in the narrow streets of Yellowstone.

Beffort looked enthralled. "If I'm hearing you right, this Shibuki spotted your men before you entered the factory yard?"

"Probably," Wyatt admitted, "because the light was turned off while I was opening the gate. But what does that mean?"

"Something that goes without saying," Beffort replied. "Namely, that Shibuki had plenty of time to escape while you were sneaking into hideout."

Wyatt shrugged. "Possibly. And so?"

"Well," Smith smiled, "it's totally absurd that a wanted man, knowing full well that he'd be chased, would deliberately chose to jump into the fire by racing across a city crawling with cops. In his place I would have gone south, toward the highways and the countryside, towards Colorado on Highway 220. See, Wyatt, what was Shibuki going to do in Yellowstone?"

"I don't give a damn! In my opinion, since my men were closing in on him, he was trying to lose them in the residential streets."

Beffort smirked. "No. Shibuki kept heading west, on purpose, from the time he left his hideout. In fact, given the head start he had on your men, he could easily have escaped by immediately turning south, north or east!"

"That's true," Akamatsu jumped in. "You yourself said that Shibuki committed suicide by taking the long, straightaway of 5th Street. In the end, west was the only direction that he should not have taken!"

Mie stubbed out her cigarette butt and said, "It's clear to me. Shibuki was trying to reach his friends. He was smoked out and chased, but he couldn't pull through. Plus, he obviously had to warn them. The transmitter, the animals—I'm talking about Royal, Gib and the monkey—and a supply of super-minibrains were in the hands of the police, right? In short, we hit the jackpot and if Madame Atomos didn't know about it, we'd be able to stop her. Why wouldn't Shibuki come to the same conclusions? What's Yellowstone like?"

"Residential," Wyatt said. "Full of houses, trees and gardens. A swanky little neighborhood."

Mie's eyes lost focus but found her husband. "Smith, I'd like to visit Yellowstone."

"Now?"

"Please."

Beffort sighed, but stood up. When Mie had that clairvoyant look, it was better to do what she asked.

Since the Mayor's decree did not come into effect until dawn, Casper was still bustling when the Befforts and Akamatsu left headquarters. It was 3:45 am, the time that Owen Bernitz had said the Green Dragon Force would arrive, so Beffort was not at all surprised to see his Malibu parked in front of the building. Owen was waiting behind the wheel. On seeing them he got out, took the cigar stub out of his mouth and said, "Hey! Got here just in time for the brawl, eh?" Owen had his own way of talking.

Yosho and Mie shook his hand. Smith gave him a friendly pat on the shoulder and said, "You couldn't be here at a better time, Owen. Madame Atomos just brought out the big guns by wreaking havoc at the circus."

"I know all about it. They're talking about nothing else in the city. Say, is all this talk about minibrains true?"

"Yes, unfortunately. Climb into the Malibu and take the wheel, Owen. We'll tell you all about it on the road."

Bernitz obeyed and dove behind the wheel. Beffort gave him directions to Yellowstone while recounting the latest events in detail. Bernitz made no comment, but he asked, "Has Wyatt ever fought against Madame Atomos?"

"No," Beffort answered. "Why?"

"Cause I think Ben Brady and his boys could've taken the Japanese alive. Gotta let them do the dirty work."

Beffort became tense. The swift development of the situation of late had completely preoccupied him so much that he had forgotten about Brady and Evans. But one thing was sure: Ben Brady had not contacted Mie.

"Say, Owen, does that mean that Brady's been in Casper all night? He hasn't given us any signal."

Bernitz glanced at Beffort with a hint of astonishment. "What? You called me at 6 pm and Brady's team took off 15 minutes later from the St. Louis airport. I'd bet my bottom dollar that Ben and his men have been here since eight last night."

"Well," Mie wondered, "why hasn't he called us?"

Owen pointed to the radio-phone and said to Smith, "If there's a hitch, maybe Stutton knows about it. You can ask him, boss. His dispatch was set up 30 minutes ago."

Beffort turned it on and spoke into the microphone: "Yellow Mask calling 6289... Yellow Mask calling 6289."

"Okay, 6289 here, boss!" Stutton sounded glad to hear his voice. "We shooting the works?"

"We're shooting the works, Ralph... Got any news from Brady?"

"No, nothing. Should I?"

"Not really. According to Owen Brady's team got to Casper last night, but he hasn't contacted us at headquarters."

"That's not like him," Stutton agreed. "Either his plane crashed somewhere between St. Louis and Casper or he ran into a member of the Atomos Organization. The first possibility can be checked easy enough. Keep the line open, I'll call the Casper airport and get you an answer double quick. Over and out."

Beffort hung the mic up and turned a concerned face to Owen, who answered the silent question by shrugging his shoulders, expressing his powerlessness more than his indifference.

"We'll wait for Ralph's call," Beffort suggested. "Take a right here and then a left. We're there. It's on the next street that Shibuki was cornered by the cops."

Not a single piece of the Chevrolet remained, but a big oil stain marked the spot of the drama. One tree had a long gash to prove the violence of the crash. Farther down the street some cartridge casings glimmered under the pale streetlights.

Bernitz stopped the car, turned off the lights out of habit and cut the engine. In this neighborhood the streets were still deserted and silent and despite the Atomos menace looming over Casper no light was visible behind the closed shutters. Naïvely, because of their fat bank accounts the residents of Yellowstone obviously imagined that Madame Atomos would not strike them.

Mie leaned forward to grab the Casper map. She shook her head and said, "Shibuki had been living in this city for more than a month and should have known it like the back of his hand. He had to know that Yellowstone was a kind of rectangle, an area cut off by the next suburb, easy for the police to surround and trap him in. Plus, Smith, do you realize that the North Platte River flows less than 500 yards from here? Now, hasn't Madame Atomos always set up her refuges near a lake or river?"

Beffort nodded. Even if Mie was taking her desires for reality, the situation in Yellowstone did, in fact, show troubling similarities with Madame Atomos' favorite sites. That Shibuki came to this precise place to be shot down while he could have beat a speedy retreat, gave even more weight to Mie's suspicions.

"According to Wyatt," Mie insisted, "Shibuki sped up when he saw the armored truck. That doesn't make sense because he had absolutely no hope of getting by it. The street is narrow, lined with trees so he couldn't get up on the sidewalk, and the truck was blocking the road..." She cut off because the radio speaker was announcing the signal 555-6289.

"Yellow Mask here," Beffort responded. "Go ahead, Ralph."

"I got the Casper airport," Stutton said, getting straight to the point. "It's confirmed that Brady's plane landed here at 7:52 and no incident was reported during the flight or on the runway. So, there's no doubt about it, boss! Ben and his men are in Casper right now."

Beffort thanked him and signed off. Brady's silence could not be explained.

Chapter XI

At the same time, Ben Brady and his men were driving a van from a tractor company into Goose Egg, a small town southwest of Casper. To tell the truth, the Green Dragon commando team had absolutely no idea that it was Goose Egg, any more than that they were in a moving vehicle.

Picked off by an agent from Rising Sun as they were coming off the plane, the ten men had been controlled by super-minibrains for hours and acted only under the impulses from the giant computer located in Riverton, i.e. in the center of Wyoming, in order to control the whole state, and under the leadership of Dr. Wataru, the main collaborator of Dr. Miwa.

After James Edward Evans, Madame Atomos was racking up points for the final round by short-circuiting the Green Dragon Force before the implementation of a defense system. Moreover, she was getting back a good number of paralyzing pistols along with their users who, if need be, could open fire on the Befforts, Akamatsu and the still-sound members of the anti-Atomos team.

The van entered a barn and a Japanese man slowly closed the heavy double doors. He was only there to feed the men, not to guard them. The giant computer in Riverton was in charge of that.

Simply put, Ben Brady and his men were beyond help now. Turned into robots, the best hypothesis that one could imagine for them was a quick death.

The Malibu was still parked in the calm little street of Yellowstone. Mie's reasoning made sense, but the three men, although Smith was already convinced, were searching in vain for objections.

Owen said, "I just got to Casper and I don't know it at all, but it's clear that if I was the Japanese, I'd never go and get myself stuck in this rat hole!"

Coming from him, an old crook, an ex-convict, the judgment held weight. There was a moment of silence, then before the debate could continue a Cadillac sped out of a nearby driveway, turned onto the street and just missed the Malibu as it headed downtown. Neither the black driver nor the bearded passenger in the backseat noticed the Malibu in the shade, but Akamatsu saw that the license plate was from New Mexico and an alarm bell went off inside his head.

"The last time Madame Atomos was heard from," he recalled, "was in Roswell, New Mexico. Strange that a car with a license plate from there is driving down this very road here, isn't it? A black driver, a bearded passenger with dark sunglasses and a Cadillac showing up less than 20 yards from where Shibuki hit a tree…"

Owen was already whipping the car around to follow the Cadillac. He found it just as it was leaving the residential zone. There was already a good deal of traffic and after Owen turned off the headlights the Malibu had little chance of being spotted among the other vehicles.

"You don't think we're barking up the wrong tree?" he asked.

"It's a risk we have to take," Beffort said. "Anyway, unless we close off Yellowstone and search the houses one by one, we have nothing better to do right now."

In front of them the Cadillac was driving fast and soon reached downtown Casper where it pulled up to

Hutzler & Sons. When the passenger got out, Owen whistled. "For a big guy, he's a big guy."

Isadori took one of the packages out of the trunk, crossed the street and entered a 12-story building. He quickly located the entrance to the basement, scrambled down the stairs while turning on a flashlight, and slipped the package between the gas pipes and the wall. When the bomb would explode around 10 am, there were going to be some pretty fireworks.

Isadori went back up, crossed the street again and settled back in the Cadillac, which sped off.

"Short visit," Akamatsu observed. "The guy must have stuck the package in a mailbox."

Beffort made no comment, just noted the address. The Malibu took off after the Cadillac, which stopped before another apartment. This time Isadori took two packages and walked through a puddle of light before disappearing inside the building that had 300 apartments.

Mie, who had the eyes of a cat, said, "He's Japanese, I'll stake my life on it! Get a good look at his face when he comes back out."

"Either way," Smith murmured, "it's a funny time to be making deliveries. I'd like to know what's in those packages. Owen, I'm going to take the wheel. When the guy comes out, take a gander at the mailboxes."

Bernitz got out, closed the door and walked off. Smith slid over behind the wheel and watched Owen strolling casually toward the building.

Even though it was 4:30 in the morning it could have been 4:30 in the afternoon. There were not too many the people on the sidewalks or too much traffic in the streets, but there was enough that Bernitz and the Malibu could go unnoticed.

After two minutes, the big guy reappeared and passed through the light again. "He is Japanese," Akamatsu confirmed. "Well, that adds a little spice to the stew."

Down the street Owen entered the building. The Cadillac drove off 100 yards and stopped again. Beffort did not budge. From his seat he could watch the Cadillac and was all ready to pick up Bernitz, who was only gone for a few seconds before he came back and said, "Nothing in the mail. Since there's no apartment on the ground floor, I don't get it! This guy didn't have time to go upstairs, ring a bell and deliver a package, not in two minutes."

"Trouble," Smith admitted. "Unless someone was waiting in the hall. Someone who knew he was coming. Note down the address, Mie, it might come in handy later. Owen, call 6289 and give Ralph the two addresses that we have so far. I want these buildings searched within the next 15 minutes and I want those packages found and checked. Three packages, right?"

"Three packages," Mie confirmed. "One at 316 Lincoln Avenue, a second at 348, same street... Watch it, Smith! The Cadillac's leaving!"

Bernitz got in touch with the Green Dragon Force dispatch, transmitted the orders to Stutton and asked about Ben Brady but received not the slightest information about his commando. He signed off, with a worried brow, more worried than he wanted to look, and brooded in his seat.

The Cadillac in front of them continued its weird little game. The huge Japanese man got out, delivered one or more packages in very big, hence very crowded, apartment buildings, got back in the car and left. He acted with almost feverish quickness, speeding up the later it became. At a respectable distance Beffort and his team noted the addresses that Bernitz relayed instantly to Stutton.

At 5:15, a quarter of an hour before the enforcement of the shutdown, Stutton reported that the first group had visited the building at 316 Lincoln Avenue. "Negative. No resident received a package and no one saw your bearded Japanese."

"Push it!" Beffort shouted. "Search the entire building from basement to roof. The package was delivered before our very eyes. We have to find it. Out!"

At 5:20, after delivering 27 packages, the giant Japanese climbed back into the Cadillac, which turned around and headed back to Yellowstone. At 5:28 the car was in front of the gate flashing its headlights. Ten seconds later the gate opened automatically and closed right after the Cadillac drove through. The headlights lit up the night behind the high hedge, then everything fell back into darkness and silence.

Inside the Malibu no one needed to say what everyone was feeling. It all stunk of Madame Atomos!

Beffort turned to Bernitz, "Call 6289, Owen, and let me talk. I need to know who's living on this property."

Isadori took off his false beard and his glasses and climbed up the stairs to the second floor. He knocked on a door, entered after being invited by Madame Atomos and found her frozen in front of a T.V. screen. The giant Japanese approached without saying a word and watched over her shoulder. The screen was dim, but it was easy to see the shot of the street outside their property, the trees around it and a big car parked along the sidewalk in front, all lights out.

"It followed me from downtown," Isadori said.

Madame Atomos sneered, "Longer than that, Isadori, longer than that…"

"Who is it, mistress?"

"The famous armored car of Smith Beffort," Madame Atomos said calmly. "In a few minutes, the sun will rise and I'll know if he's inside his Malibu. In the meantime, call Dr. Wataru in Riverton and give him the coordinates of this car. Brady and his men have to attack it as soon as possible. No paralyzing pistols! Grenades and machine guns! Go!"

Isadori walked out the door. The radio was set up in the basement, not far from the traditional escape tunnel that Madame Atomos and her men used in case of imminent danger. This tunnel led to the North Platte River where a boat was moored that would carry the fugitives to Goose Egg around Jackson Canyon and a waiting helicopter. Mie was right about her forebodings. The sinister Japanese woman would, in fact, flee on the river.

Through 6289 the information kept flowing into the Malibu, which was still parked by the suspicious property.

"The owner's name is Desmond," Stutton said in answer to Beffort's question. "He's an architect, married with four children, but right now living in Kalipell, Montana."

"So his house should be empty?"

"Sure. Especially since the guy's in the can for fraud and his wife went back to her mother's with the kids."

Desmond's adventure was unusual, but it had nothing to do with the Japanese guy living on his property. At least the architect could not be accused of aiding the Atomos Organization.

"Okay, Ralph. What else?"

"Oh, the packages. No big deal. Just enough explosives to burn down the dumps around 10 in the morning. Detonation on an acid-type timer…"

"Good God! Couldn't you tell me this first?" Beffort thundered.

"Everything in its own time." Stutton made excuses. "You want to call in the troops?"

"Of course and double quick! And send a vanload of Green Dragons to Yellowstone. Tell Wyatt to block off the area paying particular attention to the river and check all the boats. Not even a cat should be able to get out of Yellowstone starting right now!"

He hung up the mic, certain that his orders would be carried out to the letter. Then he turned to Akamatsu and Mie and said, "If this house is really harboring members of the Atomos Organization, it's likely that we were spotted tailing the Cadillac, at least at the end. I think we should be expecting some surprises."

"I couldn't agree more," Akamatsu said.

Mie frowned, "That means that we have to stay in the Malibu until backup comes. Smith, do you realize that Madame Atomos might be inside that house?"

Beffort smiled bitterly. "If she is, she knows for a fact that we're here! Cameras and microphones are part and parcel of her usual set-up. Personally I have no desire to be fit with a minibrain! And it's done quick, then everything's over! Do you realize that, Mie?"

The young lady did not answer. Owen Bernitz adjusted the mirrors, turned on the electronic sights and unlocked the machine guns and paralyzing cannon. After this he let out a little sigh of satisfaction and in an extremely rare gesture lit his cigar stub.

At that very instant Stutton's voice came over the speaker. "Yellow Mask? 6289 calling Yellow Mask…"

"I'm here," Beffort said. "What is it, Ralph?"

"A report from Washington. I quote: James Edward Evasn, director of the FBI, has just been found dead in his car where he had handcuffed himself to the wheel. Evans died of a cerebral hemorrhage. The FBI is investigating. End quote." Stutton was silent.

"Thanks, Ralph," Smith spoke in a hollow voice. "The backup?"

"On its way, boss… Say, what's all this about J.E.E.?"

"Minibrain. By the way, still no news from Ben and his boys?"

"Nothing. Hey, do you think…"

"I hope not," Beffort cut him off, "but you have to admit that there's something fishy going on. Since the beginning of the Green Dragon Force, this is the first time that we've have a defection like this, isn't it? The plane did land in Casper on time and nothing was reported during the flight. Unless Ben and his boys missed the takeoff…"

"No. I was the one who drove them to the St. Louis airport. Hold on, I have a newsflash from the police." A moment of silence, then Stutton said, "This probably has nothing to do with our affair, but in spite of the mayor's decree, a van is on the road right now on Route 87."

"Where's Route 87?"

"It crosses Casper from east to west."

"Details on the van?"

None, except that it belongs to a tractor company around here. But don't make a big deal out of it. Since 5:30 the cops have already stopped a hundred cars breaking the law. They're always guys who don't read the papers or listen to the radio or watch the tele. Over and out?"

"Over and out," Smith signed off.

He hung up, looked at the dawn rising over Casper and automatically reached for his pack of cigarettes. He was thinking of Evans…

"Cuffed himself in his car!" Bernitz spit out. "He didn't do that by himself!"

"I'm not so sure about that," Mie murmured. "J.E.E. must have realized that he was acting strangely, against his will, and tried to stop himself from committing some act he didn't want to do but that he couldn't help. So he handcuffed himself to his car. The cuffs kept him from obeying and his minibrain killed him just like it killed the animals at the Pangani Circus in their cages and the Freemont's parrot…"

She was forcing herself to stay calm, but a slight tremolo in her voice betrayed her grief and distress. Evans was a long-standing friend, a good man without an ounce of meanness.

"Madame Atomos will pay for this!" Akamatsu growled.

His remark was useless and meaningless. Madame Atomos had already so many crimes to pay for that her one life would never be enough!

Chapter XII

The van, barreling full speed ahead, had been forced to take Route 87 because of the police checkpoints. Coming from Goose Egg, that is from the southwest, it was detoured due east before turning north in search of a chink in the armor surrounding the city.

Brady found the chink at the intersection of highways 87 and 20-26. Even though spotted by checkpoints, the vehicle had miraculously slipped between the rather large gaps in the police control and was now arriving in Yellowstone on the southwest route of Center Street.

When it reached the Federal Building, the van ran into a police barricade, stopped and was instantly circled. Brady looked calmly at the machine guns pointing at him and smiled when a lieutenant asked for his papers. When he flashed his Green Dragon identification the lieutenant said, "We called you over 20 minutes ago and been given arrest orders to boot. You could've stopped a little earlier."

Brady shrugged. "Very sorry, lieutenant, but this is a work van and hasn't got a radio. I didn't know that me and my men were on the list…"

"They've been looking for you since yesterday!" the other interrupted. "It's none of my business, but you should probably inform the dispatch right away. Where you going?"

"Yellowstone. Let me through, pal, and you can tell whoever you want! I repeat, this old heap hasn't got a radio. Plus we have a mission to accomplish and every minute we're held up will fall on your head. Got it?"

The lieutenant stepped aside. "Okay. Go ahead."

The van took off and the lieutenant walked over to his jeep. He had no suspicions about Brady and his men; he was simply following the orders of Chief Wyatt by reporting their appearance. He grabbed his radio-telephone, called 555-6289 and said, "Bear 20 here on Center Street. We've just seen that tractor company van come through here. Ben Brady's driving it and his nine men are with him. Over and out."

"Wait a minute!" Stutton brayed. "Were Brady and his men acting normal?"

"I don't know what you mean. Brady was in a hurry to get to Yellowstone, but not at all worked up."

"Why didn't he give us some sign of life?"

"The van doesn't have a radio."

"Thanks," Stutton signed off and called Yellow Mask. "I just got word from Center Street. The van I talked about earlier is being driven by Brady and he's heading in your direction as we speak and his whole team's with him."

"How did he know where we were?"

"Exactly," Stutton pronounced every syllable. "He couldn't have known! His vehicle doesn't have a radio, he's not in contact with any of us and this is the first we've heard of him since he disappeared. In theory he's got my radio and telephone contacts, so he should have got in touch with me first thing. None of this is good, boss. Watch out! The van will be showing up on your street any minute now and if Madame Atomos is controlling Brady…"

"Don't worry, Ralph," Smith reassured him, "we're ready here. Where are the troops at?"

"Yellowstone is blockaded in the south and west. Men are armed and waiting in the north on the other side of the North Platte River. In the east, I mean in Casper, it's a little less tight, but there's not much of a chance that Madame Atomos would try to flee in that direction unless she wants to commit suicide. What do you figure on doing?"

Beffort did not hesitate. "I'll wait for the van and then I'll see how Ben and his men are acting. In the end, no matter what happens with Brady, I'll use the Malibu to break through the front gate here... That's when you can sound the alarm, Ralph. With the Malibu against her, Madame Atomos' only chance for safety will be to flee."

Akamatsu put his hand on his shoulder. Beffort looked up, saw the van at the end of the street and spoke into the mic, "I'm signing off, Ralph. Brady's here."

He put down the mic and stared at the work van speeding down the street. Behind the windshield Brady was smiling, waving his hand and starting to slow down.

"Damn!" Owen cursed, "He looks in good shape. We're wrong about him, boss. I'm getting out."

"Don't move!" Smith ordered. "Turn on the outside speaker instead. Before getting the go-ahead, Ben's got to answer a few questions I have for him first."

"But..."

"Be quiet, Owen! Roll up the windows! Turn on the oxygen! I'll take care of the paralyzing cannon!"

The van stopped a dozen yards away from the Malibu. Brady jumped out. His men did the same while Akamatsu remarked, "Grenades and machine guns, that's new!"

Smiling and raising his arm Brady yelled out, "Hello! We're here as backup, boss!"

"Good to see you, Ben," Smith responded through the loudspeaker that was disguised as a fog light. "I guess you came on orders from dispatch?"

Brady, or to be more precise Dr. Wataru, jumped headlong into the trap. "Stutton himself."

In the background, without trying to hide it, the members of the commando team pulled the grenade pins and tossed them. Smith instantly pressed the trigger of the paralyzing cannon and the unseen ray literally cut the group down. They dropped to the ground all together. It was not spectacular, but on exploding the grenades added sound to the silent film that suddenly rose to deafening decibels. At the same time, the bodies were thrown up and scattered. The trees abruptly lost their leaves and were decorated with bloody debris while a cloud of burning shrapnel sprayed the Malibu's armor.

More vulnerable because closer to the epicenter of the explosion, the van flipped over, caught fire and burned like a torch, melting the asphalt of the street. Smith turned on the engine, pulled away from the curb, sped around the wreckage and smashed through the gate of the suspicious property. Being extra-reinforced, the Malibu's bumpers had been designed to break through one and a half foot walls with no damage.

On being rammed the gate cracked like nutshell, folded in on itself and fell down like a carpet under the three-ton Malibu that rushed up the driveway, kicking up gravel from its puncture-proof tires.

When the monster burst onto Madame Atomos' screen the sinister woman jumped up. "Isadori! The Cadillac!"

"It's on its way, mistress, and the dummies are in place."

Outside, the Malibu was sliding around the central flowerbed when the Cadillac sprang out from behind the house. The black chauffeur was driving. In the backseat, a little stiff but very easy to recognize were Madame

Atomos and her Japanese gorilla. All of this was glimpsed in a flash because the Cadillac was rounding the other side and heading for the gaping gate.

"She' getting away," Mie screamed.

Beffort floored the accelerator, got around the big flowerbed, and chased after the Cadillac, which was already out of sight. He could not help laughing nervously. As soon as the car got within range, the paralyzing cannon would put an end to Madame Atomos' career.

In the tunnel Madame Atomos and Isadori sprinted toward the river. 500 yards! A piece of cake! They reached the end in less than three minutes, climbed a ladder, pushed open a trapdoor and came out in a small house on the edge of the water. They walked through the kitchen and into a shed where the boat was waiting on its trailer.

Isadori snuck around with surprising agility, opened a window and peeked through the shudders. He scowled. Madame Atomos approached and glanced outside. On the other side of the river, far off but clearly visible, uniformed men, armed and ready, were posted every 50 yards like telegraph poles.

"That's trouble," Madame Atomos mumbled. She had never really panicked, but since she was with Isadori her blood remained cold as ice. The Japanese giant looked made of stone. "What are they waiting for?"

Madame Atomos squinted. "You and me, what do you think?"

Isadori stepped away and opened a cabinet, revealing a wide selection of disguises: hats, crutches, wigs, beards, moustaches, etc.

"Oh!" Madame Atomos purred. "Extraordinary!"

"Thanks, mistress," Isadori said humbly. "I also have a bunch of fishing poles... Early in the morning on such a beautiful day as this, it's not so surprising to see a couple of fishermen cruising around looking for a good spot."

They got undressed, chose some clothes that fit and were quickly transformed into Sunday fishermen. With her hair was tucked into the waterproof hat Madame Atomos looked like a young boy accompanying his father.

Isadori threw two fishing poles into the boat, checked the Mercury 50 hp motor and the gas tank, then stood up, satisfied, before he caught Madame Atomos glaring at him.

"No one's living in the house," she said, "and they haven't seen anybody come in. Plus, Smith Beffort must know by now that he's chasing after dummies. We have to act quickly! It won't take long for them to find the entrance to the tunnel."

Isadori lifted her up and placed her in the boat. When he opened the double doors, sunlight flooded the shed and sparkled on the water where the launch trailer rested. Lumbering around on purpose, aware that he was being watched through binoculars, Isadori pulled out the blocks, started the electric winch and watched the cable unroll with agonizing slowness.

"Turn around, mistress," Isadori whispered.

Madame Atomos spun around so that her back faced the river. She seemed very calm, but her smile was still a little tense. From under the visor of his cap, Isadori was spying on the other side of the river. The guards were not moving. They had no binoculars. Some of them were even hiding a cigarette in their cupped hands.

The cable reeled off its last inches and the boat was finally in the water, detached from the trailer, floating. Isadori jumped aboard, pulled the cord of the outboard motor but got only a laughable burp. He tried again, heard it cough and then gave it another good yank. This time the motor rumbled like the start of a storm on a calm, quiet morning.

Isadori stepped to the front and very gingerly pressed the gas lever. The boat was moving, slowly, down the unguarded river as if it were drifting by Yellowstone. Just for show, Madame Atomos stretched out one of the collapsible fishing rods and unrolled some wire, the reel going "zeezee" at every pull. In the early morning sun it was magical.

"Hey, you! Boat!" one of the guards shouted.

Madame Atomos stopped pulling the wire while Isadori pretended not to hear. How was anyone to know that the traffic ban applied to boats as well?

"Hey, boat! Get back to your port!"

Isadori slammed down the gas lever. The boat bolted off like a bucking horse and the motor screamed through the air. The pole that Madame Atomos was holding flew overboard and the terrible woman was plastered against her seat, blinded by the spray of water and clinging to whatever she could grab. The noise of the motor drowned out the shots, but Isadori felt a bullet whiz by over his head. A warning shot!

He skid over to the bank, raced through a row of moored boats and came out the other side full speed ahead. The boat was bouncing and shaking and crashing loudly over the river, ripping through the waves, forming a huge watery curtain around it.

Shaken up and soaked, Madame Atomos glanced behind but saw nothing but a geyser on the move, splattering and fading, then rising up again to splash her full in the face and cut off her breath. She saw nothing and wondered how Isadori could steer in the infernal chaos against the unleashed elements...

She had lost her concept of time, of reality, and felt like she was freefalling in an abyss when all of a sudden everything stopped. Silence and sun. And Madame Atomos had the sensation of being carried away on a cloud. Then there was a jolt when the boat touched the bank. Isadori leaped out, lifted Madame Atomos in his arms and together they jumped into a bunch of reeds, plowing straight ahead.

Through a clearing Madame Atomos could make out the other bank where police cars had just stopped, still enshrouded in the dust kicked up when they slammed on their brakes. Farther off down the river a big boat was approaching with its siren wailing.

Groaning, swearing, a fiend of strength and determination, Isadori kept pushing forward, carrying his mistress like a feather, crushing reeds like a bulldozer. He hurtled down a slope, crossed a marsh, leaped over a guardrail and was standing on Highway 220, down from Mills, a few miles from Jackson Canyon where the helicopter was waiting. But in the reeds behind the guardrail, the marsh and the slope, the blue hats of the cops were already making dangerous headway. On their right a walkie-talkie antenna was swinging around, proof that police cars would quickly be arriving on the 220. Farther back on the river the boat was still hitting its siren and on the other bank the police cars were rushing off to find the nearest bridge.

An engine coughed and Isadori froze in the middle of the road, legs spread, holding Madame Atomos, the very picture of a survivor of a bad accident. The Pontiac came around the corner and skid to stop four feet away from the couple. The driver leaned out the window. "Need some Help?"

Isadori lurched and whacked him with the side of his hand. Then he opened the door and threw the man onto the road. Madame Atomos dove into the backseat while Isadori got behind the wheel, shifted into first and shot off. Madame Atomos parted her hair, which was all over her face, and watched a little dazedly as the countryside flew by. Since she had left the shed, her feet had not touched the ground.

Isadori sped down the highway for about five miles, then took a sharp turn onto a bumpy road, lifting his foot from the gas pedal as he did so. Hunched over the wheel he kept his eyes glued to his surroundings like a wild animal protecting its female, a fearsome killer whom only death could vanquish.

Madame Atomos took a look behind her but saw only a cloud of dust, which she knew would give the police something to follow. "Slowly," she said. "Slowly. We're safe now."

Isadori gradually slowed down more and relaxed, catching the dark eyes of Madame Atomos in the rearview mirror, but also seeing the dust cloud that was probably visible from the 220. He kept slowing down while his big hands slid over the steering wheel and caressed his cheek. His jaw finally unclenched and he could talk.

"In two minutes we'll be on the airstrip."

Madame Atomos giggled. Sometimes Isadori was like a machine running out of gas. He was terrifying in action, but he fell into an incredible lethargy when the danger seemed distant.

"Speed up a little," she said.

Isadori accelerated and steered the Pontiac through the trees, up a hill, down the other side and suddenly into a field in the middle of the forest. It was really only a clearing with a small cabin like a weekend getaway and a helicopter under camouflaged netting.

Isadori honked the horn three times as he pulled the Pontiac up to the cabin. An Asian man came out. Isadori opened the door and ordered, "Climb into your bird, Nachi, and get it started! The police are after us!"

Madame Atomos got out after him and looked anxiously into the sky. Between the field and Riverton a lot of things could still happen…

Chapter XIII

Just as he had expected, Beffort had the Cadillac in his sights very quickly and as promised he pressed the trigger of the paralyzing cannon. Like always the effect was instantaneous. The Cadillac went straight on instead of finishing the curve it was in the middle of and off the driveway into a fence. It bounced and drifted before stopping between two trees.

Beffort and his team rushed forth. When they saw the dummies and the black chauffeur slumped over the wheel, they knew that Madame Atomos had once again proven her remarkable spirit of invention. Even if up close the dummies did not look at all like Madame Atomos and her goon. One of them had a brown moustache; the other a false beard and dark sunglasses; both of them were sitting up straight in their seatbelts.

"Unbelievable!" Akamatsu bemoaned. "How could we have been fooled so easily?"

"We were expecting Madame Atomos," Mie said. "We were counting on her! Obsessed as we were, it was inevitable that we'd chase after the first rabbit that popped up."

Pale and raging Smith turned to the Malibu when he heard Ralph Stutton faintly calling on the radio. He rushed over and picked up the microphone. "Yellow Mask here! What's going on, Ralph?"

"I'm asking you!" Stutton boomed. "You were supposed to call me about Ben Brady, right?"

Smith scowled. In the heat of action he had forgotten the fundamental rule of security among the Green Dragon Force that meant that the dispatch should always be up-to-date on the situation. To coordinate diverse teams, this was of utmost necessity.

He recounted the episode with Ben Brady, then the chase and conclude by saying, "Madame Atomos and the Japanese giant are on the run, but the chauffeur is paralyzed for the next hour."

"If you'd told me earlier…"

"It wouldn't have mattered," Smith interrupted. "Madame Atomos must have fled when the grenades exploded and now she's got a good head start on us."

"Not necessarily. I'm sure she hasn't left the Yellowstone area. I'm in constant contact with the different checkpoints and they haven't reported anything at entrance to the neighborhood. I'm not giving orders, but I think you should go back to the property."

Smith hesitated and shot a questioning glance at Mie and Akamatsu who had just joined him while Owen was carrying the paralyzed chauffeur back to the Malibu.

"Madame Atomos is no longer there," Akamatsu decided.

"And maybe she never was," Mie added. "No one saw her, did they?"

Owen flung his package onto the floor of the car, stood up and said, "Anyway, we saw the bearded gorilla and he didn't just disappear into thin air. I'm with Stutton. We should go back, check out the dump and find the entrance to the tunnel." He pointed at the chauffeur and added, "This guy should know a lot, but he can't open his mouth for an hour. In the meantime we should try to nab his buddy. It couldn't hurt."

"Okay, Ralph. We're going back to the property."

"Hold on!" Stutton requested. "Something's happening on the North Platte River… A boat with two fishermen is cruising around despite the ban…" He tried to follow the course of events while relating them to Beffort at the same time. His words came in fits and starts with many long pauses.

"So?" Beffort asked. "What about these fishermen?"

"Wait a minute," Stutton sounded preoccupied. "I'm listening to the guards north of Yellowstone reporting to headquarters... hey, the boat just shot off like an arrow! It's headed upstream!"

"Who's on board?" Beffort howled.

"Don't know... It's happening fast... There you go, it's left Yellowstone and is heading towards Mills. Now the squad cars are taking up the chase... A police boat is also on the water... okay, the boat's veering off to the right bank. According to the sergeant in charge it's going to land for sure..."

"Damnit!" Smith burst out, "Who's on board?"

Stutton did not answer. Through the Malibu's speaker they could hear the faint echoes of a conversation cut off by shouting and sirens—the suspense was unbearable. Five miles from there, somewhere on the North Platte River, the Casper police were obviously involved in an important operation and Beffort was fuming because he was being kept out of it for want of information.

"Madame Atomos!" Stutton suddenly yelled. "She's just been officially identified by the police boat. Unbelievable! The pilot of the other boat is carrying her in his arms and jumping ashore!"

"Tell them to open fire!" Beffort screamed.

"Too late. Madame Atomos and her goon just disappeared in the reeds. The police boat reached their landing spot, but the cops on the other bank are blocked off, running around trying to find a bridge."

Smith became suddenly calm. On foot Madame Atomos and her bodyguard had little chance to save their hides. "Stutton?"

"I'm here."

"Give me the location of the boat."

"Between Mills and Goose Egg around the 10-mile mark on Highway 220. But don't knock yourself out, boss. Some motorcycle cops are already on their way and the highway will be blockaded in two minutes, along with Mills and Goose Egg."

"Keep me up-to-date," Beffort ordered. "I'm leaving right now."

"Okay."

When Smith got behind the wheel, Mie, Akamatsu and Bernitz were already in the car. The Malibu shot off like a cannon down Alcova Road and came out on Highway 220 just after Locust Street. Seven minutes later Beffort was leaning over the corpse of Peter Boone, salesman, whom the motorcycle cops had discovered in the middle of the road. The unlucky body was still warm and might have just been sleeping if it were not for the huge black bruise around his ear.

"A heavy club," the highway patrolman guessed. "Here are his papers. Seems most likely that this guy was going home in his Pontiac when he stopped and was killed by Madame Atomos' partner."

Smith looked at his watch. "It's been about 12 minutes since they were here. The Pontiac should be found."

The lieutenant shook his head. "Between Mills and Goose Egg no vehicle of the make has been spotted by the roadblocks or the patrols. We're going to have to search the side roads and paths leading into the woods around the 220."

Smith furrowed his brow. "That could be long and hard."

"Maybe, but at least we know one thing: Madame Atomos and her thug can only be on this side of the river, which means they're surrounded inside an impassable net."

Just when the lieutenant finished saying this, the helicopter flew low right over the river and headed due west without being spotted by the men climbing around.

This success, of course, served to identify Madame Atomos too late, but also as proof of the fantastic speed with which Isadori and Nachi, the pilot, had acted. Huddling in her seat like a worm in its cocoon, the sinister woman certainly did not regret that she had reformed an organization with only Japanese members. Almost fanatical, with an inhuman disregard of death, the members of the Rising Sun were a perfect fit for the needs of Madame Atomos, who was still a big "maneater."

The Cadillac chauffeur was the only black spot—literally and figuratively—in this impeccable strategy. The Black knew a lot about the location of the various Atomos refuges and too much about the plans of the diabolical woman who, frankly, was hoping he would die trying to escape. She was thinking it was probable and told Isadori.

He answered, "I think so, too, mistress. Sam isn't the kind to be taken alive."

Oddly, and no doubt because they were still slightly traumatized by the hazards they had recently run, neither Madame Atomos nor Isadori thought about the paralyzing ray. Moreover there was the example of Shibuki who was shot down by the police, which implied that after the death of Brady and his men, Smith Beffort no longer had a complete Dragon Force in Casper.

Nachi steered a course to avoid urban areas and highway junctions before he landed the helicopter to the north of Riverton where the country was particularly dry and arid because of its proximity to the Rocky Mountains whose high peaks vanished in the clouds. The ranch spread its hectares far from any neighbors. But there were no cattle or ranch hands to be seen and everything was falling to ruin. Four buildings surrounded the vast ground where the helicopter alit. To the right, on top of the 65-foot high tank, stood a kind of television antenna but with six satellite dishes extending from a feeder that came straight out of the tank.

Madame Atomos and Isadori got out of the helicopter and went to meet the three men waiting at the central building. "Dr. Wataru?" Madame Atomos asked.

One of the Japanese pointed toward the tank. "He's in the station, Madame. Do you want me to get him?"

"No. When he's finished, just tell him that I arrived. Come on, Isadori, we need some rest."

Isadori followed her. After the emotional ride, he knew exactly how his mistress was going to use him to vent. "Rest" was just a euphemism.

Sam, the black chauffeur, came to abruptly, like a cork bobbing to the surface, and rolled his wild eyes. He had lost contact with reality at the wheel of the Cadillac and now found himself in a strange office. He was lying on a couch, handcuffed, across from four men and a woman sitting and watching him coldheartedly.

Sam took a better look at them and his mind went *tilt*. If he was not mistaken, he was in the presence of Smith and Mie Beffort, Akamatsu and Owen Bernitz! He did not know Wyatt, but that did not stop him from turning gray. Among the members of the Rising Sun,

Smith and Mie Beffort had a frightening reputation. As for Akamatsu and Bernitz, it was better not to talk aobut it!

"Okay, Sam," Bernitz scowled. "Now that you're awake you'd better spill the beans. If you clam up, it's the gas chamber instead of an afternoon snack. We do things fast! No lawyers, no courts, no prison! Either you sing and come work for us or you hold your tongue and we snuff you! Got it?"

It was painful for Sam to swallow. He did not have the Japanese fanaticism of the Rising Sun and figured he was too young to make a beautiful corpse. Furthermore, contrary to what Isadori thought of him, he would much rather be a living traitor than a dead hero. He also knew that Smith Beffort always kept his promises. In the history of the Atomos Organization, he was not the first to sell out Madame Atomos or change sides by joining the Green Dragon Force. As a mercenary he would go wherever his interest lay. Plus, all things considered, especially the direction that the conversation was headed, Sam felt some relief in the possibility to give up crime.

"What do you want to know?" he asked.

To open up the cooperative dialogue Owen stood up and took off the handcuffs. On the psychological level, this act had an enormous effect on Sam. He gained back some color, sat up and accepted the cigarette that Smith offered him. All of a sudden, contrary to how he felt in the Rising Sun, he had the profound impression that there was no racial segregation in the Green Dragon and this was extremely comforting.

"Thanks to you," Beffort railed, "Madame Atomos got away. I have only one question to ask you and you have only one answer to give me. Where is she?"

"Riverton," Sam said without a moment's hesitation. "If you have a map of Wyoming, I could show you exactly where Dr. Wataru has the station."

"The station?"

"Yeah. That's where the big transmitter is that controls all the super-minibrains roaming around the state. But…"

"But what?"

"Madame Atomos will choose another refuge if she knows you captured me."

Smith grinned. "We thought of that. Right now all the papers, radios and T.V. stations are telling how you were found dead by sacrificing your life for Madame Atomos. Before you woke up dozens of photos were taken of you at the morgue, deader than dead. So we staged the whole thing perfectly. Look at the newspaper. Owen?"

Bernitz pulled a paper out of his pocket, unfolded the special edition and laid it in front of Sam, who saw the big headline and a picture of himself on a table in the morgue. His blood-stained clothes were in tatters, his mouth gaped open, his eyes rolled up… It was terrifying, so true to life!

Sam shuddered and Beffort spoke calmly. "It's just for show, but if you had escaped us, the police would have found you and given you the same treatment as Shibuki. Without a doubt it's what Madame Atomos was hoping for. The map, Owen."

Bernitz went to the desk and spread out a detailed map of Wyoming, then waved Sam over. The Black leaned over and put his finger on a point between Riverton and Shoshini on the southeast dotted line marking the border of the Wind River Indian Reservation.

"The station's here on an old ranch. More precisely it's inside a water tank. Madame Atomos has got a helicopter and some cars there and two weird machines that I don't know what they're for."

Beffort pricked up his ears. "What do they look like?"

Sam puckered his lips. "Nothing in particular... or at least nothing I know of."

"But still?" Beffort pressed him. "An object has to look like something, more or less, so you have to be able to make some kind of comparison. You said two machines, so you unconsciously realized that these things are put together to do something or to observe something or measure something."

Sam frowned and his hands drew an arc in the air. "The hangar was dark, but I saw pretty clearly that there were two platforms standing on four feet with a kind of rail going round... on the edge of the platforms was something written in white that I couldn't read."

Bernitz sneered, "Swear it sounds like one of those thingies put at intersections for the cops to stand on and direct traffic."

Smith looked at his watch. "We can talk about this later. Right now the most important thing to do is to surround the ranch. Do what's necessary, Wyatt, and tell your men to be discreet. Let's get to Riverton. Sam, you're coming with us."

Chapter XIV

Because of the slope of the land the ranch was not visible from Highway 789, so in order to see without being seen, a surveillance plane was sent up. Flying at a reasonable altitude with a Miller High Life advertising banner flapping behind it, the plane sent out a message to Beffort: "Two sedans in the main yard surrounded by three buildings... A Bell helicopter badly concealed under some camouflage netting..."

"Vulnerable?" Beffort interrupted.

"With mortar shells it'll crack like an egg," the quiet voice of the pilot assured. "Except for that nothing special. The place looks deserted and there's only one access road. Need anything else?"

"No, but I don't think it's normal that there's no lookout posted on the roof or the tank. Can you get any lower?"

"Not without drawing attention to myself. An advertising plane around this godforsaken land is strange enough as it is."

"Okay, forget it," Smith decided.

The plane went on its way to the north before making a wide turn. Soon it would be back in Riverton with its store of pictures taken over the ranch. On examining them they would certainly find the details that escaped the pilot and they would have the exact location of the Bell.

It was 1 pm. The sun was beating down hard, melting the landscape into waves of trembling heat. The trees had only short shadows off their trunks. Everything appeared calm and still, but teams of the Green Dragon

Force were combing the area in a long, meticulous exploration of a very wide zone. The tunnel might have been behind a rock, in a ditch by the road or next to the Boysen Reservoir that formed a lake where another boat could be waiting... Indeed, given the fact that Madame Atomos' underground tunnels often went on for miles and miles, it was almost a herculean task.

"We'll still be here tonight," Akamatsu complained.

"Time doesn't matter now," Smith replied. "Madame Atomos is on this ranch and we can't let her get out, except to come before a judge. We'll spend days on this if we have to, Yosho, but when we attack, we'll be absolutely certain that Madame Atomos has no way to escape."

"The helicopter?"

"It'll be blown up right before the attack."

"The explosion will alert Madame Atomos."

"Sure, but it'll be too late. The ranch is already surrounded by the police and the Green Dragon, even if there are some big holes. But when we go into action this afternoon, tonight or tomorrow, I'll swear to you that Madame Atomos and her men will run into a human wall. This time she won't get away!"

Mie and Owen glanced at each other skeptically and Sam crossed his fingers behind his back to ward off bad luck. Akamatsu said nothing, but privately he was sure that Smith was the only one who believed it.

The brutal death of Sam announced by the papers, radio and television had completely reassured Madame Atomos who had been thrown into a short panic by the pessimistic predictions of Dr. Wataru. Outside of his laboratory on San Esteban Island, the doctor was anxious and pathologically suspicious. All the more since

the super-minibrains had fizzled out and his giant computer showed only three lights representing Royal, Gib
and the Chapins' monkey. For a man who dreamed of
"robotizing" the USA, after five years of patient research, this was a terrible flop.

"Smile, Wataru," Madame Atomos laughed. "We're
in a tough spot right now, but tomorrow the Rising Sun
will give us a slew of subjects to control."

"Why not today?"

Madame Atomos stretched out on the couch and
furrowed her brow. "Because our informers don't know
where Smith Beffort is," she grumbled. "Well, I've been
counting on killing him first in order to decapitate the
FBI and the Green Dragon. With Beffort dead the United
States will be putty in my hands."

"We're wasting time," Wataru said.

Madame Atomos glowered at him. After living on
an island with only Dr. Miwa giving orders, this old goat
seemed to have forgotten who was boss. She propped
herself up on one elbow and said softly, "Get out of
here, doctor, and don't bother me anymore today. I'm in
charge here! Now get out!"

Wataru bowed and walked out the door. He headed
to the tank, clambered up the ladder and sat down at his
computer. Wataru was fighting in memory of Nagasaki
and Hiroshima, but he did not understand Madame
Atomos' strategy. Moreover, on becoming younger she
seemed to have lost sight of the real goal of her battle
against the Americans, as she was scaling her noble
vengeance down to a simple fight with the Befforts and
Akamatsu, thus destroying the remaining trust that
Wataru had had in her.

And then always half-nude, provocative, perverse
and depraved, Madame Atomos was giving the impres-

sion of being more obsessed with her senses than with accomplishing her mission.

Wataru took a deep breath while thinking of his dead loved ones in Hiroshima. In the end, whatever he did would do nothing but make more death and bring new suffering to life. A lot of time had passed since August 6, 1945. Wataru felt old, weary of life because he had no other ideal but the destruction and extermination of a country and its inhabitants. In his laboratory on San Esteban Island this kind of thought had never crossed the old man's mind. Back there he lived alone, researching, focusing all his energy on the fabrication and miniaturization of the famous super-minibrain that Madame Atomos thought nothing of.

Wataru heard a rumbling and looked up. Through one of the little windows on the tank he saw a red plane towing an advertising banner. In over a month this was the first time that a plane flew over the ranch in spite of being so close to the Riverton airport. Wataru watched in gloom as it soared by and made a wide turn to head back to Riverton, which was invisible behind the arid hill that barred the horizon. It was almost as if it were flying on the ground. Then Wataru glimpsed a kind of movement and a flicker of light. It was very fleeting, almost unreal, and because he was perched high up in his post he was sure that nobody else saw it.

Taking a sudden interest in the situation, the old man grabbed his binoculars and started surveying the horizon, which seemed to be concealing an unusual activity. For a long time he saw nothing but rocks and trees, then a metal rod bobbed in and out of his vision, showed up again and disappeared for good. Knowing where Highway 789 was, Wataru wondered why a car with a radio antenna was rolling through the hills, off the paved roads, staying out of sight of the ranch.

He swung around, pointed his binoculars north and sighted another antenna swinging behind a rocky hill. When he scrutinize the horizon more carefully he counted 30 antennas, not completely hidden but staying behind the hills and mounds. At that moment Wataru should have climbed down from his nest and alerted Madame Atomos. Instead of this he did not move, stood there pensively, lost in some personal reverie until he finally sat back down in his chair.

If Madame Atomos could have seen his smile, she would have understood that not everyone loved her in her organization.

At 6 pm Art Baxter showed up at Beffort's HQ. He had directed the search of an opening near the Boysen Reservoir at a highly strategic spot for Madame Atomos who always loved water to fall back on. Baxter arrived with a negative report. Beffort took note of it and Akamatsu crossed out the entire northern part of the map.

At 6:15 Hank Seurer also came in to report. "We've checked the whole area from the suburbs of Riverton to the Wind River," he said, wiping away the sweat on his forehead. "Zilch for a tunnel."

Akamatsu crossed off the western part.

At 8 pm, as night was starting to fall, Beffort looked thoughtfully at the map. The entire perimeter was crossed out, which meant that no underground passage had been found outside the zone being guarded by the Green Dragon and the police.

"Suspicious, Smith?" Akamatsu asked.

"Yes. Madame Atomos has never been so careless. Without an escape tunnel she's lost. We may have blinders on, Yosho, but I'm sure she's got an exit door somewhere."

Akamatsu shrugged his shoulders. Now he was starting to have confidence, unlike Beffort who was becoming more and more worried as the hours passed.

"Everyone makes mistakes," he said. "Plus, by reporting Sam's death we did what was necessary to remove her suspicions, didn't we? Why would she be suspicious? Sam was the only one who knew the location of the ranch." He pointed to the buildings that were visible between two rocks. "Look, Smith, nothing's moving, right?"

"That's what bothers me," Beffort admitted. "In the past, even recently, Madame Atomos never acted like this. To bury herself in a hole when she could be making the entire country tremble in fear thanks to her diabolical minibrains... it's not like her."

Sam stepped forward and said, "We don't really have time to talk about it, but there's Isadori now."

"Who?"

"Her lover, her bodyguard, her dog!" Sam said scornfully. "She leads him around on a leash and he loves her. He was the one waiting for her in Mexico when she parachuted onto runway X. This morning he was the one driving the boat on the North Platte..."

"I see," Beffort said. "You mean to tell us that Madame Atomos and Isadori are like newlyweds?"

Sam had a big grin on his face. "You're too smart for that, Mr. Beffort! If I had to use my own words, I'd call 'em something else."

Mie was grateful to the Black for sparing her.

"I think I know what Sam wants to say," Akamatsu said in a monotone. "Not too long ago I, too, went on an Atomos honeymoon. It was in a hotel and I didn't see the sun for weeks. On that level, Madame Atomos is insatiable... Well, I hope Isadori is a strong fellow."

"He's strong," Sam confirmed, very dignified.

"So," Akamatsu concluded, "let's make sure she doesn't move from the ranch, Smith. Maybe even the mortar shells won't affect her and she'll be in a nightie when we slap the cuffs on her."

Beffort did not smile. In his soul and in his conscience he thought all this was too good to be true. Even in love like a dog in heat the terrible woman was no less fearsome, sharp or shrewd.

"Sam," Beffort asked, "how many men are on the ranch besides Isadori and Dr. Wataru?"

"Three," he answered right away.

Here again the bride was too beautiful. With no means of escape, with no ultimate weapon, Madame Atomos did not even have a big enough army to defend herself. Or else Akamatsu was right in thinking that she was not wary and was counting on the Bell in case of danger..."

"When do we attack, Smith?" Akamatsu asked.

Beffort watched the skies. "In the dead of night when all the lights on the ranch have gone out. I want to have total surprise on our side. I'll head the commando team with Owen Bernitz, Hank Seurer, Art Baxter, Dan Stone and ten other men that you'll choose, Owen."

"And me?" Mie and Akamatsu spoke at the same time.

"You, Yosho will be in charge of keeping the teams on the second line ready for action while watching the roads all around, even the footpaths. Mie, I'd like you to take care of the Boysen Reservoir, the Wind River and the suburbs of Shoshoni." He turned to Bernitz. "Owen, go right now and contact Colonel Fisk. He's got the pictures from the observation plane and knows the exact position of the Bell. He can do what's necessary to set up however many mortars he thinks he needs wherever he wants so that the first round will be a bull's eye."

"If I were you," Akamatsu spoke up, "I wouldn't be so careful. If Madame Atomos and her men are killed..."

"If they're killed," Beffort stopped him, "we'll never know where the lab is that's making the minibrains and where the Rising Sun is hiding out, which is still an ultra-secret organization, even for Sam, that we know nothing about."

"Without Madame Atomos," Akamatsu stated, "the whole thing will crumble!"

"You don't know that, Yosho. There are too many people who sympathize with Madame Atomos. One of them is bound to try to take control. There is certainly some connection between the Rising Sun and the A.O.F.M.A.[1] The latter provides the money. Madame Atomos can't control and supervise everything. It has to have a director, an accountant, secretaries..."

"Listening to you," Akamatsu joked, "it sounds like Madame Atomos is running a business."

"It is!" Beffort said. "To manufacture the minibrains takes money, materials, a research lab, machines and workers. This, indeed, means a commercial organization, accounting books, pay records, etc. So if all this still exists after Madame Atomos' death, do you really think we can rest on our laurels?"

---

[1] American Organization of the Friends of Madame Atomos.

Akamatsu did not answer. Smith Beffort was right, Yosho had to agree, but his hatred of the sinister woman was making it hard for him to hear logic. In Japan there is a proverb that says, "Crush the head of the snake and don't look for the babies because without it they'll die." Akamatsu thought of nothing but crushing the head the Madame Atomos.

"Smith," he said gravely, "by arresting this woman like an ordinary criminal, you're taking incredible risks and responsibilities. She'll rot in prison for a while before going to trial. Don't tell me that the Rising Sun or the A.O.F.M.A., probably both, won't try to break her out."

Beffort lit a cigarette and smiled. "In the meantime, she'll talk, or it'll be Isadori, Wataru or one of the men on the ranch and we'll snuff out the Rising Sun, disintegrate the A.O.F.M.A. and destroy the lab and all the hideouts scattered around the USA. When Madame Atomos is in our hands, Yosho, she won't escape…"

He left it at that to show that he would run the affair as he saw fit. Then he turned to Bernitz and said, "Get going, Owen, we have no time to waste. Make sure Fisk acts swiftly. Until that Bell is torched, I won't believe we can capture Madame Atomos."

"Okay, I'm going," Owen said. "What weapons should I get for the commando team?"

"Paralyzing guns. No firearms. If they fight back, I don't want a nervous trigger finger killing Madame Atomos."

Akamatsu scowled. He knew why Smith was sending him to the back and he had to admit the precaution was warranted. If he had a weapon and was standing in front of Madame Atomos, he could not stop himself from killing her.

Chapter XV

Isadori woke up suddenly and opened his eyes in the darkened room. The night was overcast, letting no light filter through, and the silence was as thick as a wall. Isadori sat up and listened. He heard only the breathing of Madame Atomos lying in bed on the other side of the room and the annoying sound of a dripping faucet. Isadori always slept like a log, with no dreams and no nightmares, vegetative, coming out of it in the early morning... or when his instinct warned him of imminent danger.

He stood up, opened the window and peeked through the shutters. The land was dark but farther off he saw a halo moving on the horizon line. A horizon that was really quite close since the ranch was in the middle of a kind of crater...

Isadori stuck out his stubby nose and sniffed the air like a wild animal.

"What is it, Isadori?" Madame Atomos whispered, also aware of an unseen menace.

The giant turned around and whispered, "I don't know, mistress, but I have the feeling that something's changed."

Without turning on the light Madame Atomos joined him in front of the window and examined the night. To the right the glow from the Riverton street-lights was dancing on the low clouds. But it was the moving halo she stared at, digging her nails into Isadori's arm.

"Do you see that?"

"Yes. Looks like a flashlight in the hand of some-one walking…"

Madame Atomos' eyes dilated in the dark. The road was far from the ranch and the path leading to it was on the other side. In fact, in the direction of the halo there was nothing but gravel, rock and some clumps of stunted trees.

Madame Atomos went back to the bed and felt around for her binoculars. When she got back to the window she adjusted the night vision and then started when she saw a group of armed men sneaking toward the ranch. These men had nothing to do with the halo, which continued crawling behind a hill, but all the action proved to her that danger was afoot. She focused her binoculars better and recognized the tall outline of Smith Beffort, then the stocky shadow of Owen Bernitz. She grabbed onto Isadori like a life preserver. But her moment of weakness passed quickly and the next second she was the great Madame Atomos again, giving orders.

"Got tell Wataru and the others that the Green Dragon has surrounded the ranch. They can take the hel-icopter. If they act fast they might still reach our base in Big Sandy."

Isadori looked down. "They won't make it. The Bell will be shot down when Beffort spots it."

"I hope so! Like that we'll have a chance of getting through unseen. Go! Meet me in the hangar after putting on some warm clothes. Remember that it's cold on the platforms."

Isadori nodded and rushed out of the room. Mad-ame Atomos put on her pants, boots, two wool shirts and snuck off to the hangar. Once in the small building, she drew a camouflage curtain to keep out the light and flicked on a big flashlight.

The Hiller platforms were ready to go and the equipment was all there. Madame Atomos put on a black helmet and slipped into a suit of the same color. Then she sat down and waited calmly for Isadori.

The Green Dragon Force, the police and the FBI were ready for any eventuality. As for Colonel Fisk, he was waiting for Beffort's signal to send his missiles at the Bell, which was already "in his sights."

For the moment, the order was for silence and still-ness. Action was taken only by the team that Beffort was leading. An action that was still passive, stealthy, merely a slow and careful approach over the rocky ter-rain without a glimmer of light. Everything was going as planned with nothing to report, but at the head of the column Smith could not help feeling a growing discom-fort. Since the first appearance of Madame Atomos on United States territory, this was the ninth time that the forces of order had her trapped in its apparently lethal grasp and in all the previous operations the diabolical woman had always managed to break out and preserve her truly inviolable freedom.

Smith looked up. Less than 200 yards away, a dark-er spot in the dark night, the ranch looked like it was sleeping on its rocky bed. No light, no movement, death-ly silent…

"Say, Boss," Owen whispered, "what if she's hiding out somewhere else?"

"No. With those two round machines that Sam saw in the hangar here…"

Just then a man slipped and rocks cascaded down the hill. Everyone froze and Smith's thought vanished before he could finish it. Then when the last rock had stopped rolling, the team resumed its march, got to within 150 yards of the ranch and spread out around the fence of the old stockyard. The path from the ranch to the road entered here and Smith led his men over the ground that had been stamped down for centuries by thousands of hooves.

Now the team was less than 100 yards from its goal and Smith figured it was time to send in the mortar shells. He stopped everyone and raised his hand to Baxter with the walkie-talkie, who pulled out the antenna.

At that very second the harrowing scream of a rotor blade tore through the silence and a gust of air slapped Beffort who stood petrified by the sudden noise. The Bell literally jumped into the sky, dove into the clouds and soared off toward the Rocky Mountains.

It all happened in a flash, within a few seconds, and in such conditions it is hard for a man to control a reflex when his finger is already on the trigger of a paralyzing rifle with a maximum range of 500 yards. Smith was this man. The thought popped into his mind that they had no air cover, that the groups around the perimeter had orders not to fire until the mortars had done their job and that the Bell, flying at 200 miles a hour, would be out of range in no time, lost in the night.

He shot from his hit, wildly, keeping his finger on the trigger and the invisible ray swept over the aircraft that was already just a shadow. Not sure of the distance, thinking he had missed because it was still flying straight ahead, Smith yelled, "Sound the alarm, Baxter! Open fire!"

Shaken up, Baxter yelled the order and almost simultaneously hell broke loose around the crater. Amidst the din of explosions, while all eyes were turned on the Bell, no one heard or saw the two Hiller platforms flying sideways into the sky, heading north, more precisely toward Creek where a garage rented by a local partner of Madame Atomos housed a Honda 500 cc racing bike that Madame Atomos and Isadori would ride off averaging 125 miles per hour.

Knowing that the Hiller flying platforms—a relatively late model at that—were only good for short hops, Madame Atomos had once again seen to everything…

In the smoking debris of the Bell, they had just found five charred corpses, barely identifiable, but that Sam could still recognized easily enough.

"That's Dr. Wataru. That one's Nachi the pilot. I don't know the names of the other three, but they were the ones on the ranch before Madame Atomos got here."

Smith clenched his fists. Madame Atomos and Isadori were not in the helicopter and no longer on the ranch. The other surprising find was that the two machines described by Sam were not in the hangar. However, no one had passed the guards surrounding in the area and no building on the ranch had a basement so that the existence of a tunnel was not seriously considered.

Furthermore, the exploration that followed confirmed the probability and Beffort was forced to admit that the sinister Japanese woman had once again proved her diabolical ingenuity.

Mie and Akamatsu, pallid and tense, climbed out of the jeep. The latter spoke right away. "It's not possible, Smith. We were wrong. She wasn't here."

Beffort shrugged. "She was here, Yosho. In a room inside her bed is still warm and her clothes are piled up on a chair over a pair of night-vision binoculars. Since the window opens onto the hill that I was coming over with my team, the conclusion is unavoidable, isn't it?"

"If she was here," Akamatsu growled, "then she's still here! No one got through the lines and the Bell came down in flames. How do you think…"

"The two platforms described by Sam have also disappeared," Beffort him off. "They are somehow involved with Isadori and Madame Atomos, but I haven't figured out how yet. Unless they belong to some crazy new arsenal like a teleport by self-disintegration. Otherwise I don't know what they were for."

From the doorway Owen Bernitz said, "Don't sweat it, boss! I just got a message from 6289 who's still getting info in his dispatch in Casper. Around ten minutes ago a police patrol on a side road around Creek ran into the two Hiller platforms abandoned in the middle of the road. They were marked US Army, were in perfect working order and had been used recently.[2]"

Beffort felt a hole in his stomach. It was so simple compared to the usually fantastic means that Madame Atomos had at her disposal that no one had dreamed of it.

"Where's Creek?" Akamatsu asked.

"Six miles from here," Bernitz responded. "No need to say that the alarm's been sounded and teams are already searching the place house by house, street by street, and the roads are being closed all the way to the state border."

Akamatsu looked at his watch and snarled, "We can give it a shot, but do you realize that Madame Atomos and Isadori have almost an hour head start? Searching

---

[2] The Hiller flying platforms, also known as HO-1 or VZ-1 Pawnee, were designed in 1953 for the American army by Hiller Aircraft Corporation. Judged to be impractical by the Pentagon, only six prototypes were built.

the town of Creek is a waste of time. If Madame Atomos went there, it wasn't by chance. I'm sure a plane piloted by a Rising Sun member was standing ready to take off and with the head start Madame Atomos could be flying over just about any nearby state..." He sat down and concluded, "We're beaten, Smith. That's the truth."

Beffort sat next to him. There was nothing more he could do.

For Madame Atomos the fantastic ride was over.

Isadori knew how to do many things, but he was truly a champion driver on a motorcycle racing through the mountainous roads. Like in the boat, Madame Atomos had almost lost her sense of time. Nothing else existed except the dancing beam of light that flashed over the trees or on a bottomless ravine with sheer cliffs and once in a while on a brief stretch of straight, open road.

Clinging to the massive back of Isadori, Madame Atomos had a vague, out-of-body sensation, unconsciously drunk on the speed, drowned in the howling engine and the screeching tires. The monster roared between her legs, with annoying vibrations, and her nails dug into Isadori's chest as he hunched over the handlebars.

The lights of Big Sandy appeared at the end of the winding mountain road and Isadori slowed down, turned off the road before the first houses and steered the Honda up a steep path too narrow for a car to pass through. The bike climbed the hill with no problem, jumped over one last bump and pulled up in front of a chalet.

Isadori cut the engine and turned around. "We're here, mistress."

Madame Atomos unwrapped her arms from him without saying a word. She stepped off the bike and headed for the stairs. Right away an old woman appeared in the open the doorway that cast a long triangle of light into the night.

"Close the door, Kishi!" Madame Atomos barked as she shoved by her. She took off her helmet and turned around. "Is your radio working?"

The Japanese woman bowed. "It works, Madame."

"Call the Rising Sun base in Casper right now!" Madame Atomos ordered. "When you've got Yamoto on the line call me."

Kishi went into a small room next to the living room as Madame Atomos took off her black suit and boots and flopped into an armchair. Isadori entered and laid the automatic pistol, which he had kept in his belt, on the table and said, "I parked the bike and…"

"Who told Beffort?" Madame Atomos asked coldly.

The giant shrugged. Madame Atomos continued, "Someone betrayed me, Isadori! The ranch was my safest refuge and few people knew its location. Who's in charge of my security?"

"Me, mistress."

Madame Atomos stood up, an evil grin on her lips. "Who failed at his job, Isadori?"

"Me, mistress," the giant grumbled.

Madame Atomos walked up to him, grabbed the pistol and pointed it at his forehead. "So," she said softly, "do you deserve to die?"

The giant did not even blink. "I deserve it."

At that moment Kishi called from the other room that she had Casper on the radio and Yamoto on the line. Madame Atomos hesitated, then finally put down the pistol and hurried into the next room. Isadori sat down, a little disturbed, wondering if he owed his life to Kishi's interruption.

To be sure, he emptied the pistol's clip as he listened to Madame Atomos questioning Yamoto, the head of the Rising Sun. The conversation was brief and Madame Atomos came back to take her place in the armchair, apparently calm. She watched Isadori with all the tenderness that the eye of a cobra could muster, and whispered, "Sam's not dead. Yamoto has proof."

Isadori wrinkled his brow. "Well then, you think he's the one who told Smith Beffort?"

"Of course, you idiot! He was finally seen with Owen Bernitz in the streets of Creek, which means that he's joined the Green Dragon Force and is fighting against us from now on."

"We've got to kill him, mistress!"

Madame Atomos smiled. "Yes, but before we do I think he might inadvertently help us make the Befforts and Akamatsu fall into a trap. I have to think..."

She stretched out her arms, suddenly a pussycat. "Take me upstairs, Isadori. After that ride, we need some rest, don't you think?"

Isadori lifted her in his powerful arms, climbed the stairs and pushed open a door with his foot. He laid Madame Atomos gently on the bed. He knew that she was completely crazy, but he loved her like that.

"Get undressed, Isadori," the terrible woman cooed.

The giant leaned over her, put his hand on her offered flesh and stroked her tenderly.

Madame Atomos? A sweetie!

Jean-Marc Lofficier: *Madame Atomos' Holidays*

Grand Bahama, January 1976

There is no rest for the wicked.
Isaiah, 48:22

"Your problem is that you never go on holidays," said Madame Atomos.

"I beg your pardon?" replied the Yellow Shadow.

They were both relaxing in their chaises lounges on the private beach of the magnificent Xanadu Beach Resort on Grand Bahama island. The weather was perfect; the turquoise blue sea made a striking contrast with the immaculate white sand that was raked every morning by the *boys* of a palace which, once, had counted Frank Sinatra, the Rat Pack and Cary Grant amongst its guests.

A light breeze gently caressed the palm trees, which cast their shadows over the beach-goers and kept the temperature wonderfully cool for the season.

Madame Atomos delicately took a sip of her pineapple rum cocktail, which she had been nursing since she had come on to the beach to join her occasional associate. She had gestured to her usual companion, the hulking Isadori, to go and play in the water while she talked business with the Yellow Shadow. She wore a striking black bikini with as little fabric as the law allowed, which emphasized her splendid figure. But she entertained no illusion as to the power of her feminine charms over the stone-faced Mongol. Madame Atomos knew Monsieur Ming well enough to know that he was entirely invulnerable to her sex appeal.

They had agreed to meet at the Xanadu. In the past, her organization had lent assistance to the Yellow Shadow, in 1965 in San Francisco, when Ming had established his base in the underground city of Kowa, and later, in Africa, to help him spawn his deadly butterflies. In exchange, Ming had pretty much let Madame Atomos have a free rein in America and had given her financial support whenever he could.

"You're always working," explained Madame Atomos. "Constantly coming up with new schemes, which are then invariably crushed by that insolent Frenchman. This creates a permanent stress that must be very bad for your health."

"My health is fine, thank you," said the Yellow Shadow, rather testily, his robotic right hand clamping on his left to hide the slight shaking that had started to plague him recently.

"If you spent more time relaxing on holidays," continued Madame Atomos, "you would feel more rested when the time comes to launch your next offensive. Don't tell me that you don't occasionally feel like you're not as good as you used to be, or that you've been repeating yourself lately? Not that it doesn't happen to all of us eventually," she rushed to add, having noticed a quick, baleful look in her associate's amber eyes.

"So... What would you suggest?" asked Monsieur Ming after a pause.

Madame Atomos stretched like a big cat, boastfully displaying her perfect breasts and her long, smooth legs.

"Do as I do," she purred. "Find yourself a beautiful toy, a little corner of paradise and have some fun."

With a gesture of her manicured hand, she blew a kiss to Isadori who was still frolicking in the water.

"I don't think that's in my nature," sighed the Yellow Shadow with some finality. "I've come to tell you that I've experienced some financial reversals of late..."

"That Frenchman again?" inquired Madame Atomos, whose eyes pointedly stared at the Mongol's left hand which was trembling.

Monsieur Ming ignored her and continued:

"...Therefore I can no longer finance your organization. I know that you have suffered some major setbacks. However, because of my debt to you, I will give you the blueprints for a new type of quantum field generator that will enable you to build a new and better generation of transdimensional saucers."

"It's more than I would have dared to hope for," said Madame Atomos. "Thank you !"

Monsieur Ming got up. Even in black Bermuda shorts, he still looked like a dour clergyman.

"Are you sure you won't stay for dinner?" asked Madame Atomos.

"No. I'm expected in Macao."

The Yellow Shadow walked away.

Madame Atomos smiled. She had duped the Mongol, who was after all a potentially dangerous rival. Monsieur Ming had not suspected the real reason for her presence in the Bahamas.

She looked at the 13th floor penthouse of the Xanadu. For ten years, she had had various servants of hers surreptitiously administer a carefully prepared mixture of drugs to its occupant, who was also the Hotel's owner. Thanks to her efforts, he was now a full-blown lunatic, who barely weighed over 90 pounds, no longer cut his hair and his nails, and slowly agonized–but not without having discreetly transferred half of his vast wealth–$2 billion !–to her Swiss bank account.

Howard Hughes will be dead with three months, thought Madame Atomos, *and with his money, I will rebuild my organization and be even more powerful than before!*

As if she had the time to go on holidays!

ANTICIPATION

ANDRÉ CAROFF

LES SPHÈRES ATTAQUENT

fleuve noir

THE SPHERES OF MADAME ATOMOS

Chapter I

It looked like a soap bubble except that this sphere was approximately the size of a tennis ball. In the bright South American sun, the bubble reflected iridescent hues as it rose over the magnificent Amazon vegetation. The wind was blowing lightly from the west, so the bubble drifted towards the east, but in a straight line skimming over the thick treetops, which it strangely avoided touching.

In the beautiful expanse of the virgin forest, under the wide and open blue sky, the bubble was just a tiny thing, almost invisible because it was transparent, a thing of no account, which would inevitably pop with some gust of wind or against a branch or the beak of some hungry bird... distracted.

The bubble was floating around Manaos, the capital of Amazonas, a city of 350,000 inhabitants, located in the heart of the tropical forest on the Rio Negro, 20 minutes by boat from its confluence with the Solimoes, the upper waters of the Amazon. Manaos, in the north of Brazil, is rich in buildings from the rubber boom, its wooden houses floating over the river or built on pilings, often with a second story to be used during flood times. Manaos and its flotilla of small peddler boats, for the most part Indians, maneuvering in the floating port that can rise with the water level from 20 to 30 feet.

The bubble reached the outskirts of the city, hovered for a minute, then entered a humble home through a window that opened onto the black waters of the Rio Negro. The bubble roamed around the room before drifting into a corner of the ceiling where stopped moving.

Later, a couple carrying a baby entered. They were young, uneducated and uncultured Indians. The baby was six months old. Flies fluttered around its mouth while its mother, already fat and flabby, gave it her breast, humming softly. Sitting cross-legged, the man smoked a cigar stub while drinking a glass of aguadiente. He and his wife were prematurely aged, maybe a little mentally slow, and in any case alcoholic and probably syphilitic.

The bubble unstuck from the ceiling, silently crossed the room and drifted out of the window. It flew over Manaos, coasted around the Teatro Amazonas and came into a residential zone where it floated down towards a big, beautiful, neo-classic house and slipped through the narrow opening of a bay window protected from the sun by an elegant shutter. The bubble roamed around the big living room and just like in the room of the poor Indians it stuck in a corner of the ceiling and stopped moving.

The house belonged to Dr. Alvares Vargas, a renowned gerontologist whose office was in the chic area of Manaos. Dr. Vargas had inherited this house from his parents—his father was also a doctor, a gynecologist—and he lived here with his wife and three sons, also married and doctors by atavism and tradition.

Furthermore, this family of doctors naturally belonged to the elite of Manaos and they all had relatively important functions in the City Council: the father Alvares Vargas in the Council itself, the eldest son Jorge in the Events Committee, the youngest son Rodolfo in the City Orchestra and the middle son Miguel in the Sports Commission.

Maria Vargas and her three daughters-in-law presided over the city's philanthropic work, sang in the church choir and organized charity activities all year long in the ideal tradition of the family whose prestige only grew stronger through the generations.

Also through tradition they had dinner as a family every night at the Vargas' house whereas for the other meals they could do whatever they wanted. Therefore, at 8 pm the servants set the table in the center of the huge living room. At 8:30 Maria Vargas came to supervise the operation, straighten out some of the silverware and make sure that the vases had enough water so the flowers would not die, then she went upstairs to get dressed after checking that all was well in the kitchen.

At 9 pm the men met in the small salon and talked about their day while drinking imported whiskey and smoking El Salvadorian cigars. At 9:30 the women came down, hair done up, make-up put on, perfume sprinkled, and wearing their jewelry and low-cut dresses. The conversation picked up in the small salon, very polite, without loud voices and, in short, with that good, proper, Vargas upbringing that clung to them like a tumor on the flesh.

At 10 pm they sat down at the table. It was Feijoada night, a traditional dish which is, in fact, a complete meal where all the ingredients are brought together on the table. It's a kind of stew with red and black beans cooked with sun-dried meat, beef brisket, sausages, lard and pork feet, ears and tails. They are served separately with rice and green cabbage finely chopped, accompanied by slices of ham and grilled pork ribs. Alvares Vargas took a little of everything, mixed it up and seasoned it lightly with the special bean sauce with chili peppers and lime. After that, while the other members of the family were serving themselves, he sprinkled the dish with farfofa before eating it with orange slices.

For a few minutes the Vargas family ate in silence, then Maria felt that the temperature had risen considerably since she had entered the living room. At this hour when it should have been cooling off, it was pretty weird. Maria snuck a peek at the wide-open windows and then automatically looked up at the ceiling without seeing the bubble, which was still stuck in the corner and was now emitting an invisible ray.

Maria kept eating. She had not drunk a drop of alcohol, but a strange euphoria was creeping through her. Although 50 years old she suddenly felt like a young girl, wanting to escape, even just for an instant, from the shackles of respectability.

All of a sudden Alvares Vargas narrowed his eyes, put down his knife and fork and asked, "What's going on here tonight?"

Since he was looking at Jorge, his oldest son, he answered, "I don't know, but it's not bad, is it?"

His wife, Catarina, broke out laughing so cheerfully that Maria, her mother-in-law, and Teresa as well as Vitoria, her sisters-in-law, all chimed in. The men balked, then smiled, but Alvares snapped his fingers a few times and the laughter stopped.

Alvares said softly, "The servants are leaving in three minutes. Show some manners in the meantime, please... Um, don't you think it's a little hot tonight?"

Without thinking, he loosened his tie and unbuttoned his collar. Nobody found this odd, even though it was fiendishly so! Alvares Vargas was known for his sense of decorum and his respect of etiquette. He never raised his voice, never swore and never used slang, even common words.

"It is hot," Miguel said, taking off his coat and draping it over the back of the chair. "I'm dying here."

Nobody said a word. Everyone was listening to the servants who were leaving to go to their rooms on the other side of the huge house. When the sound of their footsteps had faded away, the men took off their coats and ties.

"Aye!" Rodolfo sighed with satisfaction, "There are times when it's good to live free... Father, I'm beginning to get tired of taking care of people. I think it's depressing."

"It is depressing," Jorge agreed, leaning his elbows on the table, which he never did. "Truthfully, I don't think any job is more grueling than ours. Am I wrong?"

Normally he would get booed.

"You're dead on," Teresa answered, who had always been formal and polite since she was the wife of Rodolfo. "Your brother is called away at all hours of the day and night so we sometimes go an entire week without making love because we don't have the time..."

This was said very matter-of-factly and no one batted an eyelid, even though the subject was strictly taboo at the Vargas house. To the contrary, Maria giggled before commenting without the least bit of condescendence but with plenty of good humor, "You don't know how to organize your time, my child. Me, I used to arrange things and still do, I might add, to meet with your father-in-law in his office if need be, even if we have to do it in a chair or on his exam table."

There were laughs all around and one of the sons, maybe Miguel who was the youngest so probably the boldest, yelled out, "Bravo, Mom!"

"Stop with the jokes," Alvares said in the icy voice he used on his patients when they continued to believe they were in good health. "We have to do something to stop this slavery... We don't have a minute to ourselves and we're less and less respected. Our patients aren't even grateful to us. They come to us to heal them like they were flat tires that just need a little air." He downed a glass of wine and said ominously, "I intend to set things straight, my children, I guarantee you. From now on I'm going to take drastic actions. What's the point of wasting time on hopeless cases?"

Miguel approved enthusiastically, "Finally, an idea I can sink my teeth into! Medical ethics is a worm-eaten rag. We have to replace it or we'll be done for. Let's kill the pests before caring for them... like that we'll for sure take care of the healthy ones."

While speaking he kept watching the windows and doors. He knew he was talking to his family alone and they were the only ones who could accept his ideas. They were his family, but for some time that he could not say how long, they were also his clan.

Everyone applauded except for Vitoria. She was at the end of the table, the farthest away from where the bubble was stuck. She said, "You're crazy, Miguel! If you're a doctor and you refuse to care for the sick, you become a murderer!"

The bubble suddenly formed into a multi-sided shape full of colored waves and the radiation was directed at Vitoria whose husband, parents-in-law, sisters and brothers-in-law, all stared at with budding and deepening distrust. Being the wife of Miguel, the youngest son, she was the youngest lady in the family and consequently the last to have joined it.

Alvares grabbed his steak knife, glared at his daughter-in-law through squinting eyes and growled, "Miguel just pronounced a theory of irrefutable logic. Don't you think so, Vitoria?"

He had stood up and was already approaching her, clenching the knife handle in his right fist. Vitoria suddenly felt like she was being pierced with heat waves. Her father-in-law was coming toward her, knife in hand, her husband and the others were watching on with no friendliness in their eyes, but she was not afraid.

"When you're not with us," Catarina quickly muttered, "you're against us. So make up your mind."

Vitoria smiled, revealing her dazzling teeth, and answered, "Okay, I didn't understand my dear husband very well. Now I get it. He wants to eliminate the patients before they become impatient."

Alvares tossed the knife on the table. He was ecstatic. "Ha! Now that's well said, girl! Let me hug you, my child!"

He lifted Vitoria and hugged her tightly as his hand, in a less than paternal fashion, patted the young lady's round rump. Neither she nor Miguel nor Maria found anything wrong with it.

"Well!" Jorge declared. "I'm glad we've all agreed to rehabilitate our chosen profession. However, I think the other doctors might not be as intelligent as we are so it might be better, at least for a little while, to keep quiet about the real meaning of the new way we've decided to take." He turned to his brother Rodolfo and added, "Tomorrow at the hospital we'll both do our good work, won't we? But we must be careful... Over there they don't think like us."

He started whispering to Rodolfo while Alvares continued petting Vitoria, which nobody seemed to mind. Maria was chewing a piece of meat and said to Teresa and Catarina, "We can't in good form just sit and do nothing while the men get busy. How can we help them?"

Catarina slipped off the straps of her dress. She was very hot. Since she was not wearing a bra, everyone saw her round, firm breasts. She said, "Tomorrow I'm supposed to go to the Catholic mission to give them some vaccines. Jorge, could you get me something else, some kind of virus or something?"

Jorge nodded. "Nothing could be easier," he assured her. "I've got everything you need at the hospital. Who's supposed to be vaccinated?"

"All the children at the mission. Indians, mestizos and whites. There's almost 300 of them and they're supposed to be vaccinated against smallpox."

Just then the bubble peeled off the ceiling, drifted toward the window and left the Vargas house. It had emitted its thought rays and its presence was no longer necessary.

"I'm going upstairs with Vitoria for a minute," Alvares announced as if it were the most natural thing in the world.

Vitoria smiled kindly to her husband and let herself be dragged away by her father-in-law who had half undressed her in a fit of impatience.

Jorge watched them scramble up the pink marble staircase and said, "While those two are having fun, it'd be good if someone could come with me to the hospital. The viruses are locked in a refrigerated safe... I can't open the safe and distract the guard at the same time."

"I'll go with you," Miguel offered.

"How are *you* going to distract the guard?" Rodolfo asked sarcastically. "Even if he's homosexual, you're too skinny to seduce him. You need a woman, come on!"

Catarina stood up with her bare breasts. "I'll go, Jorge, but I guess I can't go with you dressed like this?"

Her husband shrugged his shoulders. "Go get dressed properly and we'll leave when you're ready."

Catarina went upstairs. Maria looked up at the ceiling and mumbled, "To think that I was bored in this house for so many years and life is getting exciting only now that I'm old…"

Nothing meant anything to the Vargases anymore. They had only one goal: Accomplish the mission that the bubble had just programmed in them through the irresistible means of the thought ray.

At the same time, an ambulance stopped in front of a run-down building in a workingman's neighborhood. The police were already there and now a crowd of nosy onlookers was hoping to see the corpse.

"Who is it?" the doctor asked.

A policeman answered, "A woman. An Indian worker. She strangled her baby and killed her husband with a broken bottle before jumping out the window."

The doctor leaned over her. The woman's skull had shattered like a nutshell on the cement sidewalk. "Why'd she do that?"

The policeman shrugged. His work was, among other things, to step in when something unusual happened. He had no desire at all to know why some people killed others or themselves.

The next morning at nine o'clock, Catarina Vargas drove her car into the Catholic Mission parking lot where she parked it in the area reserved for teachers and medical personnel. After taking the package containing the "vaccines", she went straight to the infirmary.

Dr. Olindas and his two nurses had just arrived. Olindas was buttoning up his white coat in front of the window, admiring Catarina as she entered the mission. The young lady was ravishing and rich and despite all that she was willing to bring his needs to the attention of the medical community of Manaos when she was not busy with the elderly or the poor whom she gave clothes and food with her sisters-in-law and Maria Vargas.

Olindas went to open the door for her and they talked for a few minutes while the nurses went to tell the director that the vaccinations could start. Led by their teachers, the children lined up in the courtyard. There was, in fact, a risk of smallpox, after a few isolated cases of this terrible infectious and contagious sickness reported around Manaos. Although the general vaccination was still not mandatory, the mission preferred to take no chances, relying on the principle that if it did no good, at least it could no harm.

Olindas opened the package that Catarina brought and asked her, "Do you want me to vaccinate you, Mrs. Vargas? We've reserved a time for the teachers, the administration and nurses, including myself…"

Catarina smiled and shook her head. "Thank you but my husband will take care of it, doctor. This morning I don't have a minute to myself… I still have to visit some helpless old people. Goodbye."

She walked off, with elegance and a pleasant perfume, supple as an animal. Dr. Olindas thought that Jorge Vargas was a very lucky man.

At the Manaos general hospital, several very sick patients died in the morning. They had all been given a more or less short time to live, so it came as no surprise. Then Dr. Guaruja was called urgently to the bedside of one his patients. A businessman hospitalized for around two months after a pulmonary infarction, otherwise called a red infarction or local tissue death of an organ following the destruction of a blood vessel.

Guaruja entered room 707 and looked questioningly at the nurse leaning over the patient.

"He's not at all well, doctor. I don't understand. He was getting better, even in excellent shape this morning… I think he's going to die."

Guaruja felt for a pulse and found it very weak. The patient was cyanotic and unconscious. "There's nothing we can do," the doctor said softly. "Did he call you?"

"No, I just happened to come in, just to see if the window was open or the room too hot. We had a nice conversation and…"

She stopped. Guaruja saw he was having a heart attack and tried to resuscitate by pressing on his chest, then ordered, "Mouth-to-mouth, quick!"

The nurse leaned over, tilted the dying man's head back, pinched his nose, stuck her mouth against his and blew. For four or five minutes they fought to keep the man alive in the silent room while carts rolled down the corridors and the sounds of the city came in through the open window. In spite of years of experience, Guaruja was not used to death, this lonely, sneaky thing that struck down young and old alike. Every time he lost a patient, he lost a battle and felt even more responsible if it seemed well fought.

He straightened up and said bitterly. "It's over, nurse. Thank you."

The young lady closed the dead man's eyes and pulled the sheet over his face. Guaruja examined the temperature chart and furrowed his brow. The readings were normal. "Did you say that he was doing well this morning?"

"Yes. He even wanted to go for a walk outside and I had to raise my voice to keep him in bed. And I can say that he was in perfect health less than two hours ago because it's not yet noon."

Guaruja went to the window, opened wide the curtains and unconsciously watched the cars in the parking lot seven stories down. He heard the nurse saying, "…to talk about it with Dr. Vargas who had stopped by, but he was in a hurry and I preferred to call you."

Guaruja turned around. "Jorge Vargas?"

"Rodolfo. But Jorge Vargas was right behind him. Are you surprised, doctor?"

"Well, the Vargases have nothing to do with our wing here."

The nurse felt like he was talking just to say something but that his mind was elsewhere. Guaruja confirmed this when he asked, "Tell Dr. Mendez to come here, please. I would like to have his opinion on this unexpected death. This is the first time I've seen such a thing… maybe it was an internal hemorrhage or a ruptured aneurism…"

While talking he uncovered the body and examined the arm. He asked, "Did he get a shot this morning, miss?"

"Certainly not! I'll go get Dr. Mendez."

She hurried out. Guaruja leaned closer to examine the trace of a shot in the crook of the arm. It was barely visible but clearly brand new.

At noon an elderly man left the office of Dr. Alvares Vargas. He had just turned 70. Vargas had given him a series of exams, a full check-up as he said, and the results were all negative: no heart problems, arteries in as good shape as possible after years of good and loyal service, no cholesterol, etc.

The man's name was Peruide. He had retired a few years ago after working for an accounting firm where he was not only the expert but also the director. At one time he had worked as the Vargas' accountant. But not simply that. Alvares had tried to hide some of his earnings from the tax department and he hardly appreciated Peruide's integrity.

Peruide opened his car door, sat behind the wheel, closed the door and started the car. Then the street started swaying. His lungs stopped pumping. He opened his mouth to suck in some air, but he could not do it. He fought for a few seconds as his life passed before his eyes. He watched his own funeral, then passed out and collapsed on the steering wheel.

Miguel Vargas handed the pill to the woman. "Take this in five minutes," he said without looking at her, "wherever you are. Is that understood?"

The woman held the pill. She had been sick for a long time, suffering from coronaritis, an arteritis of the coronaries resulting in stenosis or artery spasms and possibly ending in a fit of angina. She usually took drops of 1% nitroglycerin or chewed on sugar-coated powdered nitroglycerin with poppys…

She said that she understood, paid her bill and left. She was 75 years old, but did not look it. She went down the elevator and out into the street where she bought a newspaper that she read after putting on her glasses. After walking a bit she remembered the pill she was supposed to take. In the paper they were talking about a probable small pox epidemic, a plague they believed had never disappeared, and they were warning people who had not been vaccinated or whose vaccination was too old to guarantee immunity... There were other frightening details and scary words, like the appearance of a rash, ominous outbreaks of different kinds, morbilliform, scarlatiniform or pupuric in the hemorrhagic eruptions...

They talked about headaches, back pains, stomachaches, vomiting, constipation, anoxeria... The old lady doubled over with a sharp pain in her stomach and fell to her knees. She had dropped her newspaper and handbag and was rubbing her belly trying to calm the pains and cool down the fire that was consuming her. She screamed and rolled onto her side as the fire spread throughout her body like a flaming gas spill. People ran to her aide, but she pushed them away with her involuntary kicking and jerking. Then she wailed horribly, her body twisted unnaturally and her dress crumpled up to reveal her thin, white legs. She made them scared. People are quickly scared of things they do not understand.

The old lady's body rolled one last time into the gutter and stop moving. When someone leaned over her, it was to declare that she was dead.

Maria, Teresa, Catarina and Vitoria worked as a team at the systematic extermination of the crippled elderly whom they formerly helped with so much generosity.

While her daughters-in-law kept the old from moving or crying out, Maria simply stuck a big hatpin into their medulla oblongata, their lower brainstem. Death was immediate, almost painless, and if a suspicious coroner did not think of looking too closely at the victim's neck, it was likely that the death would be put down to natural causes. It was clean, quick and undemanding. Between the murders the ladies talked about fashion, theater and make-up…

By the time it was noon, they had killed thirty old folks.

For two days the Vargases killed many sick and elderly people without being the least bit bothered by it. Then, after the normal incubation period of 48 hours, the first symptoms of botulism broke out among the teachers and children at the Catholic Mission.

Jorge Vargas had achieved a masterstroke with this because unlike other food poisoning, botulism does not bring on fever or other drastic symptoms, especially gastroenteric. At first the sick just complain of a queasy stomach, then there is some vomiting and constipation, but nothing too bad. But on the 3rd day, the children and teachers had serious eye problems. They had accommodative iridoplegia, trouble seeing things up close, mydriasis and often paralysis of the ocular motor nerve: drooping eyelids, squinting, paralysis around the eyes… Then came the drying up of their mouths, throats and nasal cavities, a lazy tongue, dysarthria and in many cases paralysis of the palette and pharynx thus making it extremely difficult to swallow. This same paralysis sometimes reached the larynx and caused a more or less complete loss of voice.

The emergency doctors called in observed a decrease in the voluntary muscle contractions presented as muscular weakness without real paralysis, motor incoordination with some strength preserved, but a decrease in tendon reflexes. Nevertheless, because the cafeteria workers suffered no symptoms even though they ate the same food as the teachers and children, the doctors could not immediately determine that it was botulism.

Their delay was fatal to 100 children and three teachers who died on the 3rd night. On the morning of the 4th day other children, two nurses and Dr. Olindas himself were in grim shape. It was then that Dr. Olindas shared his fears with his colleague treating him. This colleague just happened to be Dr. Guaruja who had just injected a mix of A and B antibotulinic serum through the IV while telling himself that it was too late.

"The vaccination," Olindas huffed.

Guaruja was listening closely. "What vaccination?" he asked.

"Small pox," Olindas struggled to speak. "I think there was an accident with it... You have to ask her... where she got the vaccines?"

"Okay, who was it?"

"Mrs. Catarina Vargas," Olinda confessed as his head rolled to the side.

Guaruja hid his reaction as best he could. Along with Dr. Mendez he had learned that the patient in room 707 along with 60 others being treated in the hospital had been murdered by an air shot, meaning an empty syringe. Unfortunately this could not be proven. Nor could Dr. Jorge and Rodolfo Vargas be incriminated for roaming around hospital wings where they had no busy being.

He called his assistant and left after one final look at Olindas for whom he was gravely worried. For a few days Guaruja had realized that this series of deaths coincided with the sudden death of the patient in room 707. Manaos was living in an unusually dark time. They stopped counting the old people found dead in their beds or the sick people who suddenly passed away in the street or in a hospital. To all this was added a small pox epidemic and now the botulism at the mission. It was too much.

Too much to put down to chance.

Guaruja was good friends with the chief of police. He found a telephone booth, dialed the number of police headquarters and asked to speak to Chief Canela. When he got on the line, after the usual small talk, Guaruja broached the subject carefully. He was not sure of anything, only had some suspicions, but if they took note of the fact that...

"Listen, my friend," Canela interrupted him, "if you have anything suspicious to report, do it. What's this all about? Who do you suspect?"

Guaruja swallowed hard. Vargas was a big word. A rock against which more than one had been broken. "Well," he said, "Dr. Mendez and I noticed that Jorge and Rodolfo Vargas..." He had started and he finished it.

When he stopped talking Chief Canela just said, "First of all, your story sounds completely crazy, my dear friend. The Vargases are upstanding citizens, but you never know. Don't mention this to anyone. I'll get someone to watch them and we'll see what turns up..."

"I hope I'm wrong," Guaruja said, deeply worried.

Canela laughed reassuringly. "Don't you worry, this'll stay between us if my men find nothing wrong with the Vargases. Only those who do nothing are never wrong, right? See you soon, pal."

When he hung up, Guaruja's hands and forehead were soaked in sweat.

Chapter II

The bubble, blown by the wind from the north, drifted gently over the Potomac. It passed the headland formed by East Potomac Park when a little whirlwind sent it in another direction, towards the Anacostia River, the Washington Eastern Power Service so that it was finally moving against the wind...

It was impossible. A round object, extremely light, cannot act like a sailboat equipped with a jib, sail, rudder and keel. However, in spite of the technical impossibility, the bubble continued forging against the wind in a way they call "close-hauled" in sailing.

It sailed around the greenery of the Mall where the Capitol Building stood facing east because they had thought that the city was going to develop in that direction whereas the contrary happened so that the building stands with its back to the main part of Washington. Here, too, was the White House, the Federal Triangle, the State Department, the most important public buildings and museums of the capital of the United States, and surrounded by Pennsylvania Avenue, 9th Street, 10th Street and E Street was also the seat of the FBI, the place where Smith Beffort had his office and his private anti-Atomos dispatch...

But it was 9:30 pm, the administrative buildings were deserted and Smith Beffort was watching T.V. at home with his wife Mie Azusa-Beffort, the ex-Miss Atomos, who had been miraculously saved from her motor-brain by an operation performed in record time.

The city and its inhabitants were calm. They did not yet know about the events in Manaos. They did not yet know that an "Atomos situation" had just been created in the north of Brazil. They were at peace.

The bubble descended in some neighborhood downtown and glided through a ventilation grill, but farther on hit a grill too narrow to squeeze through. So, it turned around and circled the building that it seemed to have chosen for a specific purpose. It was a movie theater showing a "disaster film," a cross between *The Omen* and *The Towering Inferno*. The bubble entered the dark theater and immediately stuck itself in the middle of the ceiling. Then it started emitting its dreadful thought rays.

The theater was built by the owners following the latest regulations, thus containing only 300 seats. Tonight it was half-full. The spectators could have scattered around, but besides the fact that Americans loved to live and have fun as a group, the usher had kept them together to make her job easier. It was something that no one knew, but over the course of normal showing with an average-sized audience an usher ended up walking over three miles up and down the aisles. Since this kind of theater was open full-time, offering six shows a day, it meant almost 20 miles that an usher covered on foot every day, not to speak of all the time she spent standing in the lobby or selling chocolate ice cream and candy during the intermission. To be an usher in a movie theater you had to be in good health, friendly, patient and, as often as possible, in a good mood.

The film told the story—the title was *Death Around the Neck*—about a man with a weak character, without any personality, repressed as well, who worked all year long as a salesman in a big clothes store. It was not a big budget or a very good film. Being a B-movie it showed in the smaller theaters but still got a particular audience... the same as pornos, westerns and really bloody crime films.

So, the repressed salesman without a personality, who has been assigned to the "men's" department for years, suddenly finds himself sent to the "women's" department and discovers an empty space between the ceiling of the dressing rooms and the second floor of the store. By crawling into this space he can watch the ladies undress. His desire becomes uncontrollable and one evening, just before closing, he drops down on top of a beautiful young woman and strangles her with a scarf before raping her. Once the store is empty, he gives in to his most debauched fantasies with the corpse... That is when the scenes become difficult to watch and the sensitive people in the audience leave... In the aftermath, the criminal maniac burns the body in the store's incinerator, goes home for some shuteye, then comes back to work the next day where he works through the evening, strangles another customer, rapes her, etc.

Tonight the theater had about 100 men and 50 women, which was an anomaly since statistics show that women are always in the majority during horror films.

About halfway through the film, after the bubble had been emitting its rays for 30 minutes and the action was reaching a climax, a man suddenly leaned over, slipped his scarf under the chin of the woman sitting in front of him and before she had time to react he pulled back with all his strength and strangled her to death. While he was killing, the people sitting next to the unfortunate woman tore off her clothes and in the rest of the theater the same scene was repeated 50 times, equal to the number of women present.

The usher came in to check on the room before going home and was instantly attacked by two madmen who strangled her, stripped her, raped and sodomized her in the aisle. In the dark nothing but the grunts of animals in heat could be heard as they fought over the corpses.

Now the men attacked and killed one another. There were screams, gouged eyes, throats ripped open by teeth and knives. The wounded crawled between the seats stained with sperm and blood and the excretions from the corpses.

Out in the lobby the manager was waiting for the end of the film, looking at his watch over and over again. Because of the soundtrack he did not hear the yelling and screaming. Besides, he was too used to it to pay attention to the noise. However, after a while he wondered why the usher had not said goodbye to him. He was distracted but not so much that he missed the young lady leaving. He threw his cigarette into the ashtray and went to peak into the room. The first thing that struck his eyes was the film, which was nearing its end, then his sight adjusted to the darkness and he was very surprised not to see any heads over the back of the seats. Time stood still for a moment. All of a sudden he saw a raised arm, spread fingers against the background of the screen, then human forms lying in the aisle and he heard moaning and groaning. He shuddered and got goose bumps as he looked upon the carnage. The audience had been the victim of an extraordinary accident! Something unbelievably dreadful had happened in his theater! He ran like a crazy man to the automated projection room, stopped the film and turned on the lights. When he leaned out to look through the small opening, he shrieked at the ghastly sight.

Two minutes later his trembling finger dialed the number for the police.

The bubble—but was it the same one?—stuck to the ceiling of the Palladium Room, a restaurant that included dancing with dinner at the Shoreham Hotel. It was 10:15 pm. The place was packed, the dance floor full, the ambiance very cheerful, very hot, plus the food and wine were good. The people who were there had come to have fun and forget their worries, at least for one night. Streamers rained down, trumpets blew and everyone put on their brightly colored paper hats, a ridiculous sight anywhere else but amusing in this place.

Of course, they were all a little drunk, some a little sad or glum from it, but never any unseemly behavior. The men wore suits and ties, the women evening gowns or cocktail dresses. A night at the Palladium Room was very expensive so the customers were generally well off, well educated, or just plain lucky.

Directly under the spot where the bubble had landed a few minutes earlier was a 12-person table of 6 couples: the Webers, the Gibsons, the O'Haras, the Dracks, the Wilsons and the Adams. All of them lived in Washington D.C. and the men were executives at the Weber Company, which had organized the party to celebrate its 30th anniversary.

Charles Weber was close to 60 years old, his wife as well, even though it was less visible on her thanks to the beauty clinics. They were both clearly happy about their success and to be there with their closest partners but also their friends as Charles Weber liked to say when he gave them a slap on the back. They had been dancing themselves breathless all night, which is probably why they were suddenly exhausted with their legs full of lead and their minds a little foggy.

"Wow," Maud Adams said, leaning on the back of a chair, "I haven't had this much fun in ages!"

Karine O'Hara smiled at her, winked and joked, "It's always better when we've got no kids around and our husbands don't have to foot the bill! Look at our males, dear! They can't help talking business even in the Palladium!"

May Weber guffawed. "It's a good thing they're like that. Don't complain about having hard-working husbands, otherwise we wouldn't be here tonight."

Maud Adams and Karine O'Hara looked at each other annoyed. The "boss wife" was obviously referring to the check that Charles would be signing to pay for the food and drinks.

Hedy Drack suddenly jumped into the conversation. She was a beautiful, tall woman, a Texas girl raised on a horse... They said she was an ace with the pistol and no one could match her at hitting a target with a throwing knife. She leaned towards May Weber, a dirty look in her eyes, and said with unexpected animosity, "Well, okay, then! You don't have to make us feel like your employees. It's by our work that you survive. To hell with the bosses!"

May Weber turned red with anger; the other women giggled. When May Weber jumped up, her chair fell over. "You little bitch!" she shouted. "I'll teach you to piss on my life!"

She stormed over to Hedy Drack, but the latter stuck a fork in her throat, twisted it in the wound and let out a hysterical cry. Blood spurted every which way as Hedy Drack threw May Weber onto the table, pulled out the fork and stabbed her again in the belly and the chest.

Just then Charles Weber ran to defend his wife. Someone tripped him and he fell, pulling the tablecloth and all the plates and glasses with it onto the floor. Weber stood up with a knife in his fist and buried it deep in Maud Adams' back.

All over the room people were fighting furiously for no apparent reason. Friends, sometimes relatives, using forks, knives, plates, chairs and bottles that were smashed and turned into deadly weapons.

The doorman, attracted by all the noise, came and watched on in utter amazement. The other employees and the musicians were fighting each other or the customers. The women were especially aggressive. With their hair disheveled and their dresses torn off they were relentless in their attacks on anyone at all, their nails bared, furiously, as if their lives depended on it. One of them rushed at the doorman and tackled him. They rolled on the floor in front of the coat check girl who could do nothing but sob and the woman bit the doorman in his face so hard that she tore off a piece of his cheek. The doorman, groggy with pain, socked her in the nose but she kept scratching his face until a veil of blood blinded him. Still, he managed to grab her neck and squeeze, squeeze…

Farther away, with a fork in both hands, Hedy Drack was struggling with two wild men who were trying to rape her on the table. They had already torn off her skirt and top. One of them pulled down her panties and planted himself between the young lady's strong thighs. At that very second, she managed to push off the one holding her down and with a quick fork jab she put an end to the rapist's future. With his balls pierced he started baying like a wolf in the wilderness.

The Webers, Gibsons, O'Haras, Wilsons and Adams were dead. Dozens of lifeless or seriously wounded bodies lay among the overturned tables. Peter Drack was crawling toward his wife, one eye gouged out and his skull split open by a broken bottle. The partner of the man whose private parts Hedy had just forked grabbed a chair and pounced on her as she was standing up. There was a wicked crack and Hedy collapsed with a broken neck in the middle of a group of roaring people fighting for their lives against one another.

The coat check girl finally found the strength to leave her cubbyhole. She felt like she was watching a nightmare, something unreal but which she knew was real. She met no attackers as she ran down the corridor of the Palladium Room and then into the Shoreham Hotel lobby calling for help.

It was 10:30 and guests were walking around. One of them, Mike Lippon, turned to the girl. Although he was in the shadows he could see her and right over her head he caught the fleeting but distinct image of a kind of transparent tennis ball that seemed to glow as it floated. It was coming from the Palladium and heading for the exit. Lippon thought it looked like a miniature flying saucer before it disappeared and he concentrated on helping the girl. People were already surrounding her as she stammered out her story of the atrocious scene she had just witnessed.

"We've got to get in there!" said a short-legged man who was clearly shaking with fear.

"No!" the coat check girl screamed. "Don't go in there, no matter what! Anyone who goes into that room will turn into a raving lunatic! Call the police!"

Her voice cried out with such terror that no one budged. Since the corridor leading to the Palladium Room was empty, they had no idea what might be happening on the other side of the swinging doors.

"I'm going to see," Mike Lippon said calmly. "If what she says is true, we will call the police right away."

They watched him walk down the corridor and then crack open the door. He just stood there for a minute, frozen, then he came sprinting back, terror-stricken with his eyes popping out. Without a word he ran by the group and straight to one of the telephone booths next to the elevators.

Mie Azusa-Beffort heard a bell ringing in the distance. She was dreaming that she was shooting clay pipes at a fair. When she hit one, a bell was supposed to sound, but never when she missed. She was terribly annoyed with the guy at the stand, who was the spitting image of Yosho Akamatsu... Then the bell kept ringing more than it should have in a dream and Mie knew that it was the telephone.

She reached out, turned on the bedside lamp and picked up the phone after seeing that the hands of the clock read one o'clock in the morning. She spoke clearly, "Mie Beffort here. What do you want?" She had the rare ability to be clear-headed as soon as she woke up.

On the other end of the line a voice that she knew well but that she had not heard for months said, "Sorry to bother you, Mie, I just remembered that there's a time difference between our two countries. I'm calling from my apartment in Tokyo. Do you know about Manaos?"

Smith Beffort suddenly sat up. He was sleeping in the next bed and since he had not heard the telephone ring, a mysterious premonition must have alerted him. "Who is it?" he asked.

"Yosho Akamatsu," Mie said. "Wait, Yosho, I'll give you to my husband."

She handed the phone over and picked up the extra earpiece. Smith grumbled, "Glad to hear your voice, but I would have preferred a different time. Where are you, buddy?"

"In Tokyo, at home, and I've been listening to the world news while you've been sleeping. Some trouble's been brewing in Manaos in the state of Amazonas in Brazil. Does that mean anything to you?"

"No. I've never heard of Manaos," Beffort groaned as he adjusted his pillows. Let's have it. You're paying for this call so now that you've woke us up we can talk until dawn."

"In Manaos," the Japanese began, "there was once an honorable family whose male members all became doctors by tradition. Their wives did charity work, sang in the church choir and stuff, you know the kind..." In four minutes he gave them all the facts and ended by saying, "They were arrested and freely admitted all the crimes they were accuse of. The Vargases seem to find their actions quite natural, Smith... In short, they lost their mind in a split second, or at least in one night, all of them, and turned into perverse murderers even though they acted the same."

Beffort and his wife glanced at each other. There was silence. Finally Beffort murmured, "Let's see, Yosho, it's been nine years now since *She* has shown up..."

"I know, I know," Akamatsu responded, faking nonchalance. "Maybe what happened to the Vargases is just an accident... Still, I asked for more information before calling you. The Vargases had no scars or any traces of injections."

Mie breathed a tiny bit easier. "That means that *She* didn't operate on them to implant a motor-brain in their

184

skull. And no traces of a injection means that *She* didn't use an air gun to shoot a pinhead-sized super-minibrain into them that would follow the blood up to their head."

"But," Akamatsu continued, "that doesn't mean anything. If *She* is still alive, we all know that *She* must have improved her techniques over the last nine years…"

Beffort shrugged his shoulders. "I don't believe it! It's a legend, gossip! You know, for a long time, despite the ashes found in Berlin, some people wanted to believe that Adolf Hitler was still alive and hiding out in South America. Today because of some inexplicable event in Manaos, you're talking about the return of Madame Atomos. After nine years of silence! Not likely!"

Akamatsu snickered. "You're the one talking about it, Smith," he said snidely. "I didn't even say her name…"

"Don't be a hypocrite," Beffort said. "You're in Tokyo and we're in Washington D.C. but we're all living with the same fear since that fateful day in April 1969 when Madame Atomos and Isadori disappeared from that chalet in Big Sandy, Wyoming[3]. The proof of this is that you call us when something out of the ordinary happens."

Akamatsu did not laugh. He spoke gravely. "That's true, Smith. If the terrible woman came back, it would be disastrous for humanity because it's obvious that she would have designed new weapons… But where would she come back from?"

"You can say that again. You'll see that this Manaos affair is an isolated case… Can we get back to sleep now, Yosho?"

---

[3] See *The Slaves of Madame Atomos.*

Akamatsu said goodbye and Beffort hung up the phone. Mie stared at him intensely. He said, "Calm down, calm down. This story in Manaos can't in any way be connected to Madame Atomos. She has no beef with the Brazilians. They weren't responsible for the atomic explosions in Hiroshima or Nagasaki, right? Let's go back to sleep."

He turned off the light. The room was faintly lit by the moonlight filtering through the shutters. Beffort could clearly see the black form of his wife's profile in the gloom. Her eyelids blinked, her lips were open and her breathing was labored. Mie often showed strange signs of clairvoyance. Right now it looked like she was waiting for something, like she could not sleep until it came…

The ring of the telephone startled Beffort. He picked it up at the same time that Mie turned on the light. Before he could talk, Owen Bernitz started firing away, "I'll be over in five minutes, boss. Get dressed and come downstairs! A bunch of people killed each other in a downtown movie theater and in the Palladium Room! Some guy named Mike Lippon saw something weird at the Palladium! There are close to 400 dead! I've already alerted the Green Dragon Force! In five minutes, boss!"

He hung up. Beffort did the same and caught his wife's dilated eyes. She whispered, "It's *Her*. I'm sure it's *Her*. My God, *She* killed our son, Dr. Soblen, James Edward Evans… and *She* swore to see us dead…"

Beffort struggled out of bed and got dressed with unusual slowness. Mie threw off her bed sheets and also got dressed, though she kept looking out the open window through the shutters. Beffort went to close the window and finished getting dressed in silence. Mie was just a girl and studying singing at the Takarazuka School when Mikonosuke Watanabe, a young servant of the Atomos Organization, kidnapped her in Tokyo to turn her into Miss Atomos... They operated on her and "mechanized" her. She killed and caused havoc at the instigation of the Great Brain. On a sidewalk in Palm Beach she opened fire on Beffort. The first bullet grazed his cheek, the second blew off the pinky of his left hand... The word *Hiroshima* was tattooed on her right breast, *Nagasaki* on the left, and no one had suffered more than her at the hands of Madame Atomos.

A horn honked. "Come on, Mie," Beffort said gently.

They went down the stairs, cautious by reflex. Knowing the weapons that Madame Atomos loved to use, they would now be watching their every step if the return of the sinister woman turned out to be true.

At the wheel of the powerful Chevrolet Owen Bernitz was waiting, the cigar stub still and always stuck in the corner of his mouth, a hard look in his eyes and a grim expression on his face. They climbed in, Mie in the back, Smith in the front, and the car sped off.

"How did you find out?" Beffort asked while lighting a cigarette.

"A tip," Bernitz growled. "I'd made sure to keep tabs on the whole country, you know... Well, just now I got a ring at home and they told me the audience in a movie theater had just murdered each other. Women were strangled and raped during the film... I barely hung up and a second call came in telling me that the same thing happened at the Palladium Room and this guy Mike Lippon I mentioned had seen a kind of glowing ball come out of the room. Well, first thing I did was put the Green Dragon Force on it, then I called you."

Mie leaned forward. "Where are we going right now, Owen?"

"To the Palladium where Lippon's waiting... No need to go to the cinema. Except for the manager, who didn't see a thing, everyone's at the morgue." He unconsciously puffed on his unlit cigar and sneered, "It's *Her*, eh?"

Beffort did not answer right away. Over the course of the past nine years, thousands of agents had searched for Madame Atomos in the USA, but also in every country across the five continents. In Washington, Texas, California, Florida, Ohio and Rhode Island, in all the states everyone who had fought the Atomos Organization were at the ready, watching the news from around the world, analyzing weird events, examining the photos taken by Russian and American satellites where objects a foot long were visible even though taken from 125 miles up. You could make out a license plate on the photos. When the Russians built a new building in Moscow, the Americans knew about it a few hours later. When the Americans extended a highway, the Russians knew about it in the same way... So, how could Madame Atomos build a new refuge or a factory or lab without the rest of the world finding out?

"Maybe it's *Her*," he answered, "but we can't be sure until we get hold of some irrefutable proof."

The car circled a big intersection and turned onto a street crowded with police cars and ambulances. It was stopped halfway down by blockade. An ambulance sped off with its siren wailing and a group of onlookers was unceremoniously pushed back. It felt like a major disaster zone; the air was charged with electricity... "Get out of here!" a policeman barked, twirling his nightstick. "There's already too many people!"

Beffort flashed his FBI card and the officer stopped snarling and said, "Park your car, Sir, and go the rest of the way to the hotel on foot. They don't know where to start. I've never seen so many dead at the same time."

Owen parked the Chevrolet as best he could, half-way up on the sidewalk, and they walked to the Shoreham Hotel. Medical personnel kept passing by with stretchers on their way to the ambulances. Trails of blood stained the sidewalk. Everyone was at the windows of the hotel and nearby buildings. In spite of the number of people present, the silence was impressive, ominous—they could hear a baby crying, probably woken up by its parents leaning out the window of their apartment.

"Owen!" someone yelled. "Over here!"

Bernitz waved to a skinny little man with a pointy nose who was standing at the hotel entrance and then made a brief introduction, "Holborn." Then to the skinny little man, "Where's your witness?"

Another man stepped forward. "I'm Mike Lippon," he stated firmly. "Glad to make your acquaintance, Beffort... and yours Ma'am... I imagine that you, like me, have no time to waste? Well, here's what I saw: the young lady, the coat check girl from the Palladium Room, came out of the corridor. She was clearly visible in the light while I was in the shadows and the whole lobby was reflected in the windows. I think this particular lighting scheme plus my own position allowed me to see what was probably invisible to everyone else. It was a sphere the size of a tennis ball. It was transparent, but it also glowed with color. It was drifting a little more than six feet off the ground, let's say six and a half, and it headed for the door of the hotel."

Beffort led him into the lobby because they were being constantly bumped by the crowd. When they were sitting quietly at a table in the deserted bar, Beffort asked, "So, in your opinion, this sphere was capable of controlling its movements?"

Lippon nodded, staring at Mie, whom he thought was pretty. "I can't be absolutely sure," he said cautiously. "Anyway, I am sure that the ball wasn't thrown because it curved a few times before swinging out into the street. If it wasn't controlling its own movements, then maybe it was being remote-controlled? I know a little about that, you know…" He smiled at Mie's look of surprise and continued, "No, I'm not one of those heroes from Cape Kennedy or Houston. I work in insurance, but my hobby, every weekend, is operating model airplanes, cars and boats by remote control…"

"In that case," Beffort intervened, "your eyewitness report is of primary importance. Did you have the impression that this ball, this sphere was being remote controlled?"

Lippon rubbed his chin. He had a "Cartesian" mind, so for him the "ball" had to be radio-controlled. Nevertheless, it moved noiselessly and relatively slowly, "drifting" as he said, and he did not really see how they could have stuck a motor and antenna in it, not to mention everything else needed to operate an engine by remote control…

Beffort grinned. "Are you thinking that it wasn't moving on its own, that it couldn't have been remote-controlled, that maybe it was being piloted by little green men from another planet? Don't get upset, I'm not making fun of you, Mr. Lippon. I just want to get everything out of your story as possible so we can get to the bottom of this."

Lippon nodded. "I understand. Well, I'm going to surprise you, but that last suggestion sounds less amazing than the first two. Now I remember feeling like I was watching a flying saucer… Yes, a tiny flying saucer, miniaturized if you'd like."

Mie, Owen Bernitz and Beffort stared at him without a hint of a smile.

Lippon thought it might do some good to add, "Hey, it was just a feeling. I hope you're not going to make it into some big thing?"

Mie asked gently, "Mr. Lippon, please think before you answer me. This "ball" was transparent and, according to you, glowing with a little color. In the transparency, did you see any human forms?"

Lippon was speechless. He stared at Bernitz and Beffort in turn, then his eyes came to rest on Mie's charming face and he kind of grunted before repeating in utter astonishment, "Human forms, huh?" He took a deep breath and while his face flushed asked, "Really, Mrs. Beffort, it's because I mentioned a miniaturized flying saucer that you're trying to trap me with this question, right?"

"Not at all, not at all," she defended. "Look, if it's physically possible to reduce an unidentified flying object from another world to this size, it shouldn't be too difficult to also reduce its crew. Me, I'm perfectly willing to admit this."

Beffort clapped his hands and stood up. "Okay! Thank you, Mr. Lippon, your eyewitness account will no doubt be very useful to us if there's any aftermath to the affair. Do you know where we can find the coat check girl from the Palladium?"

"She's in the hotel's little sitting room," Lippon answered mechanically.

Mie smiled at him. "Thank you and good night."

"So long," Owen Bernitz said.

"Goodbye," Beffort said.

They turned around and walked toward the sitting room. Lippon flopped back in the chair and mumbled, "Human forms in a tennis ball... No, I didn't see human forms... but then how was the sphere moving?"

He put his chin in his hands. He had something to think about for days to come.

Chapter III

The man pushed his wheelbarrow along the grooved path that wound through the forest from his field to his humble cabin. In this age when everything is mechanized, he continued to work his land by hand with a spade and a shovel and instead of spreading chemical fertilizers he used manure. Behind his cabin, protected from the wind, he raised rabbits. His chickens gave him eggs and his bees honey that he ate and sold.

He had a horse who helped him haul heavy loads and whom he yoked to a cart when he went to town to buy tobacco, oil and coffee. But a horse was nothing compared to an automobile. Especially since he was an old horse, crippled by rheumatism just like his master. Today he was not in good shape, so Old Brook decided to leave him in his stable, warm and comfortable. He knew that a horse did not always want to slave away like a mule.

He, too, sometimes needed a break. Just like automobiles that sometimes broke down. Then the drivers would come looking for Old Brook and it was the old horse who towed the cars that had 25 or 30 horses under the hood... This kind of thing happened in the summer when the area was rife with tourists. But at this time of the year, the region was very calm, that is to say totally deserted. It was the time of year that Brook liked best. He had chosen to live far from the world, in nature, among the plants and wild animals, away from all the politics, the gaudiness, the envious and especially from all the damn news about all the devils! Brook did not give a straw about knowing whether a Russian just broke his leg falling off a ladder or an Indonesian had quintuplets or a fire had just destroyed a factory in Norway...

He watched his potatoes and his lettuce grow and took care of them when he was not taking care of the chickens, rabbits, bees or his horse. He replaced a shingle here, a fence pole there. He mixed the manure and gathered the hay for winter, so even if he had had a radio or television he would not have had the time to listen or watch.

This morning, therefore, at seven o'clock when ribbons of mist were still on the ground, Old Brook was pushing his wheelbarrow to his No. 6 field. He had ten separate parcels of land on either side of the forest, numbered 1 to 10 by Brook who figured this more practical than keeping the numbers from the Land Registry. To reach them quickly, as quickly as necessary and possible, Brook found nothing better than to go through the forest so that he went back and forth over the same route and ended up carving paths that had not been there before.

Brook's wheelbarrow did not have an iron-rimmed wheel but a tire, which did not make a racket to hell and back (Brook liked this expression), and on either side of the hub two small springs that looked like nothing but were, in fact, downright shock absorbers!

He was an odd man. If he passed by a certain place at a certain time and just then a shingle fell on his head, he would say he was unlucky, that the damn shingle could have fallen a little before or after he passed... but when you think about it, nothing would ever get done if destiny took the time to prepare everything in advance and then nothing would happen.

Thus, because his horse was in bad shape, because his wheelbarrow had a tire and two shocks, because he had a small hill to climb to get to Field 6, Brook arrived without any noise from his boots or wheels or hubs to the top of the hill and amazing! He found a big, white bubble sitting quietly in the middle of his field, just to the right of his crops.

Brook was not the kind to scream or run for his gun to make them respect his land. Moreover, he was as curious as a cat.

For the moment he thought it was one of those balloons that carried a basket with people inside, but then as far as he could tell through the fog he realized that the balloon in question was too huge. He figured it must have been 100 to 120 feet in diameter.

Brook slowly let go of his wheelbarrow and crouched down so as not to be seen in case someone was roaming about. He did not like to disturb people and had no desire to talk to anyone who might, for example, be lost... The fog cleared to the left and Brook saw that the bubble was sitting on some kind of feet. There were three of them and they supported the bubble but did not keep the lower part from touching the ground where Brook could make out a kind of oval doorway and the start of a dimly lit corridor. He began to think that this bubble was not something normal and wondered how it could have come into his field where there was no road.

Then he heard a faint whistle and a cloud formed around the lower part of the bubble while the door slid closed from top to bottom. Brook was plastered to the ground. He was not really a coward, but he hated things that he did not understand. And something beyond his understanding was happening before his very eyes: little by little as the cloud rose and thickened, the bubble seemed to diminish in size and its color turned from pure white to milky to transparent.

The whistle grew louder. Brook plugged his ears because it was bursting his eardrums, but his eyes kept getting bigger as the bubble got smaller. Now it was only 30 feet in diameter and in the next three or four minutes it got so small that Brook, reluctantly, had to get up on his knees.

It was as if it was speeding off towards the horizon, but it was still there with its cloud of steam or smoke— Brook could not really say—that was also shrinking until he saw it no more. But the bubble now was the size of a soccer ball and transparent. When it had disappeared Brook sat there for a long time without moving. He dared not move. His tranquility had just been shattered. From now on he knew that something else existed...

After 30 minutes, he came out from his hiding place and walked slowly to the place where the bubble had been. The feet of the machine had sunk deep into the soft ground and in the middle of the triangle the grass was burned over a large area.

Brook turned around and started running. He left his wheelbarrow in the path and headed straight for home where he harnessed up his horse. He did not know exactly what he was going to do, but he had to go and tell someone. To hell and back!

If Sheriff Golway had not known Brook since childhood, he would no doubt have told him to go jump in a lake and advised him to drink less bourbon. But the two of them had cut their teeth at the same school with different success since Golway had become county sheriff and Brook had become nothing at all. And Golway knew that Brook did not drink and did not have enough imagination to invent such a ludicrous story.

Golway closed the file, stood up and simply said, "Okay, let's go, old pal. If this bubble left traces of its props in your field, they should still be there, right?"

"For sure," Brook said.

Brook climbed onto his cart and Golway into his jeep. A second later they were heading off to Brook's cabin where they left the cart and jeep to continue on foot into the forest.

"There they are," Brook pointed to what he called the foot marks but that Galway called the prop marks.

Golway knelt down, took a tape measure out of his pocket and measured the width and depth of the first hole, then the distance between each hole. "Well!" he estimated, "that was some machine!" Looking sharply at Brook he added, "So, you say that this bubble thing was around 100 feet in diameter?"

"More like 120 or 130," Brook corrected him.

"Then it shrank down to the size of a soccer ball?"

"Yeah."

"First it was white, then milky, then transparent?" the sheriff asked.

"Like I said. I know it sounds like a bunch of hogwash, but I'm not making any of it up, I swear. What do you think, sheriff?"

Golway took a deep breath. "Well! I think you're damn lucky to still be alive! Last night in Washington D.C. some people slaughtered each other in a dance room and a movie theater... I heard it on the radio right before you came to my office. A witness said that he'd seen a kind of sphere the size of a tennis ball coming out of the dance room and go flying off, turning and moving all by itself. It was transparent."

Brook finished rolling his cigarette, licked it, then lit it with an old lighter. "Doggone! It's not normal, huh?"

Golway shook his head and pointed at the marks. "You're going to cover these up with a tarp. They have to remain intact even if it rains. I'm going to contact the authorities. You got a rifle?"

"Yeah."

"Get it and keep everyone away from field. Don't tell anyone anything. If you handle things right, a bunch of papers will offer you a fortune for the exclusive on your story. I'll come back in the morning. You keep quiet, right?"

"Yeah, I will. Cat's got my tongue. I'll go back to the cabin with you to get my rifle and some tarps."

They left the field and the sheriff climbed into his jeep and drove back to town. He was disturbed. Terribly disturbed. During the whole ride back he kept checking his mirrors and watching the sky through the windshield. He had seen a film whose title he could not remember, in which a UFO flew over a car and shot a ray down to turn off the engine and radio. As the hood of the jeep kept banging in the wind, he could not get rid of the feeling that someone was taking potshots at him. He did not start calming down until he was halfway home and out of sight...

Out of sight of what? He wondered. And the anxiety returned. Just because I can't see the hill doesn't mean I'm safe from an attack by extra-terrestrials.

He sped up, even in the turns...

The small, yellow man flipped the switch and launched a call from the spaceship, "Cosmos XII here, calling Central... Do you read me?"

A few seconds passed, then the response came, "Central here, I hear you loud and clear, Cosmos XII, where are you?"

"North of Randolph in Maryland. We had to land in a field after a little damage to the B6 transformer and our detector is signaling that we were spotted."

"Did the repair require you to return to your original size?"

"Yes."

"In that case," Central commanded, "you have to liquidate whoever saw you. Use the thought inductors to make it look like an accident. But under no circumstances go back to the original size. Is that understood, Cosmos XII?"

"Understood," the little yellow man responded. "Over and out."

"Over and out. Check in after the operation."

He switched off communication, turned on the inside line of the size-changing vessel and sent a series of instructions in Japanese, the same language used during his radio exchange with Central. The spaceship immediately banked into a turn and headed south with all the power of its 16 atomic reactors. On the ground everything was gigantic, but the Cosmos XII team was used to the gigantism. When you shrink to 128th your normal size, a fly becomes a flying fortress and aphids turn into fighter-bombers.

Golway had come out of almost the last turn. There were only three left before he could speed up again on the long straightaway into Randolph. He was planning to get to his office and immediately call Yellow Mask, Smith Beffort's code at the FBI, which all the law officers in the United States had known for years. In case of an emergency (and Golway figured that this was one) any officer was authorized to communicate with Yellow Mask without needing to wade through the holy hierarchy.

Golway was entering one of the last turns when all of a sudden a transparent tennis ball started floating in front of him outside the windshield, just 20 inches from the sheriff's face. But it was a strange transparency in the sense that its internal structure was made up of opaque objects, obviously very tiny, that made it look like a living molecule.

He panicked and slammed on the brakes to put some distance between him and the ball, but it was no use. When he floored the accelerator next, he had the same result. In fact, the ball seemed to be stuck there for good. Golway thought he was a goner, that the thing would attack him as soon as he stopped or got out of the car. Then, out of nowhere, he had an idea and told himself that he would trick it good if he took a back road through the woods. Impregnated by the thought rays, he had no chance to survive. He cut his own path through the woods to where there was nothing but a rocky ravine and, with a pleased grin on his face, he drove his jeep into the chasm.

When the car crashed 200 feet down below, its gas tank exploded and the car went up in flames. The spaceship Cosmos XII made a quick U-turn and headed back to Old Brook's field.

Brook had just put the third and last tarp on the ground. He had them weighted down with stones to keep them from blowing away, figuring that he had done his best to complete the task that his friend the sheriff had given him. He backtracked to the edge of the forest, popped two cartridges into his old over and under shot-gun, pulled his hat down over his eyes and waited quiet-ly for Golway to return.

When you live alone in the forest, you do not react like an ordinary citizen. You get weird habits. Brook often talked to himself. He listened carefully, also, to the noises in the fields or in the bushes and his keen eye caught the slightest movement. He was no hunter, but he tried to perk up his usual fare when he had a chance to shoot at some game. This is all said to justify his reaction when the semi-transparent ball suddenly material-ized in front of him, around ten feet from where he was sitting.

A city man would have instantly come up with a slew of questions, quickly recognized the danger and probably panicked and run any which way. Brook did nothing of the kind. Because he lacked imagination, he did not think that the ball was a tiny spaceship or that they could disintegrate him with a ray. He simply thought that it was the time to act because if he waited for the ball to become as big as a building again to try something against it…

He lifted his gun, got the ball in his sights and fired his two cartridges.

The shots hit their target and it crashed 60 feet away. Brook reloaded his gun and advanced toward the ball, which was now riddled with lead and looked a little like a cracked egg. Then one part of it dropped off and Brook was astonished to see little bugs spilling out. He put on his metal-rimmed glasses and bent down…

The little bugs had two legs, two arms, a chest, a head and were wearing yellow suits. Some of them were dead, others were running through the grass while the ball started crackling as if a series of short-circuits were firing inside its now opaque shell.

"Men," Brook muttered. "Tiny little men…"

He did not understand a thing, but he felt vaguely like something really extraordinary had just happened and he was responsible for it, so he better not stay there. He grabbed his knife, cut off a piece of tarp, folded it into a kind of pocket and stuffed the wreckage and the yellow corpses inside. Then he caught all the little men trying to run away. They felt like fleas in his big hands and when he was finished he could not swear that he had not crushed a few while picking them up. Brook closed the pocket tightly with his handkerchief, picked up his gun and went back to his cabin. Instead of waiting for Golway to return, he decided to go and see him. Since there was only one road to Randolph, he could not pass by the jeep and his initiative would certainly make things easier for the sheriff.

Beffort and Mie followed Lieutenant Hasting. They went up some stairs and entered the morgue. On a table, covered by a sheet, lay the body of Sheriff Golway.

Lieutenant Hasting introduced the Befforts to Dr. Robbs, the coroner who had done the autopsy on the cadaver. By chance, Golway had been thrown from the car on impact and his body was recovered intact near the burned out shell of the jeep.

"Fractured cervical vertebrae," Dr. Robbs explained as he lifted the sheet. "He died on impact and we would have believed it was an accident if Mr. Brook hadn't come to see Lieutenant Hasting… I didn't find anything in particular, I mean Golway didn't have any device in him that might have controlled his will."

He looked spaced out. From Washington, when Beffort had been told what had happened, he had asked to see if Golway had a motor-brain in his skull. Robbs was young, logical, and was uncomfortable accepting ideas or events that were too out of the ordinary. Especially after hearing that Brook claimed to have harvested some really weird crops... Lieutenant Hasting had not denied nor confirmed it, but they were talking about tiny extraterrestrials.

Beffort thanked him and took Mie and the lieutenant outside. When the three of them were in the police car, safe from meddling ears, Beffort could finally question Hasting. His voice was ice cold. "So, you saw Brook when Golway wasn't here and then you called us. Are you sticking with your story?"

Hasting nodded gravely. He felt like he had aged years in the last few hours. His voice was hoarse. "I didn't make anything up, you'll see in a minute. It's unbelievable! Golway told me about a huge spaceship that Brook had seen shrink to the size of a tennis ball. I didn't believe it. I thought it was an optical illusion or that Brook had hit the bourbon too hard... Then Brook shows up with his sack. He poured it out on my desk and I saw these tiny little yellow men and the debris from their ship..."

He was acting nervously, like he was not himself. He stammered and balked under the great emotion. He took a turn too fast, making the tires squeal, and continued.

"At the time I didn't do anything. Then I started worrying about Golway, remembering his instructions in case something happened to him and I called your number at the FBI... Since you got here I haven't been back to my office. I hope everything's okay there."

Beffort cast a sidelong glance at him. "What precautions did you take?"

"About what?"

"The little men, of course."

Hasting ran his hand over his face. "Sorry, but I'm not exactly myself today. Golway was run into a ravine with his jeep and Brook says he, too, was attacked by this space ball... I wonder if Golway and Brook weren't victims of some kind of ray?"

Mie jumped in. "That's likely, Mr. Hasting. I suppose you're afraid you might not be completely in control of you will? If that's the case, you're wrong. It's obvious that Brook destroyed the spaceship with his shotgun, otherwise he couldn't have captured the crew in his sack and brought them to you. Plus, these little men aren't exactly extraterrestrials. We think that Madame Atomos is behind all this."

The car swerved to the right. "Good God!" Hastings said. "That's why you're so bent on keeping the whole thing a secret, isn't it?"

"We want to avoid a panic," Beffort responded. "We're still not sure about anything. Madame Atomos hasn't shown herself in nine years. She might be dead, but she might also have devoted all these years to preparing for her return. Anyway, it's better not to talk about it, even if it's just to force Madame Atomos to tip her hand. She's too proud to attack us incognito..."

The car stopped in front of the administrative building. Hasting pulled the handbrake and looked up at a second floor window. "Brook's up there in my office. I put him in charge of watching the little men after we put them in a big pot. Crazy, isn't it?"

Beffort did not answer as he got out of the car. "Let's go, Hasting. If we're dealing with Madame

Atomos, crazy things are going to keep boggling our country and the rest of the world."

They entered the building and walked through the first floor where plainclothes and uniformed policemen were bustling around. No one paid any special attention to them, but from the tension in the air Beffort realized that the secret was not as private as he hoped.

On the second floor, Hasting knocked at a door and said, "You can open up, Brook."

"Is that you, lieutenant?"

"Yes, open up," Hasting repeated.

A locked turned, the door swung on its hinges and Brook stepped aside to let Mie, Beffort and Hasting enter. The latter, after locking the door behind him, asked, "Everything okay, Mr. Brook?"

The old man had a skeptical frown on his face as he looked at the pot on the desk. "I guess so. Nothing's moved for a while, like they're all cooped up in that big part of their ship."

Beffort and Mie leaned over the pot. No little man was visible. On the other hand, they could very clearly see the inside of the ship that was, indeed, the size of a tennis ball. Its surface was riddled with holes from the two gunshots fired by Brook; one of its walls had fallen off and the lead had caused irreparable damage to the structure and crew of the vessel.

Beffort looked at Brook and asked, "When was the last time you saw someone walking around outside the ship?"

"Ten minutes ago or so. Then I went to take a look through the window to see if the lieutenant was back and when I came back the little men were hiding. I think they gave up trying to climb out and skedaddled over the desk."

"How many are there, Mr. Brook?" Mie asked.

Brook scratched his scalp. "Frankly, I don't know, Ma'am. They're really tiny, you know. No bigger than a pinhead if it had four limbs and a head. You really got use your imagination to think they're people like us. When I captured them in my field, I felt like I was holding grains of sand in my hand. There were some dead ones, too, but they were carried back into the ship by their friends. Damn! To think that this thing was as big as a building!"

Beffort straightened up, his forehead wrinkled in concentration. "Mie," he said, "we're going to wrap up this pot and everything inside and you're going to take it to Washington for tests. Six G-men will go with you. You'll also call Akamatsu to let him know that we need him. Take Hasting's number, too. His office will be our dispatch as long as we're in the area."

Mie nodded and asked, "What do you intend to do in Randolph, Smith?"

Beffort looked at Brook, grinned and said, "I'm going to live with Mr. Brook for a little while. If I'm not mistaken, the disappearance of the spaceship should alert some headquarters somewhere and it'll be worried when it doesn't come back... I'll keep the suitcase."

Smith and Mie understood each other. The suitcase contained two paralyzing pistols taken from the enemy nine years ago. In spite of all the time that had passed, they were in perfect working order, reservoirs full of the mysterious charge that no laboratory had time to analyze before it vanished...

"It's not very comfortable at my place," Brook said. "I'm just warning you, Sir."

"Doesn't matter," Beffort retorted. "I hope you have a supply of cartridges?"

"Plenty and then some, since I make them myself," Brook assured him.

"Perfect! Now I just have to buy a gun and if another ship flies into your area looking for the one you shot down, we'll give it a mighty warm welcome! Lieutenant, my wife is in your hands. Don't forget to have the G-men escort her. See you later, Mie. I'll call you at the bureau tonight."

The young lady raised her eyebrows. "Mr. Brook has a telephone?"

Beffort looked a little testy. "Hasting will lend me a car equipped with a two-way radio, don't worry. You and Akamatsu stay ready. I'll give you hourly reports if need be. See you."

"Bye," Mie watched him leave with Brook.

When Beffort got an idea in his head, he ran headlong toward his goal and nothing could hold him back from going all out.

For 48 hours no incident was reported in the United States. Yosho Akamatsu was staying in a hotel in Washington D.C., but, in fact, he spent almost all his time in the office of the Yellow Mask at the FBI with Mie, listening to Lieutenant Hasting or Smith Beffort.

In the meantime, specialists had examined the wreckage of the "tennis ball." It was, indeed, a flying machine, some said a spaceship with atomic reactors, navigating instruments and a bunch of machines too miniscule, even under a microscope, to say for sure what they did. Every time they tried to take something apart, it broke and nothing was left but crumbs for the birds.

As for the little yellow men, their corpses were found in what looked like a dormitory. They had apparently committed collective suicide, but since it was impossible to autopsy such tiny bodies, it remained a puzzle. Nevertheless, one thing was certain and unquestionable: they were Japanese.

On the morning of the third day Beffort and Brook took their guns and made the round of the woods, passing by the field where the foot marks were still visible. At Beffort's request, Brook had taken off the tarps so that the marks and the burnt grass could be seen from a distance.

Brook lit his cigar and said, "Why do you want to attract them here?"

"To limit the battlefield," Beffort muttered. "You've no doubt heard about Madame Atomos?"

"Yeah, sure… Don't tell me that awful woman has come back?"

Beffort leaned on a tree. The weather was beautiful. No drop of rain had fallen in more than two weeks and the air had a rare purity. Insects rose up in the sunlight, starting to buzz and the forest hummed with countless sounds. 20 miles from Washington they were far from the pollution and din of the city, as far as if they were standing in the heart of Arizona.

Beffort answered, "We're not sure, Mr. Brook, but there's a strong probability that it's true. She's had nine years to manufacture shrinking machines that could transform its crew along with it and no one can say what she's got in store for us. It could be that she's found a way to build a base on the moon or another planet, but it could just as well be that she's sitting in the Amazon or right here…"

"Here," Brook said. "You mean in this field?"

"In this field, in the forest, in Randolph or somewhere else… Did you ever wonder why the spaceship landed in this spot?"

"Sure, I wondered," Brook said, "but couldn't find an answer. Maybe it broke down?"

Beffort nodded. "I think so. Some damage would have forced it to return to normal size and that's how you came to spot it. But I also think that your land was on its route, see? A route that it had to take to get back to its base after spreading panic in Washington."

Brook shook his head. "Could be. And so? I mean where does it get by knowing that?"

Using a branch Beffort drew a circle on the ground. To the northwest of the circle he marked an X and explained, "The circle represents Washington D.C. and the X is this field. If you draw a line starting in the circle and passing through the X, you can see it's heading northwest at exactly 330 degrees, towards Pennsylvania, Lake Ontario and the deserted areas of Ontario…"

Brook spit out a bit of tobacco.

Beffort continued, "Madame Atomos has always like setting up her bases around water, get it?"

Brook nodded and at the same time he and Beffort heard a shrill whistle.

Chapter IV

Brook swung around, his eyes scanning, but the whistling seemed to come from all directions.

"What is that?" Beffort asked, his finger already on the trigger of his gun.

"I don't know," Brook grumbled. "The last time I heard a whistle that loud, the sphere was covered in a cloud of smoke and shrinking before my eyes. Better watch out!"

Beffort examined the field from the underbrush where he and Brook were squatting, but he saw nothing suspicious, although it was true that the sphere would be hard to spot if it were flying over the trees in its shrunken form. A tennis ball, especially a transparent one, could hide in the leaves and branches and sneak up on its victims. Beffort felt a shudder run down his spine. The audience at the movie theater, the dancers in the Palladium, the Vargas family in Manaos had completely lost touch with reality after the sphere showed up. Sheriff Golway, even though he knew the road to Randolph perfectly well, drove his jeep over a cliff...

"I don't see anything," Brook mumbled, gripping his shotgun. "But the sphere ought to be getting bigger now, right?"

Beffort gritted his teeth. Brook's reasoning was simple and logical. When he heard the whistling before, the sphere shrank, so naturally he deducted that this whistling phenomenon would happen in the opposite case.

"Let's move out," Beffort ordered, "we're too vulnerable here."

They backed into the cover of the trees and took the path back to the cabin. The whistle became no softer, in fact it seemed to grow louder the farther they got from the field. Then there was a crash of broken branches, trees fell down in front of Beffort and Brook while a glimmering dome appeared above the treetops in front of them.

"The bubble!" Brook shouted. "Look at the smoke!"

Beffort stopped short. The dome was white, getting bigger every second and emitting a huge cloud of steam or smoke.

"Turn around!" Beffort said. "Our guns are useless against a machine like this and I 'm afraid they're going to start chasing us any second now."

They ran down another path, Brook leading the way, into the depths of the forest. But Brook had old legs and was quickly out of breath. Beffort figured they must have run more than half a mile when Brook waved to him that he could go no farther. The whistling was quieter, but something droning was moving nearby now. It progressed slowly, with its weird, mournful noise, like human breathing mixed with a kind of sickening rumble.

Without a sound, frozen in place, Beffort and Brook tried to locate the Thing through the bushes and tree trunks. It was close but still invisible, as if it were hiding in order to surprise them. And in the background was still the whistle coming from the sphere, which must have reached its full size by now. Brook slowly straightened up. He was not scared of what he understood, but he was afraid of everything unknown.

"Let's get out of here," he huffed as beads of sweat ran down his forehead. "If we stay here, we'll end up like Golway."

"Stay calm," Beffort whispered. "You can see that they haven't spotted us yet. It must be some kind of detection probe, some machine with an electronic eye. As long as we don't move…"

"I can't stand it!" Brook cried, walking off. "Stay if you want, but I'm going!"

Beffort tried to grab his legs, but Brook dodged, turned and ran down the path without looking back. Beffort started to follow him, but at that very second, a kind of articulated, telescopic tentacle appeared, crawling over the ground like a snake. Beffort saw its probing head fit with microphones and cameras. It moved swiftly, hissing and humming, equipped as well with a cannon that looked a lot like Madame Atomos' disintegrating weapons.

Beffort flattened himself on the ground, held his breath and did not move. The tentacle passed 30 feet from him, then abruptly shot out in the direction Brook had taken. Beffort promptly crawled backward, leaving his gun behind, and scrambled up a rocky hill that, he hoped, would screen him off from the hunting tentacles. When he reached the top, he suddenly saw Brook foolishly entering a clearing. The old man was already dead tired again. Beffort saw him turn around when the tentacle snaked out of the forest and reach for him, its probing head off the ground, threatening, its battery of mics and cameras working to identify him. By reflex Brook did as he should have. He shouldered the shotgun and fired twice. In answer, the tentacle shot its disintegrating ray. Brook was instantly illuminated, then his form melt-

212

ed along with his gun and in a split second the man and weapon were wiped off the face of the earth.

Beffort clenched his fists and clambered down the hill. He ran for cover in the trees, not knowing exactly where he was going as long as it was far away from the sphere. At the same time he was also running away from Brook's cabin and the car he had borrowed from Lieutenant Hasting with the paralyzing pistols inside and the radio whereby he could alert Mie, Akamatsu and the Green Dragon Force.

He went deeper into the forest to escape the fearsome tentacle, but the farther he went the more isolated and therefore the more vulnerable he became.

Beffort was in good physical shape and he had what could be called experience in the anti-Atomos fight, but he had enough common sense to know that time was not on his side. From what he had seen, the tentacles could move very fast over a long enough distance that they were probably coming out of a machine being driven by men. Brook was spotted when he started running. Therefore, Beffort should hole up, hide and stop moving as long as he figured danger was afoot, that is to say as long as the sphere remained its original size without attracting attention.

Randolph and the area were not in the desert. A number of airplanes flew overhead and the sphere must have been very visible from the sky. If a pilot or member of the crew saw it, there would be untold consequences.

Beffort heard the droning again and right away dove into a thick bush. A tentacle had found his trail! The probing head, its mics and cameras, could not have the nose of a bloodhound and track its prey for miles and miles, so there had to be something else, a much more sophisticated tracking system that he could not evade…

Beffort lay motionless. The wide eye of the probing head came directly at him, bobbing clownishly. It was equipped with five microphones and as many cameras. It was triangular and its point was extended by the terrifying disintegrating cannon. Beffort knew that no escape was possible, but he had a hard time fighting against the desire to run helter skelter into the trees to get away from the tentacle.

The probing head hesitated, went around a tree, came back toward the bush and stopped 15 feet from Beffort. The droning turned off but the breathing sound continued with its animal rumbling.

Gritting his teeth, frozen stiff, Beffort struggled in the desperate face-off. He was directly in the camera's field of vision, so if it had not yet seen him, if the mics had not yet detected his breathing, it would be a miracle...

Then the head straightened up a little, advanced slowly and stopped just three feet from Beffort. The unforgettable voice of Madame Atomos spoke, "Hello, Mr. Beffort. I have been waiting for this moment for years, but I didn't think our destinies would meet so soon, especially under such circumstances."

She laughed and the probing head shifted so that Beffort was targeted by only one camera. And Madame Atomos continued, "You haven't really changed. We haven't seen each other in nine years, but you don't have a wrinkle more... I hope your wife and Yosho Akamatsu are doing well? Come on now, get out of that bush!"

Beffort stood up and brushed off the leaves that he had thought would save him. He noticed that the probing head also had a little speaker and the disintegrating cannon was still trained on him.

He said, "My wife and Akamatsu are in good health. Me, too, as you see. And you?"

The probing head moved a few feet backward. "I'm in perfect health, thank you… You surprise me, Mr. Beffort! Am I correct to assume that you were expecting me?"

Beffort nodded. "The Vargas in Manaos, the movie theater, the dance hall, already almost a thousand dead. Who else could it have been? How many victims will you need this time?"

There was silence, then a male voice said, "Please follow my detector or I will be forced to paralyze you. In the first case you will go to a helicojet that will pick you up a hundred yards away. In the second, after the jolts and tremors and all the physical unpleasantness, I will come grab your limp body and the result will be the same. It's up to you, Mr. Beffort."

"I'll follow your detector," Beffort grumbled.

The probing head recoiled and the droning resumed as the telescopic parts swished closed, one after another. Beffort walked forward as the detector backed up. After the hundred yards he heard a faint whistling and when he looked up he saw the helicojet over the trees. The tentacle retired completely into its housing under the helicojet and a kind of basket lowered while a loud speaker ordered, "Please get in the basket, Mr. Beffort. And be smart, don't resist. You are in my power."

Beffort grimaced as he climbed into the basket and was immediately lifted up. He knew that any attempt on his part to escape would fail and that Madame Atomos would not touch a hair on his head. He was her "favorite enemy," without whom the sinister woman's vengeance would lose all its spice. In her enormous pride, Madame Atomos needed a public. Beffort, Mie and Akamatsu

215

were this public, the witnesses of the technical miracles that she had accomplished over the years in the mad hope of one day conquering the United States or, at least, of making the Americans pay for the atomic explosions in Hiroshima and Nagasaki... Madame Atomos was fully aware that a battle was won on land and by occupying it. Now, she did not have the necessary troops for such an occupation, or so Beffort thought based on his experience in the anti-Atomos war, and therefore she had to be satisfied with sowing terror.

But after nine years of retirement had the terrible woman discovered a way to defeat the Americans by subjecting them to thought rays?

The basket entered the helicojet, a panel closed and Beffort was buried in darkness. When the reactors hissed and the machine flew off, Beffort sat down, forcing himself to stay calm. He was the prisoner of the Atomos Organization and in all likelihood Madame Atomos would do all she could to transform him into a robot and force him to serve her. At worst, she would let him go after exposing him to the thought rays so that he would work for her while still being the head of the Yellow Mask section of the FBI.

Beffort gritted his teeth. He had to escape at any cost.

Akamatsu looked at his watch, checked the electric clock on the desk, but said nothing. Mie cast a sidelong glance at him and said, "It's past noon and Smith hasn't given us a sign of life since last night. Is that what's bothering you?"

Akamatsu took time lighting his cigarette. In spite of his many and long stays in the United State, he still smoked his Sensei, whose sharp odor made his fellow

Japanese wrinkle her nose. He spoke calmly, "It doesn't bother me. I know Smith well enough to know that he's got a good reason for not calling us…"

Mie examined the board on which she had written the times of her husband's phone calls. Beffort had a precise and regular character. Except during the night, from 10 pm until 6 am, he called every three hours, even just to say that everything was okay and nothing happening.

Mie murmured, "If we don't get a message in the next 30 minutes, I'm climbing into my car and going to Randolph. Lieutenant Hasting knows where Mr. Brook lives, he'll take me there."

Akamatsu blew a smoke ring at the ceiling. He was very good at making smoke rings. "If you do," he warned her kindly, "Smith will not be happy. He was adamant that no one disturb what he considers to be the eve of battle."

"I don't care if he chews me out," the young lady answered in the same tone to hide her growing anxiety. "We have rules. He has to respect them if he expects us to…"

Then she lost it, suddenly, and jumped up, pushing her chair back. "That's it, I've had enough! We all know that something happened and we're pretending like it's nothing! I'm going to Randolph right now!"

Owen Bernitz stood up. "If you're going, I'm going with you, but we should wait a little while. Maybe his radio's broken."

"No! If his radio's broken, he would have gone to Randolph to call us. He knows that silence would kill me, so he'd do whatever he could to contact me if he's not in trouble. I'm going."

"One minute," Akamatsu begged. "Let's call Lieutenant Hasting first. What's his number?"

Mie gave it to him. Akamatsu dialed the number and listened to the phone ring on the other end. Mie grabbed the other line. "I know the police have to eat like everyone else, but why aren't they answering? Shouldn't someone be there all the time?"

She had been extremely touchy ever since the shadow of Madame Atomos was looming over the United States again. Because they were still not answering the phone, she said, "And what if some tragedy struck Randolph, what if there are no survivors to tell the news?"

At that second the phone picked up and a male voice barked, "Police here. What do you want?"

"I want to speak to Lieutenant Hasting," Akamatsu said.

"The lieutenant isn't in. Leave a message or call back later. Which is it?"

Akamatsu furrowed his brow. Being the chief of the "Atomos" sector of the Japanese Tokkota, he was particularly sensitive to the relations between the police and the "users." He said coldly, "I've decided that you're going to go right now and do whatever it takes to put Lieutenant Hasting on the line. I need to talk to him. It's an emergency, top priority, understand?"

People who are used to giving orders are always very well understood by those used to following them.

"Who shall I say is calling?" the man asked in a different tone.

"FBI. Washington D.C. Special bureau Yellow Mask. Find the lieutenant, I'll stay on the line."

"Very well, Sir, I'll be right back."

He could hear the telephone drop on the table, then silence. Mie kept the other line glued to her ear. "If Hast-

218

ing isn't there," she reckoned gravely, "it's a bad omen. He should stay in his office, shouldn't he?"

"Not since Smith has a car and a radio at his disposal," Akamatsu responded with feigned calmness. "You should stop being melodramatic, Mie, your husband knows Madame Atomos and her methods too well to get trapped like a child."

The young lady shook her brown hair. "No, no one can foresee what Madame Atomos will do. Up until today, every one of her attacks were unprecedented and she's done it again today by showing that she can shrink men and objects in an incredible way... Smith was expecting something, probably a second spaceship around where Brook lives, but something unforeseen has obviously happened..."

Akamatsu and Owen Bernitz snuck a peak at each other. There was not much they could do to reassure Mie. She was totally clear-headed and making no illusions about Beffort. Her analysis of the situation was right and the two men shared her point of view.

After five minutes of waiting, Akamatsu learned that Hasting had gone to Brook's. When they were able to reach him on the radio, the lieutenant let them know that he would use the stronger radio in Beffort's car to call Yellow Mask when he got to his destination.

Akamatsu hung up. "Let's wait. Thanks to Hasting, we'll have some fresh news."

Mie sat down, stood back up after a minute and paced across the room. She could not stand still and her feverish activity only increased as time passed. Akamatsu and Bernitz had often seen her in a state like this. Every time a serious event happened, she seemed to have some kind of sixth sense. She went to the window and looked out at the sky as if it held the answers to the questions she had. Then the light on the two-way radio blinked and Akamatsu flipped a switch.

"Hasting here calling Yellow Mask."

"I'm listening," Akamatsu responded.

"I'm in front of Brook's cabin right now. They asked me to call you. I guess you're worried about Mr. Beffort's silence since last night?" Akamatsu confirmed this and Hasting continued, "Everything's okay inside the cabin. The car is parked in front but no one's answering the honking horn. Moreover there are a bunch of felled trees around two or three hundred yards from here. You should come out here as soon as possible, Yellow Mask."

"We're getting ready to leave for Randolph," Akamatsu said, "but we're going to leave the car and take a helicopter now. Where's Brook's cabin with respect to Randolph?"

Hasting gave directions, adding that he would light a fire so the column of smoke could guide the pilot. Akamatsu signed out and followed Mie and Bernitz who were already heading for the door.

Beffort felt a jolt, the humming reactors turned off and he knew that the helicojet had just landed. From other sounds he knew that the people in the cabin were preparing to leave, but the panel stayed closed and the basket absolutely still. Beffort waited nervously, listening carefully. He was in the dark and could see only the luminous face of his watch. Given the brief time that had passed, it was clear that the helicojet had only traveled to the ship, the huge sparkling sphere that had crushed the trees when it grew back to its original size, which Beffort, deep down inside, was more and more reluctant to call a spaceship.

A long moment passed without anything happening, then the basket jogged a little while the panel slowly slid open, letting a ray of gray light enter the helicojet.

"Come down, Mr. Beffort and follow the lighted arrows," a nasally voice said.

Beffort slipped through the opening of the panel, found a ladder waiting and reached the ground. When he was standing, the ladder rose up and the panel closed. Beffort examined the craft. He was a traditional design in the sense that it did not have a rotor but reactors. It was a spherical shape resting on three supports…

"Move forward, Mr. Beffort, " the nasally voice ordered. "Follow the lighted arrows. The vessel is technically too complicated for you to use for personal ends. Advance and follow the arrows."

Beffort looked around. Because of the lack of light, he could not make out the dimensions of the room or the cameras that were spying on him. On the other hand, he saw the lighted arrows dotting the floor. A rubbery floor, completely smooth, probably make of plastic. He walked over the arrows and crossed the room. When he approached a wall, it automatically opened to let him through and then closed behind him. He went down a corridor until he came out in a kind of cabin furnished with a comfortable cot, a drop-leaf that served as a table, a sanitary facility and a closet.

On the table sat a plate covered with a spotless napkin. Beffort heard the cabin door close. Inside was lit by a dull, indirect light that made it feel like dawn. No window, no visible ventilation system… Beffort sat on the cot and picked up the napkin. On the plate was a meal of cold cuts, a piece of cheese and an apple. Beffort grinned as he dug in. Even if Madame Atomos came from somewhere else, she did not turn her nose up at earthly food.

Beffort knew that he had been drugged when he woke up with a pasty mouth and a nauseated stomach. His watch showed 2:30 am or pm, he had no way of knowing without looking at the sky or being able to evaluate the lapse of time since he collapsed after eating.

The plate had disappeared and Beffort realized after a minute that he was not in the same cabin. They had transported him into a bigger room and laid him on a bigger bed. On the other side of the room were two plush armchairs and a third less comfortable with a kind of very sophisticated hairdryer on the back. Beffort sat up. The second he put his feet on what looked like a carpet, the door opened and two men dressed in yellow suits came in.

They grabbed Beffort, sat him under the hairdryer, strapped his hands to the arms of the chair and left without saying a word. Beffort shook his head to clear the fog that was clouding his brain and looked up at the helmet above him. He saw holes, electric wires, fixed electrodes and others that pivoted, but since he did not recognize the machine, he gave up trying to solve its mystery. Then the door opened again and Madame Atomos entered, gorgeous in white fur hugging her ravishing curves, smiling and self-assured, her magnificent brown hair floating on her bare shoulders. Beffort did not move an inch.

Madame Atomos swished over to the nearest armchair and dropped gracefully into it, saying, "If my memory serves me well, the roles were reversed the last time destiny brought us together in the same room. I was your prisoner in a police station, wasn't I, Mr. Beffort?[4]"

"Exactly. You were over 50 years old, wrinkled, scrawny and a smile like a gargoyle. Someday the effects of your disintegration journey are going to wear off and you'll turn back to the way you were before with a few more years added to the works. The awakening will be painful, dear Madame."

Madame Atomos smiled. "Always so pleasant... I would have been dead a long time ago if your eyes were pistols. I wonder how you would like it if I forced you to make love to me, Smith?"

Beffort grinned. "A man can rape a woman, but the contrary is not true. You forget that it's much easier to open your mouth than to stretch out your arms..."

Madame Atomos puckered her lips briefly, crossed her legs and casually swept a loose lock of hair from her face. She had really become a splendid creature whom any man would go crazy for.

She said, "Look there, Smith, to your right."

She waved and a metal panel slid open, revealing a huge bay window. Beffort squinted at the strange landscape before him. The plants were huge, of an unknown species, and so thick that he could not see the horizon.

Beffort asked, "Where are we?"

Madame Atomos' laughter rang out. "Somewhere in the United States. These plants are nothing but common grass and if they look so huge to you, it's only because we've become so small."

Beffort gritted his teeth. Even if he thought he had nothing to fear, he could not help breaking out in a cold

[4] See *Madame Atomos Spits Fire* in *The Monsters of Madame Atomos.*

sweat on imagining himself no bigger than an apple seed. He looked straight into Madame Atomos' black eyes.

She spoke scornfully, "My revelation doesn't surprise you much? Do you know what became of Cosmos XII?"

"What are you talking about?" Beffort said casually. "I hope you're not talking about that tennis ball that Old Brook pulverized with his shotgun?"

The terrible woman's eyes narrowed. In a low, hoarse voice she said, "I should have known you were in on it when our detector picked up your genetic code around where the Cosmos XII lost contact with Central! I am fully aware that we're rather vulnerable in the 128th reduction, but I didn't think it was that bad! A shotgun, you say?"

"Two shots," Beffort confirmed without hiding his deep satisfaction. "Old Brook informed the authorities, who informed me, and we picked up the wreckage of your machine, but the whole crew decided they preferred suicide… Your first failure in this new round, dear Madame. And I'm sure it won't be the last."

Madame Atomos controlled her anger, even found the strength to smile. She pointed at the helmet above Beffort and said, "Do you know what this machine does?"

"No, not at all and I won't hide the fact that I don't care. Unless, of course, you only captured me to tell me the secrets of this ship?"

The smile on Madame Atomos' face grew larger. "It's not to tell you what they are, my dear Smith. During this operation against the United States, I intend to wreak havoc in your house. This helmet is a thought inductor."

She shifted in her chair, pointed to a corner of the ceiling and explained amiably, "The object you see up there is a photographic lens. Do you see the relation between the helmet, the lens, you and me?"

Beffort furrowed his brow. A growing fear was gnawing away at him.

Madame Atomos continued, "When the adorable little Mie Azusa gets dozens of photographs of us in tender embraces, what do you think she'll do?"

"It'll never happen?" Beffort rasped.

Madame Atomos stood up and approached Beffort. She touched the helmet and it immediately started to hum. She went back to her chair and explained, "The thought inductor was programmed by me while you were sleeping, Smith. I will unstrap you and you will take me in your arms and carry me to the bed where we will make love. After that you will pass out and when you awake, because you will remember our embraces, you will hate me even more. But no matter. I will have satisfied my whim and during our labor of love the camera will have snapped entire rolls of film. Wouldn't you call that a skillfully plotted vengeance, Smith dear?"

Beffort did not respond. The inductor was starting to work. Gentle warmth was washing over him as he repeated to himself that all of this would be for naught. And Madame Atomos was certainly bluffing when she said the pornographic pictures would be sent to Mie...

Madame Atomos was attentively watching the emotions on Beffort's face. For an instant she had doubted the power of the inductor, but to see her mortal enemy staring at her lustily filled her with pleasure. She stood up, unfastened the belt of her robe and let it drop to her feet. Beffort leaned forward. Madame Atomos looked like something out of a dream and he desired her like he had never desired another woman.

Madame Atomos unclasped her bra and her firm, luscious breasts sprang out, tantalizing. She had an unnerving laugh as she slipped her see-through panties down her shapely legs and spun around to show that her back side was as worthy of admiration as her front. Beffort struggled in his straps. He could not talk, but his expressive attitude was more eloquent than words. Madame Atomos teased him with a few lewd poses while keeping an eye on her victim's groin. She was getting excited by the game and felt the irresistible need to be loved, to be taken like a girl.

She turned on the camera system. From now on a picture would be taken every 30 seconds.

"Well, Smith dear, do you still say you don't want me?"

"I want you!" Beffort panted. "Unstrap me!"

Madame Atomos sauntered up to him, freed his hands and backed up to the bed. Beffort ripped off his clothes, took the sinister Japanese woman in her arms and dropped her on the bed to cover her body with kisses. With her eyes closed Madame Atomos felt every groping touch with supreme pleasure.

When he entered her, she arched her back to offer herself to him and in her sensual delight dug her nails into his back...

Chapter V

Beffort regained consciousness very quickly, almost immediately, certainly not normally. The thought inductor did not work like a drug that a body takes time to get rid of. Here he recovered without a hangover, like a diver coming back to the surface and seeing the bright sunlight after the darkness of the depths.

Beffort sat up carefully. He did not feel sick, his mouth was not pasty and knew exactly where his fatigue came from. As he had been told, he remembered his amorous fling with the lethal Japanese woman down to the last detail.

In bed, Madame Atomos was demonic. Her excesses bordered on pure madness. She was insatiable. Beffort bore the mark of her bites and scratches. During the deed, controlled as he was by the inductor, he had given himself body and soul. Now it all seemed insane, unreal, inhuman and bestial.

He stood up. They had apparently brought him back to the cabin, but the folding table was not there. Beffort looked at his watch. It was 5 pm. Now he was certain. Having seen the day through the bay window he could no longer confuse it with 5 am. Therefore, it was the same day. Beffort shrugged his shoulders in dismay. What did the time matter? Or the day? He was a prisoner and as far as he could tell, shrunken to the size of the yellow men from the Cosmos XII!

Madame Atomos could leave him in this state indefinitely and reduced herself every now and again to join him. With the help of the thought inductor she could do with him as she pleased. He belonged to her; he was her slave...

Beffort groaned. Sooner or later the ship and its crew would have to return to its normal size. In the past, those who carried a motor-brain in the head were "free" for one hour every day to regenerate. A human organism cannot, in fact, endure such constraints without serious consequences. As for this shrinking, it was certainly the same thing.

A question mark remained, nevertheless.

Beffort searched his pockets, then lit a cigarette. They had left him his clothes and personal effects. This did not mean much, except that he was not yet part of the Atomos Organization whose members wore yellow suits.

"Get ready to leave your cabin, Mr. Beffort," the nasally voice said through an invisible speaker. "We're coming to get you in three minutes."

Beffort nodded automatically and after this involuntary movement he wondered gloomily whether he was himself or the thought inductor was controlling him. For example, he remembered the lovemaking with Madame Atomos, but not the moment he got dressed or how he got back to the cabin or exactly when he had passed out.

He crushed out his cigarette, threw it in the toilet and walked to the door when someone turned the lock from the outside. It swung open and Isadori filled up the doorway, strong, incredibly muscular and on his guard. He was Madame Atomos' servant who had saved her life several times. So, to thank him the terrible woman had made him her lover, her beast of pleasure, so that he was devoted body and soul and would die for her.

Beffort had caught a glimpse of him two or three times, always when Madame Atomos was about to be captured. The man was a wild animal, a brute. His brain must have been the size of a pea, but his astonishing ferocity was exactly what made his actions so exceptional. Isadori did not recognize danger; he charged like a bull, demolishing everything in his way. In Yellowstone, nine years ago, they had seen him flee carrying Madame Atomos like a feather, growling like a monster of strength and determination through the woods and marshes, pulverizing reeds like a millstone. They saw him climb a cliff, hurtle down slopes, cross a raging river, jump over a barrier and end up on Highway 220 down from Mills, a few miles from Jackson Canyon... He stood in the road, legs planted, Madame Atomos in his arms, like they had just survived a terrible accident and when a concerned driver pulled up to them he killed him with one punch to steal his car and disappear with Madame Atomos who had not touched the ground for hours...

Although Beffort was tall, but he barely reached his shoulder. Isadori was not armed. There was no need. "Move it," he ordered.

Beffort walked out. The Japanese man's eyes were like two daggers ready to stab. He must have found out that Madame Atomos had "offered" herself to Beffort, who had the feeling that if someone had to kill him, Isadori would willingly do the job and strangle him slowly, with the same pleasure that his mistress felt while making love.

"To the right!" Isadori barked.

Beffort went down a new corridor. He did not even try to tell the difference. In the ship all the corridors looked alike, all the cabins as well. Anyway, they were certainly watching to be sure that he would never get near the cockpit or an exit or any place that opened onto the outside.

A wall slid open before Beffort and he entered, followed by Isadori, a room where Madame Atomos was sitting in a big armchair. She waved him forward. "Come and sit down, Mr. Beffort. Yes, facing this wall. We're going to watch a captivating sight."

Under Isadori's watchful eyes and Madame Atomos' cold stare, Beffort sat in an armchair. She obviously had no wish to talk about what happened between the two of them in front of Isadori. She said, "We're in Washington right now, in a room that you will no doubt recognize. But I won't say any more because I don't want to spoil it for you. Look at the wall."

Beffort sat back and after a minute he could start to see through the wall. There were strange forms grouped around a kind of vaguely shaped ring. Then the wall became completely transparent and Beffort was stunned to see huge paintings. There were eight of them: the landing of Christopher Columbus in 1492 by John Vanderlyn; the embarkation of the pilgrims at Delft Haven by R.W. Weir; Washington resigning his commission as commander in Chief of the Army at Annapolis in 1783; the surrender of the English Army by Lord Cornwallis at Yorktown in 1781; the surrender of Burgoyne at Saratoga in 1777; the signing of the Declaration of Independence at Philadelphia in 1776, these last four by John Trumbull; the baptism of Pocahontas at Jamestown in 1613 by John G. Chapman; and finally the discovery of the Mississippi by De Soto in 1541.

Beffort squinted. He, or rather Madame Atomos' spaceship, was in the Capitol building!

"We're really here, Mr. Beffort," the terrible Japanese woman said ironically. "We're sitting in the dome of the Rotunda, almost 200 feet up, and since we're a different size, reduced to 128th normal to be exact, everything looks huge to you. Cosmos I is no bigger than a tennis ball, but you know all about that, don't you?"

In spite of himself Beffort clutched the arms of his chairs. He was dizzy. The Capitol Rotunda, seen under such conditions, was something out of a fairy tale. And the visitors squeezing into its 96 feet were giants, monstrous humans whose hair looked like tree trunks.

"You will get used to it very quickly," Madame Atomos assured him with absolute calm. "In a few minutes you will see all these people become puppets in my hands when I turn on my thought inductors."

Beffort looked at her. "Why come to the Capitol?"

Madame Atomos smiled. "Because there's a session right now of the House of Representatives. We're going to disrupt the session to entertain me a little and to convince you, once and for all, that my power is limitless."

Beffort looked back outside. Now the Cosmos I was gliding along the ceiling of the old House of Representatives, now the National Hall of Statuary, a semi-circular room filled with the statues of famous Americans; then down a corridor on the south side until they reached the House Reception Room where they were stopped by a pair of closed doors.

The nasally voice said, "We can't enter the room, Madame. What should we do?"

Madame Atomos thought for a second and answered, "Stay here. Someone will end up opening the doors."

Cosmos I hovered in the air, but still next to the ceiling and in the shadows. Beffort gritted his teeth. Madame Atomos had an ultimate new weapon, or nearly so considering the fact that a load of buckshot could

231

bring it down pretty easily in certain cases. Beffort saw the bailiffs and sheriffs keeping watch. No one was suspicious and there was no way to warn anyone… Beffort knew that a dreadful tragedy would play out in the chamber. Madame Atomos had come here with a specific goal: to make a big splash… In the chamber, during big sessions, there were 435 congressmen. If this session was important, everyone would be present.

"The door's opening," Isadori warned and Madame Atomos cast a menacing look at him.

Cosmos I was already moving, sneaking through the open door and drifting into the 135-foot long room. Beffort was stunned. The Republican seats, to the left and in front of the Speaker, were all full. The Democrats, to the right, had a few empty seats but on the whole there must have been 400 congressmen.

Cosmos I went to cling to the ceiling, in the very center of the room, and it sat still. Beffort was very pale when he turned to Madame Atomos. "What's going to happen?"

"They're going to fight with each other. Republicans against Democrats, like cats and dogs, and in front of the cameras when they're supposed to be voting on a law to limit the violence seen in movies and television." Her smile was angelic and she added, "What a perfect setting, don't you think, Mr. Beffort? It's almost 6 pm. Millions of Americans, 90 million if you consider the number of sets, are about to witness a bloody battle thanks to CBS, NBC and ABC. There will certainly be casualties and many seriously wounded. The strongest will survive and be voted in again the next election."

"You're completely crazy!" Beffort shouted as he stood up. Isadori simply leaned a little on his shoulders and he sat back down.

Madame Atomos grinned. "I'm completely crazy, you say? And you Americans, how would you call yourselves? When you dropped the atomic bombs on Hiroshima and Nagasaki, wasn't that an act of madness? You've made films about the Nazi atrocities in the concentration camps, but why haven't you made films about the atomic bombings? Millions of people atomized, cities razed and more than 30 years later children being born crippled and retarded. Who are the crazy ones, Mr. Beffort?"

Beffort shook his head. "Vengeance has its limits," he said. "The Nazi criminals were tried and executed. You can't be mad at a people forever for a crime committed by its citizens under exceptional circumstances. It's no longer vengeance you're seeking but your own ambition to terrify my fellow citizens! Admit it!"

Madame Atomos turned away. Her mouth was tense, her face frozen.

Isadori leaned harder on Beffort's shoulders. The Japanese was unbelievably strong. He murmured, "Shut up or I'll break your arms."

Beffort kept quiet. There was nothing he could do... for the moment. If he made the slightest move, Isadori would knock him out. If he kept at it, Madame Atomos would shut him up for good by turning the thought ray on him and just like Vargas in Manaos, he would lose his free-will and personality to become an instrument of the Atomos Organization to be used at their pleasure.

"The inductors are on, Madame," the nasally voice announced.

Madame Atomos said nothing, but her eyes narrowed. Beffort whispered a question, "Why don't we hear any noise from the room?"

Madame Atomos gave a sign with her hand. Two seconds of silence and then suddenly the room was filled with an incredible commotion, unbearable screaming and shouting. Beffort plugged his ears. Madame Atomos made another sign and all was silent again.

She told him, "You understand, I guess... When we're in the 128th reduction, sounds take on excessive proportions. Our eardrums can't listen without being damaged. That's why we use detector probes when we have to listen to the outside world. So, just be satisfied with watching, Mr. Beffort. Even without sound it deserves a good look!"

Down below, far below, the congressmen were clearly heating up. Even without sound it was clear that the session, which had kept up its usual decorum until then, was suddenly turning nasty. On the Republican side a congressman was yelling and gesticulating wildly at one of his Democratic colleagues who was responding in kind. The Speaker was standing up and trying to calm everyone down. The television crews were busy doing all kinds of things. What was happening was far from normal, especially since the vote for the law against violence had already been agreed upon and they were only waiting for it to pass with practically no discussion at all before going before the Senate.

Beffort watched all this in dread. He rapidly got used to the optical shift caused by the 128 reduction and now that his sight could calmly take in the enormous size of the people and things, he was able to judge the destructive effect of the thought ray. Apparently no one could resist it. Madame Atomos just had to select whatever programming she wanted and the irradiation would do the rest.

The Republican congressman, with nothing more left to say and being egged on by his colleagues, suddenly climbed over the railing and marched toward the Democrat with whom he disagreed. The latter did the same, marching to meet his adversary, and the two men faced off at the halfway point. In a fury the Republican sent a fist into the Democrat's chin. The latter landed a right hook. The Republican bent over and the Democrat knocked him down with a shot to the neck. A dozen other Republicans reacted right away and rushed him but he was backed up by his Democrat friends and in a few seconds it became an all-out, messy brawl.

Unbelievably, the Speaker climbed down into the arena and the cameramen abandoned their posts to join the fight and because the doors were closed no one knew what was happening...

Beffort snuck a peek at Madame Atomos who just sat and watched. He was sure that she was making this demonstration just to convince him of her power. As for him, she must have had some specific plan. Beffort watched the window. The congressmen were fighting each other with more and more savagery; blood was flowing; the Speaker was lying in a corner with a fractured skull and someone was destroying the cameras with a broken chair.

Beffort turned away. This negation of the human individual was a frightening spectacle. His hatred for Madame Atomos had no more limits and if Isadori were not there he would probably have strangled her on the spot.

To the north of Randolph the search teams had just given up because twilight came on. The twenty or so men requisitioned by Lieutenant Hasting climbed into a van and left.

Akamatsu put down his hunting rifle in the helicopter that he himself would pilot and said, "I think it's useless to continue searching this sector. What do you think, Mie?"

The young lady nodded. They had proof that the gun had been bought in Randolph by Beffort. Hasting had found it in the forest after following the footprints of the two men. One of the tracks stopped abruptly in the middle of a clearing as if the person had sunk into the ground or flown away. The other track, probably Beffort's because that was where his gun was found, made it hallway back before disappearing on the edge of another little clearing where a rectangular object had left its print in the soft ground.

All this was hardly reassuring. In both cases, Brook's and Beffort's, it looked like they were faced with inexplicable disappearances, unless they accepted the intervention of the Atomos Organization in which case anything was possible, even and especially the unimaginable…

"I think so, too," Mie responded. "On the other hand, it seems necessary that one of us stay here."

Owen Bernitz agreed. Chomping on his unlit cigar stub he said, "I'll stay. The boss will come back here for sure if he's physically unable to get to Washington." He looked around, stared at the place where a group of trees had been uprooted and added, "I have the feeling that Madame Atomos isn't too far from Brook's cabin. If you give me the authorization, I'll bring in a full team from the Green Dragon Force."

Mie and Akamatsu gave their assent and Bernitz got on the radio right away. If all went as Bernitz wanted, 50 men, armed to the teeth, would be there in less than two hours.

Once back in the Yellow Mask office at the FBI Akamatsu and Mie sent out a general search order for Beffort and Brook. Besides the men from the Green Dragon Force not mobilized by Owen Bernitz, hundreds of policemen, police informants, agents from the FBI, CIA, DIA and NSC, and various executive agencies were now on constant duty to do what they could to find the two missing men.

The Yellow Mask office was the ultimate information center. News from all the states came in here. That was how Mie and Akamatsu found out that the congressmen had just had a brawl, Republicans against Democrats, in the chamber of the House of Representatives. They counted 10 dead and more than 100 wounded. The cameramen were mixed up in the incredible event, the Speaker had been stoned by the wild congressmen and they did not know why or who to assign responsibility for the collective madness.

Akamatsu stubbed out the cigarette he had just lit and grumbled, "Signed Madame Atomos. Without a shadow of a doubt. If we don't find a way to stop her, she'll go to the White House and force the President to start an atomic war."

Mie shook her head. "No, precautions were taken by Smith a while ago to counter any eventual attack by Madame Atomos on our leaders. Before leaving for Randolph he passed by the warning center. The White House and all the main military bases with missiles are already super-protected against bubbles, spheres and balls of all sizes so that even a mosquito couldn't get through the defense set up around all the strategic places."

She sat down in front of the radio and telephone and added, "Madame Atomos can't take us by surprise anymore like she used to. A large-scale attack against the security of the country is beyond her now. But she can still commit mass murder, assassinate politicians, terrorize a city or region... But she has to be careful not to be captured. She's accused of crimes against humanity, which equals death if she's arrested, even 20 years from now since this kind of crime has no statute of limitations."

Akamatsu rubbed his chin and its scratchy stubble. Everything was in place to find Smith Beffort and Brook. The President's safety along with the important politicians and generals and the military bases were guaranteed. They only had to hope that Beffort would give them some sign of life very soon... Here Yosho Akamatsu started to have doubts. Beffort had disappeared 24 hours ago, which meant that he was either dead or Madame Atomos' prisoner.

The second probability was by no means good, but the first...

Cosmos I left the Capitol building. Its walls clouded over again and Isadori led Beffort back to his cell.

Now, while the ship soared to its base, Madame Atomos, completely nude, stood on her tiptoes, arched her back and stuck out her chest. Isadori stood in a corner of the room admiring her. "When we've finished with Washington," Madame Atomos murmured softly, "we'll attack New York."

Isadori shook his head. With her keen eye, Madame Atomos knew that she had lost none of her beauty. She twirled around and walked up to the giant, leaning against him like a wall. "Fondle me. It helps me think."

He put his big hands on her ivory skin and caressed her. Madame Atomos closed her eyes and a little smile crossed her sensual lips.

"Tomorrow," she cooed, "you'll tell the Rising Sun to go into action with Cosmos V, Cosmos VI and Cosmos VII. They'll start with the department stores, police and fire stations, highs schools and universities. In the afternoon they'll attack the postmen, taxi and bus drivers, and the employees of the telephone, gas and electric companies. Tomorrow night at this time Washington will be totally dark, without gas or electricity and all traffic will be paralyzed..."

She paused when Isadori stroked a sweet spot and she clenched her teeth as his hand became more insistent. She knew that he was playing her like a violin, that this was his way of dominating her, but even using all her willpower, she could never overcome her senses inflamed by violent lust.

Then Isadori's desire became concrete, flagrant, and Madame Atomos felt the heat, waiting for it, her flesh quivering. She swung around and embraced him. He wrapped his arms around her and bent down toward her parted lips.

"Take me," Madame Atomos gasped, flaring her nostrils.

Isadori was a good servant and a remarkable lover. He did what his mistress asked of him, coldly, like a technician, careful to suppress his own desires in order to better satisfy those of his partner. Usually ferocious and authoritarian, Madame Atomos became extraordinarily submissive in the arms of a man who was worthy of the name. Isadori knew her well enough to sense the moments when the terrible woman needed domination and violence. Tonight was one of those moments and the Japanese used his strength to conquer her mock resistance as she played the raped virgin, just for the fun of it. All this was purely animal, but it was perfectly suited to Madame Atomos' temperament, which pushed every game to its very limits. Beaten and pawed, enslaved and treated like a whore, suffering the "final outrage," she finally pushed Isadori away, telling him with the cold glare in her eyes that playtime was over and he had to get out.

Another man, less familiarized, would have left. Isadori, instinctively aware of his power of persuasion, crushed her under his weight and decreed the needs of man with unfulfilled desires. Madame Atomos struggled, bit, scratched and threatened, then in a fit of rage sank into her sea of lust once again. In fact—and both of them knew it—the game had just begun...

But while Madame Atomos reveled in her debauchery, things were moving forward without her and not necessarily to her advantage. You can't be everywhere at the same time. Madame Atomos should have known this and instead of surrendering herself to bedroom acrobatics, she should have been worrying about the eventual reactions of Smith Beffort after the scene he had been forced to watch in the Capitol.

Despair gives men new strength and necessity makes them imaginative. Beffort, locked in his cabin and condemned to an imminent doom, was ready for anything when two men in yellow suits, probably Japanese kidnapped by the Atomos Organization in Japan or the American group of Rising Sun, opened the door to bring in a plate. Beffort knew that he had to take advantage of the least opportunity. Moreover, he was dealing with men exposed to a thought inductor and so without the necessary reflexes or initiative to react to a violent attack.

Beffort hit hard, with deadly force, a double chop, amazingly fast. The man in the doorway fell like a tree. Beffort jumped on the other and hit him on the neck with the side of his hand. He heard something snap. The man let out a weak scream, dropped the plate and collapsed, blood gushing out his nose.

Beffort dragged the two bodies and stuffed them in the closet. He promptly cleaned up the plate and the mess, threw everything under the cot and peeked into the corridor. Now the hard part began. He had not thought about it because he figured on improvising every step of his way in the ship. Surrounded by enemies, not knowing which direction to take, he did not like his chances of escape, but he still preferred to get it over with as soon as possible rather than be robotized by a thought ray.

He stepped out, closed the cabin door and locked it. He did not know how long it would take them to start searching for his victims, so he had to act quickly, do anything at all but do something. In all probability the structure had several levels but no more than three or four considering the space needed for the cockpit and atomic engines, not to mention the inductors, the helicojets, etc.

In theory, the cockpit should be in the upper part of the sphere, which always remained horizontal during its flight, which meant that the reactors and inductors and the exits would be located down below with the landing gear where Brooks had seen an oval door and the beginning of a corridor.

Beffort ran and reached the place where Isadori ordered him to turn, but this time he continued straight ahead. Since the corridor was circular he could run into members of the Atomos Organization at any moment. If this happened he would dive into them and kill or be killed. But he arrived without incident at a landing. Stairs went up and down and to the left was an elevator. Beffort pressed the button and bit his lips while waiting for it to come down from the upper levels. When it arrived, he stepped in and pressed the bottom button, even though it bore no marking. The elevator dropped like a rock, slowed down gradually and the doors slid open by themselves.

Beffort went down another corridor feeling like he was on the same level as before because they were so much alike. Since the start of his flight he had seen no one and heard no voices or sounds. He did not even know if the ship was on the ground or, what was worse, what size it was.

Beffort froze. Two feet away a man in a yellow suit, armed with a disintegrating gun, was standing guard in front of a wall with the oval shape of a concave panel fitted with a kind of folding ladder. Beffort stepped back behind the curve in the corridor just when the meager light grew brighter and a horn started blasting. He stepped farther back. He did not know what all this meant but on the other side of the bend the guard had just moved and his shadow was etched on the ground. Beffort turned to run in the opposite direction but found himself suddenly faced with four guards. One of them raised his paralyzing pistol. The green ray hit Beffort in the chest. He felt a sharp pain, his strength drained out and he stood frozen in the middle of the corridor, incapable of the slightest movement and his mind stuck on his last thought.

The guards lifted him up and carried him away like a bar of steel.

Beffort came out of it abruptly. His muscles softened up and his mind replayed the images of his capture. The first thing he saw was the shaven head of Isadori, then other hazy forms that, as his sight cleared up, turned out to be Madame Atomos sitting behind a desk flanked by armed guards.

Isadori lifted Beffort up like a feather and plopped him in a chair across from Madame Atomos, who looked stern. He sighed and sat more comfortably before aiming his eyes at those of the sinister woman.

She said, "You killed two soldiers of my organization, Mr. Beffort. We weren't threatening you, you were well treated and we even granted you certain favors that more than one man would have been thankful for..." She leaned forward and raised her voice. "You deserve to die immediately and I am ready to accommodate, but Isadori has asked me for the right to hunt you and I have accepted. Nevertheless, you have the right to choose your own death. Do you prefer a cyanide capsule or to play the rabbit for Isadori and his team?"

Beffort shrugged his shoulders. "I guess I'll have no weapons to defend myself and the hunt will have no time limit... that it will be out in the open, far from anywhere I might be able to hide? If you answer yes to these questions, then I choose the cyanide."

Madame Atomos looked over his head at Isadori and asked, "Are you prepared to give him a weapon, to set a time limit, say for example at night in Rock Creek Park in Washington so he might find a hiding place? If you can come to an agreement, I give my consent right now. What do you think?"

Isadori stepped forward and without taking his eyes off Beffort said, "I'm ready to give him a weapon and to limit the hunt to three hours in Rock Creek Park tonight. But on one condition…"

Chapter VI

Cosmos I landed in the middle of Rock Creek Park, which was closed at night. On its three supports the ship was not higher than the treetops. A group got out: Madame Atomos and her four bodyguards, Isadori and his hunting party of six men armed with clubs and spears, and Smith Beffort carrying an old sword.

Madame Atomos grinned. "It is one in the morning. The hunt will last until 4 am unless, of course, Mr. Beffort's corpse is brought back here before then. Go, Mr. Beffort, you have a two-minute head start."

Beffort turned and ran toward some bushes. He was only eight inches tall whereas Isadori and his team were in the 92nd reduction. Even though running at full speed, Beffort was aware that he was covering only inches of ground. Every stride was hardly bringing him any closer to the edge of the paved path. He glanced behind him. One minute had already passed and he was still in view of the ship. He swore, tried to speed up and finally reached the grass that even though it was mowed short, made him feel like he was in a wheat field.

The one condition imposed by Isadori, that the hunt take place in this size, was of considerable disadvantage to Beffort because even if he managed to escape, he would stay this size! But it was better than swallowing a cyanide capsule even if salvation was a problem... Isadori and his six team members seemed well trained in this kind of sport. Moreover, they were more heavily armed than Beffort, especially with their bigger size, and they could constantly surround him.

Beffort lunged through the grass and into a bush before he turned around. The two minutes were up. Back around the ship Isadori and his acolytes were running forward. The moon was bright and although zones of shadow lay across the paths in the park, the night was too well lit for Beffort to take advantage of them. He continued to the south. He knew the park well. His goal was to get as close as possible to the edge of the park near Klingle Road NW. If Isadori and his men did not catch him in the meantime, he would venture into the city and try to reach the FBI headquarters.

But this was just a plan, a kind of impossible dream. At eight inches tall Beffort did not see a bright future ahead. He was running through a nightmare landscape of giant plants. Every pebble was a big rock as he tripped over the gravel. When he ran into a six-inch high wall of cement he had to get a running start to scramble on top of it. His sword was cumbersome, but it was his only weapon and he had to hang onto it at all costs.

He ran quickly down the cement curb, under some arches and then jumped down into more grass planted with trees. Behind him he heard the shouts in spite of the distant noises of the city. Isadori and his men were hot on his trail and Beffort wondered how they could follow him with such precision.

He ran faster, still to the south and reached the north fence of the zoo where he hesitated to enter. To go into the zoo was to set off on a safari. He could, by mistake, wander into the big cats territory, or a birdcage… His eight inches would make him an easy prey. They could crush him with a paw, stab him with a beak…

"There he is!" Isadori yelled. "Everyone with me! He's by the fence of the zoo!"

Beffort turned around. The Japanese was on the cement curb, just beyond the arches and shaking his spear wildly. Two men jumped up on the curb while three others were to the right, farther back, hopping through the grass trying to see Beffort, who slipped through the fence, past a thick hedge, and ran along a little canal that wound its way across a lawn between thickets of pine. Nothing moved around him, but Beffort guessed that eyes were following his race. A giant bird got scared and soared off screeching and flapping its huge wings. When it flew into the light Beffort saw that it was just a sparrow.

He stopped to catch his breath under a thuja. Once in great shape before he was captured, he now felt weak from lack of regular meals. His situation looked suddenly hopeless. Well trained men were hunting him and even if he did escape he saw absolutely no way that he could get back to normal size without the help, voluntary or not, of Madame Atomos.

Something rustled on the other side of the thuja. Beffort brandished his sword and silently stepped back as he spied the triangular head of an adder. The reptile was no more than 20 inches long, but for Beffort it was like a python.

The adder crawled away slowly, lifting its head often, no doubt searching for prey. Beffort stayed out of sight by turning around the thuja. Then another movement caught his eye near the canal he had come from. It was one of Isadori's partners. He was moving quickly, staring at a box of some kind, and amazingly was coming directly towards where Beffort was hiding. His club was stuck in his belt and he held a spear in his left hand. He was so focused on the box that he did not see the adder slithering towards him through the grass.

Beffort clenched his teeth when the reptile un-wound and struck. Its fangs sunk into the man's body and bones cracked. The man screamed weakly, flapping his arms, then just like that he was dead and the adder carried him away. Beffort ran, trembling in fear and hor-ror. The fate of the man would be his own if he was not careful about his surroundings.

"Here!" Isadori shouted. "He's heading for the main path! Don't let him get there!"

Beffort made a dash and reached the cement, but at the same time a hunter also came out of the grass a few feet away. Beffort could not turn back or risk a blind flight through the zoo. He chose to fight and rushed at the Japanese. If he could knock him out of the way the zoo exit would be a straight shot. He had been pushed past Klingle Road by the hunters, so his goal now was Cathedral Avenue.

"He's right here!" the Japanese yelled. "You can get him from behind!"

Beffort aimed his sword. The Japanese lunged with his spear, but Beffort blocked it and grabbed the spear with his left hand. With the sword in his right hand he swiped but missed. He held on tightly to the spear that his adversary was trying to pull back and struck again. This time he made contact, lightly, and when he try to strike again, harder, he lost his balance, let go of the spear and rolled on the ground.

The Japanese had an evil smile as he lifted his weapon and tried to plunge it into Beffort's chest, but he rolled away, right into the place that his adversary want-ed to keep him away from. Beffort jumped up and in-stead of getting back in the fight he headed full speed ahead to the zoo exit.

"He's escaping!" the Japanese yelled.

Beffort had left him standing there. He sprinted down the path as fast as he could. On Cathedral Avenue there were streetlamps, buildings, parked cars and others, though few, driving. Apparently none of this changed anything. Where Beffort was going, Isadori and his men followed but the fact that he was in a city street, in a "civilized" area, was a great boost to the fugitive's morale. He ran through the gate, continued past the admission booths and did not turn around until he was on the sidewalk.

Isadori and his men (now down to five) were running after him. One of them, no doubt the one Beffort had slightly wounded, was limping and falling behind his partners. Beffort struck him off the list of hunters. Thanks to the adder and a lucky blow from his sword, he only had to deal with five enemies now. Beffort winced. It was all relative! He was feeling more confident because five men, including the daunting Isadori, seemed like nothing to him.

He took off again on the edge of the sidewalk next to the tires and through the yellow puddles of the curved streetlamps on Cathedral Avenue. A little ways down he turned around again and furrowed his brow because Isadori and his quartet were gaining on him. They were physically faster than him after not eating much and feeling the effects.

Beffort jumped off the five inches of sidewalk and waded through the water in the gutter. He slipped under a Buick that was leaking oil from its crankcase, avoided the puddle, looked right and left and then made a daring dash across the street. He was halfway across when a car came, headlights on, a growling monster at a frightening speed. Beffort was paralyzed as he watched the wheels coming at him. The tires hissed, the bumper gleamed, the chassis shook and everything combined to make a hellish racket for an eight-inch tall man whose eardrums were especially fragile.

Beffort bent over and was knocked down by a gust of air as the car sped over him. He rolled for what seemed like forever and ended up in the gutter across the street, under another parked car, in another oil leak and fumes of gas. In all the excitement he had held onto the sword. He stood up, climbed onto the sidewalk and resumed his flight along the endless building fronts. Amazingly there was not a single open door or cellar window, nowhere he could find refuge until Isadori and his men gave up the hunt.

Nevertheless, he was hoping he had lost them when he crossed the street. Then he caught sight of movements on the road and he had to change his mind because the five men were still following him. Beffort clenched his fists. It was unbelievable! He kept running along the buildings under the streetlamps that worked against him because they revealed him to his pursuers.

Isadori and the others crossed the street at an angle trying to cut some of the distance, but the move was fatal to two of them when a second car showed up. Turning from another street, lights blazing, it was on the group quicker than the first car had been on Beffort. Isadori and the two closest men had time to reach safety under a parked car but the two slower ones were run over... When the car was down the street, there was nothing on the road but two flat, shapeless blotches, barely even red.

Beffort started running again. His enemies were getting wiped out in unexpected ways but the survivors were still on his tail despite his changing directions and his tricks. There was something miraculous here! Then all of a sudden Beffort remembered the box that had fascinated the man attacked by the adder. A receiver! And if his enemies were carrying receivers that meant that he was emitting a regular "beep-beep!" So wherever he went and whatever he did, Isadori would always find him!

With shaky legs Beffort stopped in the corner of a doorway that was unfortunately closed. He was wearing a transmitter, otherwise called a "beeper," emitting a regular signal on a specific frequency that allowed Isadori to follow him. Since they had not touched his clothes or his personal effects, it had to be the sword. Beffort examined it, found the hilt a little loose and un-screwed it. It was hollow and contained the device that had a thin wire connected to the blade to serve as an an-tenna, a long-lasting battery and a small box that was the actual transmitter. Beffort threw the box into the gutter, screwed the hilt back on and continued his flight.

Because of this stop, Isadori and his two acolytes had gained ground and were only a few normal yards behind him, which translates into 100 yards or so at 92nd reduction. Rested from the short break, Beffort was ready to widen the gap and when he reached the corner of Calvert Street, his pursuers were only just passing by the place where he had dropped the transmitter.

Beffort sped up on Columbia Road, crossed the street again, moved under the parked cars and took an alleyway where he could catch his breath and hide be-tween two garbage cans overflowing with stinking trash. From this position he could watch Columbia Road that Isadori and his men had seen him run down. The hunt had lasted one hour and 12 minutes and Beffort was sur-prised to have covered so much ground on his little legs. But he had not stopped running and that accounted for it.

Time passed. Isadori and his two partners did not show up. After ten minutes Beffort was convinced that they had given up. He breathed more freely and looked at his watch; it was 3:20. He was about to leave when a disturbing shadow stretched across the sidewalk. Beffort stiffened up. A cat was approaching, flapping its tail against its sides, its ears pricked up. It was on the prowl, moving silently and swiftly. It froze for a second and then headed straight for the garbage.

Beffort knew that he was the prey it was hunting. The cat must have seen him, or caught his scent, and was getting ready to pounce as if he were a mouse or a rat. Beffort shuddered. The cat was far more frightening than Isadori and his team! He could not hope to escape by running or climbing any more than by hiding behind the garbage cans. In fact, he would have needed a mouse hole to have a chance of escaping its sharp claws. To Beffort, the cat was a monster, its yellow eyes glistened evilly in the shadows and compared to its paws his sword was a ridiculous toy. However, the cat was his one and only chance for survival.

He backed up against the wall. Between the first garbage can and the wall was a narrow space and the cat could not attack from the rear. Time was unreal, like in a cartoon, but Beffort lived it with such dramatic intensity because he was betting everything on this episode that was unforeseen by Madame Atomos.

The cat advanced and immediately stretched out its paw. Beffort yelled and stabbed the sword between two claws, pushing with all his strength. The four inches of steel stuck; the cat huffed in fear and pain, jumped back and shook itself before licking its paw. Soaked in sweat, shaking from head to foot Beffort knew that he would not have the strength to withstand a second attack. He was exhausted, worn out. His fear had vanished but his courage was drained. After this cat there might be another, unless a dog took up the chase or a car ran over him... There were so many dangers that he could not imagine of them all.

But the cat left, crossed the street and disappeared into the shadows. Beffort wiped his forehead with his sleeve. His watch showed 3:50. Time had passed blindingly fast between the garbage cans. Soon Washington would be waking up, the crowds would come out in the streets with the taxis, buses and cars and all this would present new dangers.

How would a normal individual act when faced with an eight-inch tall man? Beffort preferred not to think of it because it all depended on the level of intelligence of the individual in question... He left his hiding place, keeping an eye on the shadow where the cat had disappeared and was relieved when nothing moved. He walked off, paying close attention to everything and keeping a firm grip on his sword that even against a man in the worst-case scenario might be effective. But he would rather not have to use it.

Between the street where he was and the FBI headquarters there was approximately five miles. Beffort started jogging, his elbows tucked in, the sword firmly held under his arm, and the nightmare in full swing. He entered a residential zone; a dog barked behind a fence that Beffort thought was ridiculously low. He went by and watched the maddened dog that followed him on the other side of the fence, fearfully keeping an eye out for a hole that the animal could slip through. Farther along at an intersection a police car passed by with its siren wailing and he had to plug his ears. He did not understand why sounds were three times louder in his condition, but someone more knowledgeable about the matter could probably explain it to him.

30 minutes later he was still jogging and without coming across any serious obstacles he reached the intersection of Vermont Avenue ad Massachusetts Avenue. He had just covered over a mile. His watch showed 4:20. At this pace, as long as he did not run into any problems, he would be at the FBI at 5:50. He moved on, taking the smaller roads rather than Massachusetts Avenue that would have saved him time but where he would have to face crowds and garbage men and cars going in and out of Union Station. Even on the side roads people were on the streets. He was almost crushed by a building manager bring the garbage cans out late.

At 4:50 he got stuck at a gas station where he could not cross and he could not go back. The cars kept coming to fill up at the 12 pumps, so the attendants came and went non-stop. To the right was a commercial building. Beffort had passed it with no problem, but now the sidewalk behind him was blocked by a cleaning van and its gear. To the left the street was full of parked cars and the traffic for the gas station.

Beffort lost his head and panicked. He clambered onto the ledge of a cellar window and climbed onto a horizontal bar. Gas fumes were choking him; headlights blinded him. Then he glanced into the black hole of the basement and his blood froze. Down below, not far away, two gleaming eyes were staring at him. He jumped onto the sidewalk and ran between the car tires and treacherous feet of the gas station attendants. He slipped on a spot of oil and fell headlong as a vehicle turned to enter the automatic car wash. The huge tire rolled right next to him. He got back on his feet, covered in oil, his clothes sticking to his skin and in sorry shape, but he was still carrying the sword… and alive.

At 5:20 he was hurrying down the gutter on H Street, 30 minutes away from his goal. The sun had risen and he still had a mile to go. The hardest for sure! Because now Washington had woken up, the shutters had banged open, the milk was being picked up with the newspapers tossed by the delivery boys in front of the houses while cars and motorcycles sped out of the garages and onto the streets. Beffort was walking under the parked cars, sprinting rather in order to get through the danger zone. He was starting to get the hang of it, but he was exhausted. For his size he had accomplished an enormous feat by keeping a pace of two and half miles per hour. Now he was paying for the effort. His three-inch feet, his frenzied running, jumping sidewalks and constantly being on alert made him tense and nervous the whole time.

He was falling to pieces on the inside, coming apart at the seams, wanting nothing more than to find a hole somewhere and sleep for hours. His goal had lost its importance because as time passed he became more and more anxious about his future. How would he get back to normal size? Without an answer this question gnawed at him more than any other. Madame Atomos' new threat against the United States took a backseat even though thousands of lives were at stake. He blamed himself for being selfish, self-centered, self-involved, but his anxiety remained and he could not be concerned about anybody but himself.

Then, to his great surprise, he realized that he had changed direction for a while. He had turned his back on E Street and was heading for Judiciary Square that became, for some unknown reason, his new goal. He had to get there. It was vital. He tried to find the reason for this change but could not and gave up thinking about it. He was like a cork being carried away on the waves. And he was glad for it. Some part of his brain was taking over and he did not have to do anything.

The dangers on the street were no longer dangers. His size did not bother him because thanks to it he could things that his fellow men could not. Before, he called these people "normal." For a little while now he thought that this meant nothing since the worth of a human being depended not on his size but on the quality of his neurons, etc.

Like out for a Sunday stroll he went down F Street and then crossed 7th, 6th, and 5th Streets before reaching Judiciary Square where he slipped through the gate...

At the same time, almost at that very second, Bert Law was leaving the square by the same gate. He was part of the Green Dragon Force. Like all members of the anti-Atomos Organization, he had received information about the disappearance of Smith Beffort. Every member was supposed to be searching in his area. Bert Law lived right next to Judiciary Square, where he had just been exploring. Law was happy to follow orders seeing how he had little imagination. In the somewhat esoteric hierarchy of the human species, he was a "receiver" and not at all a "transmitter," meaning that he took orders perfectly and carried them out to the letter, but he became completely inactive and useless when he had to act on his own initiative.

Well, Bert Law looked down to push open the gate without pinching his finger in the rusty hinges, which happened too often, and to his utter amazement, clear as day, he saw a little man who started running (no doubt trying to get away from him) and brandishing a sword!

Law stumbled, slipped and fell flat on his face, his nose just a few inches from the little man who (can you believe it?) was the spitting image of Smith Beffort!

"Don't touch me!" Beffort screamed.

Law heard the warning, but only faintly because the volume of Beffort's voice was proportionate to his size. Still, it shocked Law and while Beffort ran off, it took him a minute to gather his wits and stand up.

Then he went after the strange, oily and angry creature and just as he rounded a bush where Beffort had disappeared he heard a weird, high-pitched whistle. Law looked up and saw something rising from the bush. It was spherical, with four reactors, measuring around 20 inches in diameter and through a plexiglas dome Law could see the little man who looked like Smith Beffort and two other men in yellow suits.

"Hey!" Law yelled to a guard in the square. "Look at that!"

The guard turned around, "What do you want?"

Bert Law pointed to the sphere that was already speeding off into the sky. "That thing there! That saucer! It's got little yellow men inside and a guy that could be the brother of Smith Beffort! I swear! It's crazy, amazing! I saw Beffort like I'm seeing you. He was carrying a sword and his clothes were covered in grease. He was no bigger than this."

The guard looked into the sky, but he saw nothing because the sphere was out of sight. He looked back down at Law and said, "You ought to not drink before noon, pal. If you keep going like this, you'll be seeing pink elephants crawling up the walls of your room. Go on, go home and get to bed."

Law left without saying a word and headed for the FBI headquarters. He figured that if anyone was going to believe him, it would be them.

Bert Law said nothing as he watched Mie and Akamatsu with a worried eye. They had listened to him without interruption, without showing any emotion at all. Law did not know what they thought of his story. He thought it might be useful to add, "It's the truth. I never drink and…"

"We believe you," Akamatsu said. "Our silence comes from the fact that your story confirms our fears. It turns out that Smith really is a prisoner of the Atomos Organization. Eight inches tall! Good grief!"

Mie looked surprisingly calm. She asked, "You said that his clothes were covered in grease and he was holding a sword that he threatened you with?"

Law nodded. "He screamed 'Don't touch me!' before running off to the bush. I must have scared him. He probably thought I was going to crush him or I had fallen on purpose to snatch him up."

"I would give my right eye to know if he went into that bush to hide," Akamatsu murmured, "or if he had a rendezvous with the sphere? In the first case he would have been captured, but in the second he wasn't acting on his own…"

Mie stared at him. "Don't mince words, Yosho. From the start of Mr. Law's story, I figured that Smith was being controlled by Madame Atomos. We can't do anything for him. If he can't get free by himself, it'll be exactly as if he were dead… Don't look at me like that, okay? It's a possibility I've thought about since he disappeared."

Akamatsu nodded somberly. All the trials and tribulations had hardened the young lady. Now she looked things in the face, with clinical clarity, and even if she was upset, she had the utmost restraint not to show it.

Bert Law spread his hands and spoke humbly. "There you go. Can I be of any more use to you, Mrs. Beffort?"

"No, thank you, Mr. Law. No one can do anything in such a situation. Go home and stay there. If I'm not mistaken, Madame Atomos is going to strike hard today in Washington."

Law left, frightened, in a hurry to shut himself in and bolt the door. When he had gone, Akamatsu slammed his fist down on the desk. "How can we help Smith?"

"We can't help him," Mie repeated, quietly stubborn. "I know it and you know it, too. We can only wait and hope that something happens."

"What could happen?"

"I don't know... But I'm confident and don't ask me why, Yosho. I think Smith will come back very soon... Yes, very soon."

Akamatsu looked away. If Mie fell apart, he could do nothing but go back to Japan.

Smith Beffort opened his eyes and as happened before he was conscious right away. First he examined the room. He was lying on bags, of cereal it seemed, in a corner of a dark room with a high ceiling and concave walls. An engine rumbled nearby and he heard strange hissing. The air smelled vaguely of gas, hot oil and from the walls that he could barely see came quiet thumping.

He was wearing his suit, shoes, shirt and tie, but even though he remembered falling in the puddle of oil and the sorry state he was in before, his clothes were clean and well-ironed. His wristwatch had stopped on 12—the two hands were one.

Beffort felt his face. They had washed and shaved him, as well as shining his shoes. His pockets contained his personal effects, but he looked in vain for his sword... At that very second he realized that nothing looked out of proportion. Therefore, he was still eight inches tall and was certainly on board the Cosmos I. How did he get back here?

He searched his memory and recalled running through the streets of Washington DC, particularly in the gutter on H Street. He remembered the fatigue that had suddenly hit him, then his memories faded and he was completely unable to cross the void that separated his vision of H Street from this moment.

Out of habit he looked for his cigarettes. Where he usually kept them he found the pack balled up. So, he had smoked all his cigarettes... That surprised him because he did not remember.

He stood up. His legs were stiff but in good enough shape. The place looked nothing like his cabin in the Cosmos I. In truth, he felt like he was in a hold where they kept food and bottles of wine, beer and alcohol. He opened one. It was walnut oil. Beffort stood there thinking. He had never imagined that Madame Atomos' men ate cereal and walnut oil.

He glanced toward the center of the hold and saw crates, more sacks and other bottles, all pretty indistinctly because the light was dim. He wondered why they had stuck him here. Was it some new, cunning scheme cooked up by Madame Atomos? Was Isadori behind it all? What did they want him to do? What were they expecting from him?

All of a sudden he felt like he was on the wrong wavelength. He was out-of-sync. Something had happened that he did not understand. He was living in a movie and had missed the most important scene. Hesitantly he went through the hold toward a distant ray of light. The engine kept rumbling along with the whistling and thumping on the walls. The air smelled more and more of gas and hot oil. He walked into the heat, then stood still, squinting. The Cosmos I was not hot or cold; it was air-conditioned. Therefore?

A siren went off and made him jump. A gruff voice said, "Idiots! The bastards always gotta cut us off! One of these days I'm gonna sideswipe one of them and drive 'em off the road! Sam, hit the siren again!"

Three more screams from the siren followed. There was another flood of swearing and the floor tilted. Beffort hung onto a crate that was firmly anchored down. Water splashed from one end of the hold to the other. For a split second a seagull appeared in the hatchway. Thanks to the daylight filtering into the hold Beffort spotted a metal ladder. He staggered up to it, grabbed hold and started climbing, trying not to think about anything. At the top he pushed open the hatch and scrambled onto the deck of the boat like a devil crawling out of hell.

The owner of the boat looked at him, wide-eyed, his teeth clamping down on his pipe. Beffort looked around. The boat was sailing in the middle of a bay with other boats racing around. "Where am I?" he asked.

"In Oakland, of course," the owner said. He paused a second and added, "You could maybe tell me what the hell you're doing on my boat? Sam! Come and take a look at this guy!"

A sailor the size of a closet turned around. Beffort sat down and put his head in his hands.

Mie and Akamatsu could not bring themselves to leave their headquarters. If Smith were going to signal them he would call Yellow Mask first. However, Owen Bernitz had informed them that one of his men who was checking out the forest around Old Brook's cabin one more time had sighted a sphere not far from an abandoned quarry. Bernitz was wondering if this quarry, hollowed out by crumbling tunnels and too dangerous for anyone to want to visit because of the falling rocks, might not be an Atomos refuge.

Akamatsu had given him the green light and suppressed his own desire to go to Randolph because he did not want to leave Mie alone and dejected. Washington was reporting a number of apparently inexplicable events: gas, water and electric company employees, taxi and bus drivers, firefighters and policemen, postmen and telephone workers were walking off the job without warning and organizing meetings to present their childish demands. In the department stores, high schools and universities, fights were breaking out for no good reason. They were breaking windows and looting stores since there were no police.

A bad wind was blowing through the city. Mie and Akamatsu knew that Madame Atomos was making it blow, but without the information that Beffort could provide, they did not know what to do to stop the onset of general insanity.

At 4 pm the telephone rang. Mie picked up automatically. Since early afternoon they had been calling non-stop from all over Washington and by now the young lady was blasé. But this time she pricked up her ears because the call came from the FBI office in Oakland, California, 3,000 miles away, six hours by plane, 56 hours by train and three days by car.

"Mrs. Beffort?" a tentative voice asked.

"Speaking. Who is this, please?"

"Jim Freemont. Maybe I'm bothering you for nothing, but I received instructions to inform you of even a minor incident…"

Mie cut in, "Is it about my husband?"

"Well," Jim Freemont said, "that's why I'm wondering if…"

"Listen, Mr. Freemont," she cut him off again, "please make it brief. We need the phone lines here at Yellow Mask because hundreds of calls have been coming in since noon. Speak up, I'm listening."

"I can't make it short," Freemont objected. "It is about your husband, but according to the owner of the boat, what happened is too extraordinary to… Say, Mrs. Beffort, is your husband wearing a brown suit?"

Mie's heart skipped a beat. "Yes. He's also wearing a white shirt, a reddish-brown tie and Havana loafers."

There was a pause. Freemont continued in a different tone, "I just received a radio message from a boat called the *Santa Rosa* that's sailing in the San Francisco Bay right now. The owner told me that your husband is on board. He gave a description of him and his clothes that we could identify, but…"

"But?" Mie asked with a frog in her throat.

"Uh… this is where things get weird, Mrs. Beffort. The owner of the *Santa Rosa* says that Mr. Beffort went back into the hold, wouldn't come out and when they went looking for him he was gone… I think I should add that it's a small boat… Should I pursue the investigation, Mrs. Beffort?"

"No," Mie decided. "Thank you, Mr. Freemont."

She hung up and turned to Akamatsu who had listened on another headset. They stared at each other in silence. Words were useless. Beffort had been seen in Judiciary Square by Bert Law very early in the morning. When Law saw him, he was eight inches tall, carrying a sword and his clothes were stained with oil.

Now they were seeing him 3,000 miles away from Washington on a boat where he had no business being. He was wearing the same suit as in Judiciary Square but it was clean. And the owner of the boat had given a normal description of Beffort at six feet tall...

They could say nothing... or they could bang their heads against the wall.

Chapter VII

During the evening the electricity in Washington was cut; gas and water dried up. No operator answered the telephone and it was impossible to get any information. There were no more buses or taxis. The radio did not work and the television was broadcasting uninterrupted musical programming.

Gangs formed spontaneously in neighborhoods or with friends. Passers-by were mugged, gravely wounded or killed if they resisted. Women were molested and raped. In front of the White House the police had to open fire on a screaming group of armed people to keep them from climbing over the gates. The people fought back and the police had to call for backup so that a real battle began in the Mall, next to the Ellipse, around the Lincoln and Washington monuments. They were also shooting at each other by the Capitol, in the port and in the residential areas.

In a few hours thousands of men, women and children lost their lives. Houses were burned, shops and banks pillaged, planes at the airport were set on fire and trains stopped by barricades laid across the tracks. What passed amounted to a civil war, but everyone was fighting for himself. A friend at eight o'clock became an enemy at nine and people stopped recognizing their own family.

A woman killed her husband, two children, father and mother and then in the height of excitement she joined a gang of hoodlums who tore off her clothes and raped her before leaving her to die on the campus of Harvard University.

On Rhode Island Avenue two groups ran into each other. On one side were the taxi drivers and on the other the bus drivers. They beat each other with pickaxe handles, but since there were more bus drivers they won the skirmish. Once the fight was over, they carried the dead and the wounded onto the roof of a six-story building and threw them off. Down below, someone splashed gasoline on the bodies and set them on fire.

Around the cathedral a gang of dockworkers caught six priests and hanged them from a balcony. Next to Anacostia Park, in a neighborhood as residential as it gets, several bank presidents, CEOs, property managers, lawyers, judges, doctors and surgeons formed a "disciplinary committee." Armed with hunting rifles, knives and iron bars they got in their cars and went to attack other bank presidents, CEOs, property managers, lawyers, judges, doctors and surgeons, accusing them of unfair competition.

The streets and sidewalks were piled with the dead and in the long trails of blood lay jewelry and food and everything else from the raided stores.

At Union Station a train pulled in. The passengers knew absolutely nothing about what was going on in Washington. As soon as they stepped onto the platform they were ambushed by a gang of heavily armed convicts escaped from prison who wanted to leave the city in all the confusion before the police could get them back in custody. The passengers were robbed and killed. There were rapes and unheard of atrocities and finally someone launched the train against the stop blocks so hard and fast that the train crashed through the station, ran over people, demolished the walls and pulverized the cars parked in the lot.

Secretly, almost invisibly because it was sailing around at 128th its normal size Cosmos V, Cosmos VI and Cosmos VII fired all their thought rays, spread death and desolation and transformed the city, which was reputed to be the calmest in the United States, into a battlefield.

But this was not enough. Other orders were given and Cosmos VII headed for the Bolling Air Force Base located on the shores of the Potomac, not far from St. Elizabeth's Hospital, between the Naval Air Station and the Naval Research Laboratory. Except that Bolling Air Force Base, like all the military bases in the US, was on alert and defended against an Atomos attack according to Smith Beffort's orders before he left for Randolph.

Cosmos VII found the base deserted. Not a single plane. Not a single man. Cosmos VII flew lower to examine the buildings, but it was already on the base's radar. When it was in range two cannons opened fire. Specially charged with fragmentation explosives, automatically aimed at the objective by the radar operators, they could not miss their target. Cosmos VII received the two hits head on and was literally turned to dust.

At the same time a red light went out on the control panel of the Atomos flagship. Without Madame Atomos present, since she was resting in her cabin, Commander Yamoto thought it wise to send Cosmos V to see what had happened. Furthermore, he ordered it to fire its thought inductors at the military base after programming them to Plan 2800, which had been drawn up by Madame Atomos long before the attack against the United States started. Plan 2800 would have compelled the pilots to take to the air with their planes fully fueled and their guns fully loaded for the fighters, with bombs and missiles for the bombers, and flying in formation they would attack the White House and the Capitol, shooting and bombing the city, etc.

Cosmos V arrived over the base, blipped onto the radar screens and just like Cosmos VII was shot at close range and disintegrated in mid-air.

A second red light went out on Commander Yamoto's control panel. He tried in vain to call the two ships, so in desperation decided to disturb Madame Atomos. The situation was serious. In all appearances the Atomos Organization had just lost two ships that, added to the loss of Cosmos XII, would critically destabilize its striking power, not to mention the loss of men and material…

Owen Bernitz preferred to go it alone with a flashlight and the rifle bought by Beffort. In the night the quarry was eerie, full of shadows and holes that he had to step over trying not to kick any rocks down the steep slope. Bernitz made no illusions about the success of his expedition. He knew by experience that Madame Atomos preferred the highlands to multi-level terrain and she would much rather be near water than on dry land.

He was going to check out the quarry just to ease his conscience, out of friendship to Beffort, whom he was particularly attached to, without telling anyone for fear of looking ridiculous when he came back empty-handed. He had almost told himself that it was impossible, that a woman like this terrible Japanese would never set up her headquarters in a quarry tunnel where some unforeseen accident could bury her, but the fact remained that a sphere had been seen nearby and another had been shot down by Brooks in the same area.

Owen Bernitz was very careful in using his flashlight. He only turned it on when he could see nothing at all and covered the head with his hand so just a splinter of light filtered through. And he turned it off as soon as he found his footing.

To reach the entrance to the tunnels, he had to go along a narrow ledge. From a distance it looked dangerous, but up close it was less so, as long as you did not fall off and crash 100 feet below. Bernitz stepped carefully, chewing his lit cigar stub, with the rifle on his shoulder and the cartridge belt around his waist. It was almost 10 pm, kind of late for such an expedition, but Bernitz had wanted to leave the encampment without being noticed.

He got around 30 feet from the entrance to the tunnel when a whistling sound nailed him to the wall. He looked up and thanks to the moonlight clearly saw the little sphere as it descended into the quarry. It was the size of a tennis ball.

Bernitz froze, held his breath, but the sphere just passed by and was swallowed up by the dark mouth of the mine. Bernitz could not believe his eyes. He stood there, unsure of what to do. Wisdom told him to turn around and alert Yellow Mask about his find, but if he left, would the sphere disappear before he got back?

Better to stay put there to run away… Bernitz continued along the ledge until he finally stepped into the entrance under a rocky overhang. The moonlight did not reach here, so Bernitz turned on his flashlight. There were two tunnels. He flipped a coin in his mind and chose the right. Rifle in hand he went down the slope and noticed that the shoring was new and made of metal, which clashed with the old oak beams that were rotted away by time.

Bernitz advanced with caution, listening hard, the flashlight clenched in his hand, shining only a thin beam of light. He walked for ten minutes or so, which seemed like forever to him, before he saw the faint light at the end of the tunnel. He became even more cautious, creeping from one pile of rubble to another. His rifle was ready. But the light remained as faint as ever without varying its brightness.

Bernitz slowly covered the last few feet separating him from the end of the tunnel, which stopped abruptly at a 150-foot drop. Bernitz saw a huge cave. Eight spheres, maybe 100 or 120 feet tall, were sitting there on the supports in the shadows of a passageway. Retractable ladders came out of the ships. In the back of the grotto were metal barrels and in a kind of watchtower stood a guard.

Bernitz stepped back silently. He had just discovered the refuge of the Atomos Organization! It was a stroke of luck, but Bernitz figured that Madame Atomos could not have put just one man in a watchtower to guard her fleet. There must be something else. Microphones, cameras, a system to disintegrate him as soon as he stepped out of the tunnel... Just like Beffort, Mie and Akamatsu, he had fought against the sinister Japanese woman for too long not to fear her usual means of protection.

He went back the way he came, trembling at every step, until he reached the opening and with huge relief he got back on the narrow ledge. His expedition had lasted one and a half hours. He had spent 30 minutes in the tunnel, so it would take another hour to reach the camp set up around Old Brook's cabin. By the time he alerted

Yellow Mask and got the FBI to send in the troops, tanks or airplanes, the eight spheres might have left the grotto. But it was risk he had to take, no getting around it. Alone, Bernitz could do nothing. He hurried away from the quarry and ran as fast as he could through the forest so that he arrived at camp in 50 minutes. Some men were sleeping in the cabin, others in tents.

Bernitz sat in the car, switched on the radio and sent out, "Green Dragon here, calling Yellow Mask."

He repeated this three times without an answer, but it was midnight. One more time and Mie came back right away, "I hear you, Owen. What do you want?"

"I don't know exactly. Maybe an H bomb, maybe tanks, bombers, whatever makes a big bang, but quick! I've just located the hideout of the Atomos Organization in the quarry I talked about earlier this evening. Eight spheres are sitting there, so we have to destroy it before they take off as tennis balls."

"Where's the quarry?" Yosho Akamatsu asked curtly. Bernitz told him and Akamatsu said, "We're going to bring in the planes. Bombers will take off from Bolling Air Force Base in a few minutes. They'll bomb the hell out of the quarry and everything around it. You'd best get your men out of the area, Owen."

"Okay! Say, do you think that maybe Mr. Beffort is in one of the spheres?"

"That's possible," Akamatsu answered, "but Smith was seen in Washington this morning and in Oakland this afternoon. No one knows where he really is. Plus, if he was in my place and I was in his, I'm sure he'd order the bombs. There are more than 100,000 dead in Washington, Owen... Get your men out of there! Anything else, Owen?"

"No. If the bombers target the ground west of the quarry the grotto will cave in and the spheres will be buried under tons of dirt and rock. Do it quick!"

He cut off. Akamatsu looked at Mie who was already giving orders to the commanding officer at the Bolling Air Force Base. The young lady bore the responsibility. If her husband was a prisoner in the grotto and he lost his life in the bombing, she alone would be guilty.

Owen Bernitz and his men went over a mile to the south. Except for Old Brook, no one lived in the area. Randolph was farther to the south; Mill Village around the same distance to the southeast and Woodmont to the west, a good distance from the quarry, so there was little to fear of any possible civilian casualties.

Six minutes passed by before a rumble could be heard in the sky. Coming from Washington, twelve superfortress bombers appeared, sparkling in the moonlight, a symbol of the defense of a nation that was proud because it was used to conquering.

The bombers passed over Owen Bernitz and his men and continued toward the quarry. They spotted it, banked a wide turn and came back more slowly while a series of flares lit up 300 feet off the ground. Then glistening like rain a string of bombs dropped out of the holds, disappeared in the forest and exploded one after another.

The ground shook under the feet of the Green Dragon team. They saw flames and dirt and rocks fly into the air. Birds soared up and in a flurry of wings flew off. The impacts hammered the ground and the shockwaves were certainly felt for 20 miles and maybe in Randolph some windows were shattered and walls cracked. The bombers emptied their holds in three passes and then flew back toward Washington where they could certainly hear all the explosions.

Bernitz whistled softly. "Well, I don't know how many tons they dropped, but one thing's for sure, they didn't hold back. Let's hit it, boys! We're going to check out the damage!"

They went back to Old Brook's cabin and continued walking through the forest. Bernitz was out in front, but even though he had been certain he could find the quarry under any condition, he was suddenly unsure what direction to take in the totally devastated land. It was nothing but bomb holes, huge craters strewn with trees and rocks. A rain of debris drizzled down on the surrounding forest whose branches were powdered with dust. More dust was still floating in the air, barely visible but very breathable and its microscopic motes stuck in their eyes.

The men walked through the infernal landscape. Bernitz stopped on a small knoll and gazed around with an uncertain look on his face. "I don't see the hill. Are we by the quarry, Baxter?"

Art Baxter grimaced. "We're on it, right on top of it! The bombers leveled the ground better than a hundred bulldozers! There's no more quarry, no more hill and, I hope, no more spheres of Atomos Organization!"

'We'll see about that…" Bernitz mumbled.

They searched for a while among the craters, uprooted trees and broken rocks kicked up from under the earth. Bernitz wanted to find some wreckage from a sphere or a corpse in a yellow suit… Instead of this one of his men almost tripped over a steel tube sticking out of the ground like a cannon. It was about six inches in diameter and was not a gas or water pipe, yet it looked like it went deep underground. Bernitz dropped a small rock down the tube. They heard it roll on and on and on...

"What is this tube?" Bernitz wondered aloud, anxiously.

"An old pipe," Art Baxter said calmly. "Don't forget that we're over an old quarry and an old mine..."

Owen Bernitz scowled. "Old quarry, old mine, okay. So it should be rusted, but this tube's pretty new. It doesn't look good to me, Art. Let's get back to the cars. We have to tell Yellow Mask about this."

He turned around, wrinkling his forehead, lost in thought. Six inches in diameter: a tennis ball could fit through easily...

Chapter VIII

Smith Beffort opened his eyes and was immediately deafened by the noise of the city. Gangs of people were surging back before the army charging forward with bayonets and throwing tear gas grenades. The air smelled of fire and powder. The street was strewn with cartons, crates, new clothes, cans and food. The store windows were broken, burned cars were smoking, people were running, panicking...

Beffort was sitting in a car parked on the sidewalk in front of a closed gate that apparently held a parking lot inside. The doors of the car, which Beffort did not recognize, were locked. It was black Chevrolet with beige, imitation leather seats.

Beffort looked around, confused. When he had lost consciousness he had been chatting with the owner of a boat, the *Santa Rosa*, that was sailing in the San Francisco Bay. Neither he nor the owner nor the sailor with him knew how he could have ended up on the boat. The *Santa Rosa* had not docked in three days. Around noon, it had made a short stop in the Oakland port to fill up with gas, but the owner was sure that Beffort could not have gotten on board then. So, since the mystery could not be cleared up, Beffort went back down into the hold to try to find a clue that might give some explanation...

Now at one in the morning he was back in Washington DC, in a car that did not belong to him, in the middle of some mess that looked like a riot. He was wearing the same clothes, but after checking in the rear-view mirror, the collar of his shirt was no longer white. Except for this, he felt rather rested.

Someone knocked on the window. It was a policeman, carrying his nightstick, wearing a helmet and holding a shield. Beffort lowered the window.

The cop looked at him, raised his eyebrows and said, "I've seen your picture recently. Are you Mr. Beffort?"

"Yes, I'm Smith Beffort."

"The FBI has a missing persons alert out for you. You should call your wife right away... Then you should get indoors somewhere."

Beffort nodded and pointed to the soldiers. "What's happening?"

"The policeman stared at him in astonishment. "How long have you been in this car?" he asked instead of answering.

"I don't really know. I was hoping you might be able to help me out with that. What street is this?"

"Oakland Street," the cop informed him. "As for your car, I can tell you that it would have caught my eye if it was here on my last round. It's 1:05 am now. I came by around 12:45. How did you manage to get here through the police blockades, the army and the barricades set up by the gangs?"

Beffort looked away. If he told this guy the truth, that he did not remember a thing and he was thousands of miles away a few hours ago, he would be taken for a madman. He answered, "I guess they drugged me. The car must have been in this parking lot here. Just before I woke up someone brought the car out to the curb so you could find me... Can I get to the FBI without running into trouble?"

The policeman shook his head. "I'd better go with you. Things are starting to settle down, but there are still some lunatics out there on the roofs. They have rifles and pistols and they shoot at anything that moves."

"Why are they doing that?"

"The tennis balls," the cop said. "Seems stupid, huh? But people go crazy whenever they pass by. I heard a bunch of stuff, for example that the boys at the military base shot down two of them. A little while ago some bombers hit a bull's eye outside of Randolph. It really blew! You should've heard it!"

Beffort opened the other door. "Get in. We'll try to get to the FBI safe and sound."

The policeman pulled his regulation .38 out of the holster. "If it's all the same to you, I'll climb in the back and keep the windows down."

Beffort shrugged. The policeman sat in the backseat and rolled down both windows. Beffort started the engine, let off the handbrake and headed for downtown. They ran into a few blockades set up by the police or army, but thanks to the cop's uniform, they let them pass without asking for ID.

Washington was in full swing. There were bloodstains pretty much everywhere. Ambulances were rushing to the hospitals, sirens were wailing and all headlights were turned on. In every street, big and small, cars were overturned and burned. Firemen were putting out the fires in some homes. Beffort noticed that the firefighters were not getting around the city in their vehicles. He made a remark to the cop who told him, "These guys came from Alexandria and Arlington. Me, I came from Brentwood. The firefighters and cops in Washington were on strike, so we had to replace them. You arrived after the battle, Mr. Beffort. If you saw the mayhem at eight o'clock!"

Beffort said nothing. He arrived after the battle, that was a fact. But it was not his fault. He had been manipulated by Madame Atomos. When he was running around at eight inches tall, a helicojet had probably shot him with a thought ray on H Street, under the parked cars, holding his sword and soaked in oil. Duly programmed, he had changed direction and was sent to Judiciary Square where, he vaguely remembered, a man had tried to capture him. He had escaped and climbed into the helicojet... Then he had that episode on the *Santa Rosa*... How to explain it!

Anyway, he was free now, his normal size and a stone's throw away from the FBI headquarters. Unbelievable!

He stopped on E Street where everything was calm. Because it was around the Capitol Building, the State Department and the White House, the army and police had cleared out the area.

Beffort turned around and said to the policeman, "Thanks, but I don't need you anymore. Take the wheel here and do what you can to get it back to its owner."

The cop smiled and holstered his weapon. "My name's Gary William. Don't forget it, please, Mr. Beffort. They promised a reward to whoever found you."

Beffort got out. "Okay. You can count on me," he assured him wearily. "Goodbye."

He left as the policeman took his place behind the wheel. Beffort entered the federal building like he was walking into a factory. No one was holding down the fort. The guardroom was empty and the lights out. He walked into an elevator and closed the door. While the car rose up, he was thinking that everything was like a dream. Since he had woken up on Oakland Street, he had seen nothing normal. They were fighting each other in a pillaged city; Gary William came out of nowhere to escort him; the FBI building was abandoned…

Even his own freedom was bizarre. He wondered if it was really like he wanted to believe. Madame Atomos had never given anything to anyone for free. The elevator stopped, Beffort stepped out and headed for the office of Yellow Mask. When he pushed open the door, Akamatsu and Mie were speechless.

Beffort spread his arms out and said, "Yes, it's me… Don't ask me how I got back to Washington. I have no idea."

"Smith!" Mie said. She ran into his arms and snuggled against his chest.

Akamatsu stood up, smiling. "Well, well! You'd have to be a psychic like your wife to believe you'd come back. This morning you were a tiny man in Judiciary Square. This afternoon they saw you on a boat in Oakland. And now here you are, fresh as a daisy and apparently in good health. You are in good health, aren't you?"

Beffort sat down. "I hope so, Yosho. I don't know exactly how or why, but the fact is that Madame Atomos let me go after bringing me back to normal size. I'm worried. Madame Atomos has never done any favors for anyone…"

Mie rubbed his shoulders. She, too, was worried. Her husband did not have his usual forceful energy. His attitude was distant and cautious. His voice, which was usually warm and strong, sounded strangely murky.

"You'll have a full medical check-up," she said with feigned enthusiasm. "Where are you coming from?"

Beffort asked for a cigarette, lit it and took several puffs while watching the teleprinter click away. He seemed a little lost. Akamatsu saw he was having trouble getting his bearings.

"I came from Oakland Street," Beffort said. He told them what had happened after officer William "found" him.

Akamatsu walked over and straddled a chair. "It's very unusual," he murmured. "Do you remember the *Santa Rosa*?"

"Yes, I was there, just like I was in Judiciary Square this morning with a sword in my hand, the size of a doll and terrified by other men..."

"Tell us, dear," Mie continued rubbing his shoulders and neck, "about when you were with Brook after you contacted us for the last time."

Beffort told them, his eyes closed and the cigarette hanging loosely between his lips. He talked about the disintegration of poor old Brook, about his own capture by the tentacle probe, about the cabin in Cosmos I, about the love scene that Madame Atomos had forced him into... He felt Mie's hands tighten on his neck, but the young lady made no comment. Beffort continued with his escape attempt, Isadori's hunt, etc.

When he finished Akamatsu shook his head. "Crazy! This woman is stark raving mad! Damn, I wonder why she let you go?"

Beffort grinned. "We'll deal with that later, Yosho. To know for sure, we'll have to ask her."

Mie jumped in, "Maybe she'll never be able to give an answer, Smith. Owen Bernitz found a grotto where the ships were hiding out. The air force bombed it earlier... not long ago." She had lost her notion of time.

Beffort asked, "Has he confirmed that the ships were destroyed?" He sounded skeptical.

Akamatsu scowled. "No. But they found a six-inch wide tube, brand new, sunk into the ground at a 62-degree angle... Two-inch thick steel that didn't bend or snap under the tons of debris... Bernitz said that a tennis ball could fit through with no problem."

Beffort crushed out his cigarette and commented in a monotone, "That doesn't surprise me. Madame Atomos has too much experience to let herself be trapped so easily. Eight spheres... At the start there were 12... Brook shot down one. William told me two more were wiped out at the military base. So, there's still one missing?"

"The one you were in when they brought you to the San Francisco Bay," Akamatsu explained. "By the way, I guess you've made the connection between the boat off the coast of Oakland, California and the boat on the sidewalk of Oakland Street?"

Beffort nodded. "Madame Atomos' orders were misunderstood, but it's true that her Organization is mostly made up of men irradiated by the thought inductors. In other words, they're kind of like living robots."

He sneezed and searched his pockets for a handkerchief. He found one along with a photograph that was obviously cut out of a science magazine. It showed the Earth, the Moon, Mars, Venus and Mercury. On the back of the picture they had pasted two smaller pictures, probably cut out of the same magazine. They were of the two sides of the moon.

"Why is that in your pocket?" Akamatsu was curious.

Beffort shook his head. "I don't know." He looked closely at a cross made with a permanent marker in the

Sea of Tranquility. He said, "This is odd. As far as I re-member, this is where men took their first step on anoth-er planet..."

"The team of Apollo 11," Mie said. "It was on July 21, 1969. They decided on the flat terrain of the Sea of Tranquility. Neil Armstrong stepped out at 3:56 am. It was exactly where this cross is... Relax, dear. The more I massage you, the tenser you get."

Beffort and Akamatsu glanced at each other. Mad-ame Atomos never did anyone any favors. If she had slipped the photograph into Beffort's pocket, it was for a specific reason, to show him something without having to tell him.

The hardest thing, obviously, was to find out what.

Beffort took an unbelievable number of medical ex-ams. They analyzed him, tested him physically and men-tally, then finally told him that he was in good shape and could go back to work.

In the meantime, directed by Akamatsu and Bernitz they had searched the quarry, the area around it and un-der the ground with a fine-toothed comb, i.e. a bulldozer and scraper. The tube, according to Bernitz, went down to the grotto where the eight spheres sat on their sup-ports.

Akamatsu lit a Shensei, offered one to Bernitz, who refused, and with his characteristic calm said, "The eight spheres escaped through the tube, Owen. From the first bomb, maybe even before, they shrank down and flew off. We could have saved ourselves a lot of bombs."

Bernitz kicked at the dirt. They had not found the smallest piece of metal, even though they had dug down almost 175 feet. "Maybe I made some noise when I was hightailing it out of there," he said gloomily.

Akamatsu shrugged. "Maybe, but who knows. I'd put my money on an alert system capable of detecting danger before it got too close. Madame Atomos and her damned technicians found a way to shrink things and men. How do you figure we could conquer them with the feeble weapons we have?"

"Brook had nothing but an old shotgun," Bernitz objected.

"That's the exception that confirms the rule. Besides, when we figure out how to block an Atomos attack, there are already thousands of casualties. Come on, Owen, we should get back to Washington."

Bernitz took one last look behind him. It could be that the spheres escaped through the tube, but it could also be that the five tons of bombs…

"Hold on!" Akamatsu said, squatting down. "This is a strange piece of metal, don't you think, Owen?"

Bernitz squinted and examined it. It was just barely concave, dull on the inside but shiny on the outside. It was around four inches thick and felt rough and very dense.

"Steel?" Akamatsu asked.

"More like cast iron," Bernitz figured.

Akamatsu tried to mentally reconstruct the dimensions of a ship. He held up the metal, gauging its curve. "A sphere," he concluded. "It measured around 12 or 13 feet in diameter when it exploded. We're staying, Owen! Bring the bulldozers over. They haven't dug here yet. Damn, if the eight spheres are buried under our feet…"

Owen Bernitz headed for the bulldozers, resigned to fate. Every time Madame Atomos disappeared, she made it so that they could not tell if she was dead or alive. However, this metal piece of the sphere found by Akamatsu would lead them to believe that…

In Washington the Befforts were studying a map of the Moon. Men had walked on it. Madame Atomos could very well have set up her lair there...

Michel Stéphan: *With the Compliments of Nestor Burma!*

Paris, 1960

It was a morning like any other at the Fiat Lux Agency (confidentiality guaranteed). I was trying to break the Laws of Physics by stretching my legs as far as I could on my desktop, while keeping my posterior still comfortably stuck in my chair. The sound of my secretary Hélène typing on her battered Underwood was music to my ears. I wondered if she was really trying to catch up with the mail, or if, like me, she was just pretending to work. My hands comfortably tied behind my head, I let myself become lost in fundamental existential questions like that.

"Have you taken a look at the Floutard file?"

Hélène's voice pulled me out my reverie and I almost fell off my chair. I realized that she had come into my office without me noticing. Either she was very silent, or I had fallen asleep. I managed to avoid the humiliating fall and grabbed the green folder she was thrusting at me.

"The Floutard file?" I repeated, pretending to know what she was talking about.

"Yes, the Floutard file," she said again. "That's the bald guy who thinks his wife is cheating on him with the former Maître D' of *Picratt's*. You're the one who did all the surveillance."

"Oh, right! Now I remember him."

"Well, the file is closed and ready to be sent to the cuckold with the invoice. I just need your signature."

"Hélène, you're an angel!"

"That's not all. There's a woman in the waiting room who wants to see you."

My smile froze. All my generous thoughts towards Hélène flew out of the window.

"A client is in the waiting room and you didn't show her in?" I exclaimed. "Do you know how many customers we've had this month? Are you trying to bankrupt the man who feeds you so lavishly?"

Hélène looked at me with the same cool expression as usual, but I thought I could discern a slight hint of annoyance, or perhaps condescension, in her eyes. She did not even try to apologize.

"If I had a new typewriter," she went on, "I'd have more time to take care of the clients."

I was about to respond to her unjustified attack when I heard a slight cough coming from the threshold. The woman in question had decided to not wait for the end of our family tiff and had let herself in. I admired her initiative—as well as her tall, lithe body and elegance. I hastened to offer her a chair. That back-stabbing Hélène seized the opportunity to slip out of the room and I found myself alone with the woman. She neither sat nor responded to my smile, but instead politely offered me a rather dry hand to shake.

"Monsieur Burma?"

"Just like it says on the door," I said. "Please, do sit down, Madame…?"

To my great relief, she responded:

"Leni Riefenstahl. The name might mean something to you?"

"Yes," I replied, trying desperately to remember if I had had any dealings with the German movie industry during the War.

My thoughts lingered for a brief moment on a Belgian actress whom I had met in Bordeaux who was now working as an extra on an Emile Couzinet film. Leni Riefenstahl was in a different class entirely. Judging from the perfect cut of her suit, and her beautifully-manicured nails, she was more likely to be featured in *avant-garde* cinema as opposed to the last séance at the Midi-Minuit.

"As you know, I'm a filmmaker—or rather, I was. Today, I'm a photographer. I've just returned from the United States where I've sold photos of the Masai tribes of Africa to *The National Geographic*..."

"This is very interesting," I said, "but surely you haven't come here to sell me pictures of whirling dervishes?"

She made a frown that quickly turned into a small smile, the first I'd seen cross her lips. Fraulein Riefenstahl must have been very beautiful once and, despite the fact she was now over 50, she still exhibited a certain charm.

"No, of course not, Monsieur Burma. I've come to you because I heard you were both capable and the soul of discretion."

"Has my reputation spread to America?"

"I'm prepared to pay you 3000 francs to meet someone, give him the confidential documents I have here, and, most especially, not ask any questions."

"But why...?"

"I said, no questions, Monsieur Burma. Is the fee adequate?"

"Could I at least know where I'm supposed to meet this guy?"

"Certainly. Rue de Tolbiac, in front of the café *La Petite Vitesse*, in 24 hours.

Leni Riefenstahl deposited a briefcase on my desk, disturbing my precious pile of paperwork.

"Wait a minute," I said. "I want to know the contents of that thing. I won't do anything illegal, even for 3000 francs."

She pressed on the suitcase's two snaps and the lid opened as quickly as a jack-in-the-box, revealing a sheath of papers written in a language unknown to me.

"OK, at least, it won't blow up in my face. And it doesn't look like there's any illegal merchandise in there. I suppose these papers could be top secret documents on the German V2, program, but the war has been over for more than a decade now, so they can't be worth very much today," I said, with a snicker.

Obviously, she didn't find my joke funny.

"Are you willing to take the job, Monsieur Burma?" she asked.

I nodded. She then handed me an envelope full of crisp, new banknotes.

"You can count them, if you like."

"No need. I trust you," I replied, pocketing the money.

From the window, Hélène and I watched Leni Riefenstahl's tall figure disappear around the corner. I had resisted the temptation to count the money in her presence, but as soon as she left, I did. The count was indeed correct.

"Leni Riefenstahl!" said Hélène, admiringly. "She's a great woman. I bet she's gone through tough times since her days in Berlin..."

"I'm all in favor of forgiving, but not of forgetting," I said, stuffing the money into my wall safe.

"Come on, Nestor. She was vindicated after the War, and she had a tough time getting any recognition from her peers."

"Maybe, but she still broke bread with Hitler."

"She's a great filmmaker. No one can deny the undeniable qualities of her *Triumph of the Will*."

"I'll never watch any anti-smoking film," I replied, happy to finally have had the last word with my secretary.

The next day, I stood as instructed in front of *La Petite Vitesse* in the 13th Arrondissement. I'd been waiting for 15 minutes when I saw a black sedan stop across the street. A man—an Oriental—got out. Judging from the size of the car and its dark-tinted windows, I figured he hadn't come alone.

He seemed rather harmless. Having spotted me, he beckoned to me and instructed me to get inside the car. If life had taught me anything, it was to not get into a car full of dubious-looking strangers, so I shook my head and offered him the briefcase. But suddenly, a pair of hands grabbed the case from inside, while the man standing outside shoved me into the back.

Before I realized what had just happened to me, I found myself in the back seat of the car, facing, as I had guessed, several other Orientals. It was like a casting call for a Yellow Peril movie. I didn't have time to defend myself or try to get out. I just felt a dark veil come over me, my sight grew dim and I slowly sank into unconsciousness. My last thoughts were for mother, Hélène any my new mattress at home, not necessarily in that order.

I had slept like the proverbial baby, a deep, restorative slumber and woke up in a good mood, all things considered. I found myself in a luxurious room that would not have been out of place at the Hotel George V.

A change of clothes had been neatly folded over a genuine Louis XV chair positioned near the bed. They weren't the clothes I'd been wearing when I'd been kidnapped. They were much too nice and smelled fresh. They were the type of clothes one might have worn for an evening soirée in Neuilly. I have absolutely nothing against duds like that, and they fit me pretty well, but in my business, they would be a handicap. Can you imagine me dressed like that tailing a punter through the streets of Belleville?

I got up and instinctively looked for my pipe, which seemed to have disappeared, like the rest of my personal effects. That irritated me a little, but I grudgingly put on the new clothes and, now dressed like a notary on the town, I decided to take a good look around.

Surprisingly, the door wasn't locked. What I found on the other side left me speechless: a vast corridor lined with mirrors, with high ceilings, lit by a series of crystal chandeliers. It looked like a miniature Versailles. There were doors on one side and French windows on the other, but not a single human being in sight. I looked through one of the windows and saw a large park with symmetrical alleys lined with endless rows of trees, all perfectly trimmed. In the center was a basin whose dimensions were that of a bird bath for giant rocs.

I found my way to the ground floor by walking down a grand staircase. I noticed that, despite the opulence of the house, it was largely unfurnished. But since I wasn't there to play real estate agent, I continued my investigation. I turned right into a salon where I immediately saw a man, dressed in a tweed jacket, who stood by a side window, looking outside.

I coughed, hoping that he would turn around and notice me, but he didn't react. I walked towards him and tapped him on the shoulder. He then turned to meet me. He was a funny-looking little man, with a round face, and kind, intelligent eyes. His hand came out to shake mine. It was a firm and friendly handshake, which I took as a sign that he was trustworthy. I was about to ask his name when he beckoned me to look outside.

"Do you see it?" he asked.

I approached the window and looked at the gravel path alongside the mansion. A Renault 4L van was parked right in the middle, clearly unattended. I was surprised not to find a more luxurious vehicle like a Citroën DS or a Mercedes in such a place, but its ordinary, streetwise look somehow made it a more reassuring sight.

"Do you see it?" he repeated.

I nodded, a thousand questions buzzing through my head.

"I checked it out this morning," the man continued, with an accent which I clearly identified as British. "For three hours, I turned the engine on and off. I checked under the bonnet, in the boot, under the chassis... There is no trap. The car is in perfect working order and the gate outside is open. We only have to drive it and go."

He stared at me and laughed, waving a set of car keys.

"Because, you see, Mr. Burma, the keys were on the mantelpiece!" he said, pointing at the fireplace. "I found them there this morning."

"You know my name?" I asked.

"I knew Leni couldn't come. She sent word that she was sending someone in her place—you. But I'm afraid you might be too late…"

I was going to ask him to explain himself more clearly when he feverishly grabbed me by my arm.

"You do know how to drive, don't you, Mr. Burma? I'll tell you everything once we're out of here."

I sighed and took the keys from his trembling hands.

Five minutes later, we were inside the 4L. As I was about to start the engine, I noticed that my new companion seemed increasingly agitated and panicky. I could see beads of sweat on his forehead. I wasn't unhappy about it because I thought it might make him more malleable.

"Don't make that face!" I said. "You told me you checked every inch of this car yourself. Besides, if there's a bomb somewhere on board, we won't even feel the explosion!"

I turned on the ignition. The 4L's engine started the first time and, a few minutes later, after driving through an impressive metal gate that had been left wide open, we found ourselves on a small country road. My companion kept looking behind us to see if anyone was following us, but we were alone as far as the eye could see.

"Stop fidgeting!" I said. "No one's following us. Now I'm waiting for the explanations you promised me. Start with who you are, and what you were doing in that empty castle."

There was a moment of silence during which I imagined my companion was marshalling his thoughts. Then, he began to speak, at a much greater speed than the average man. But, despite that and my rusty English,

I managed to understand what he said, even if it wasn't always easy.

"I'm a British astrophysicist. I live in Highbury in North London. Three years ago, I was asked by the Americans to join a small taskforce to combat the greatest terrorist menace bent on attacking America the world has ever seen. I, alone, managed to infiltrate that organization and discover some of its best-kept secrets..."

The first thought that crossed my mind was that he needed a good psychiatrist, but I restrained myself and let him continue.

"That organization is named Atomos, after its leader. For a year, I have been working for them, while secretly passing along information to the OSS using Leni Riefenstahl as a conduit. I've risked my life every day. The Atomos Organization is merciless when it comes to punishing traitors. Eventually, I couldn't take the pressure anymore, and I told my superiors that I wanted out. Using a third-party organization, SMOG, an exchange was arranged. The Atomos Organization would let me go in exchange for some information SMOG has collected on the mysterious 'Black Knight' satellite that was detected two years ago. Leni gave you that information and, in exchange, the Atomos Organization let me go."

"Your plan worked perfectly, it seems. Your terrorists even left us a car in perfect working order. So what are you afraid of?"

"You don't know the Atomos Organization, Mr. Burma. In the last year, I've learned much about them, their plans, their secret bases inside the United States. I know enough to allow the Americans to deal them a fatal blow before they're ready to move ahead. What if they found out that the deal with SMOG is phony? That dreadful woman will never let me live with all that knowledge in my head!"

"Woman? Atomos is a woman? You're kidding me?"

"It's not funny, Mr. Burma. You don't know her as I do. And I envy you your ignorance. When Madame Atomos' minions brought you here last night, I believed the exchange was on. But this morning, finding the castle where I'd been working in isolation until now deserted, with this car waiting in the garden... It was all too much. I know Madame Atomos. She likes cat and mouse games. It amuses her to let me believe until the last moment that I've gotten away, and then..."

At that moment, I saw a small café, no more than a truck stop, coming up on the side of the road, just as we were approaching a village.

"I tell you what—how about stopping for a drink to lift your spirits?"

The little English scientist nodded. I parked the car alongside the café, we got out and went inside. I ordered two Calvados, which were promptly served by a gruff, taciturn man with a rubicund face.

After finishing his drink, the little man's face looked less pale and pinched. He seemed more relaxed and appeared to have regained some confidence.

"I'm supposed to meet my superiors at a *lieu-dit* called Bel Air, five kilometers east of Senlis. Our rendezvous is at noon. Can you take me there, Mr. Burma?"

"You'll be there early!" I replied.

As we approached the rendezvous, my companion grew more silent, if not downright gloomy. I was just happy at the thought of being able to return to my office after delivering him into the hands of the spooks.

Just ahead of us, I saw several army vehicles parked on the roadside. Then, everything happened very quickly. I hardly had time to stop before a squad of soldiers surrounded the car. Two men, dressed as civilians, but who had the unmistakable look of being in charge, opened the door on the passenger side and let my friend out. The way he reacted to them and their friendly greeting reassured me that this wasn't a trap an Atomos Organization trap.

"Thank you for everything, Mr. Burma," said my companion as the soldiers took him to an armored vehicle, presumably to start his debriefing.

The two civilians came towards me next. One of them was well known to me.

"We owe you a sizeable debt, Burma," said Bob Morane. "This is Hubert Bonisseur de la Bath, from the OSS," he said, introducing the other man.

"You've done a great service to the United States, Mr. Burma," said the OSS Agent. "Thanks to you, we will soon have the information we need to bring down the Atomos Organization before it can do evil."

"So what the little guy told me was all true?" I asked.

"The 'little fellow' is one of the greatest astrophysicists in the world, Nestor," said Morane, smiling.

"But if that Atomos Organization is so powerful, and your scientist so valuable, why did they agree to this exchange? Why didn't they neutralize him before we got away?"

"You're correct, Mr. Burma," said the OSS Agent. "Perhaps we have overestimated their capabilities, or…"

Suddenly, a soldier came running towards us.

"Sir! Sir! Come quickly!"

Morane and Bonisseur de la Bath followed him. After a few seconds, shrugging, I decided to go and see what was going on.

There were only a few people outside the armored truck which was full of electronic equipment. Inside, sitting on a fold-out chair, was my erstwhile companion. But he now looked dramatically different.

There was nothing in his eyes but emptiness, a void so profoundly intense that it froze my blood. This man, who had had one of the best minds in the world, had become a moron. And the worst part of it was that he recognized me. I saw him making inane, smiling faces and uttering friendly grunts and snickers at me. What, at another time, might have been funny was now unbearably tragic.

I understood that he would never speak again and that the world would soon hear from Madame Atomos in a big way.

"Did he have time to say anything?" I asked.

"Nothing," said the OSS Agent. "Apparently, it happened just as he was about to speak."

"We found traces of a drug we can't identify in his blood," said a man dressed like a doctor. "We believe he was poisoned less than a couple of hours ago."

The Calvados! My friend had been right: Madame Atomos liked cat and mouse games...

Nobody said anything. Everyone was still in shock. After a moment, I managed to speak:

"I didn't know him very well, but he was a swell guy. I never learned his name..."

"Professor Bean," said OSS 117. "But he didn't like the title, so we just called him Mister Bean."

Xavier Mauméjean: *A Day in the Life of Madame Atomos*

London, 1972

Mayfair, 10:30 a.m.

Madame Atomos woke up.

Ever since her body had been rejuvenated by the effect of her multiple teleportations, she enjoyed life as she had never before done.

She now looked forward to her occasional days off in her posh Mayfair flat. Somehow, the delicacies of life tasted much more succulent since she was once again young.

She felt the silk sheets against her flawless, naked skin as she stretched, and purred like a kitten.

Under the almost scalding water of the shower, she thought about the day ahead.

Check in with the Gardener in Berwick Street. Tea at Biba's. Meeting with Sinclair at the Depository Bank of Zurich in the City. And, of course, the night was full of promise.

Madame Atomos wrapped herself in a *yukata* kimono and went into the kitchen to make a cup of tea. Lapsang Souchong, naturally.

In moments like these, she valued her privacy, tolerated no interruptions, wanted no servants to interfere with her. Even her loyal, hulking Isadori had been instructed not to disturb her. Madame Atomos wanted to be alone to reflect on her life, and the mayhem and destruction she would soon inflict upon America.

The living room was white. White walls, white carpets, white bamboo screens, white enameled furniture and an original 1918 Malevich White-on-White. Even the London sky was milky white this mid-morning, the sun barely breaking through the cloud cover.

Madame Atomos sipped her tea sitting on a silk cushion while contemplating a *shogi* problem on the low coffee table. She was aiming to disable her opponent's *yagura* defense–perhaps reach a *jishogi*–when, suddenly, a single sound, a *taiko* note, rang clearly and loudly in the room.

Madame Atomos delicately put her cup of tea back on the saucer.

The note rang again

She sighed, then pressed a square on the *shogi* board. A heavily accented Japanese voice that seemed to emanate from nowhere broke into the silence of the room.

"Hai, Mistress! This is Shoichi Yokoi. Hydra Bruderschaft has taken over our secret base in Guam."

Madame Atomos sighed again. Since Baron Strucker's disappearance after Hydra Island sunk, Madame Hydra had done everything she could in the Pacific to rebuild her empire.

"Madame Hydra will want to avoid scrutiny; they will remain discreet. Do you have a cover story?"

"Yes, Mistress," said the voice. "I will say that I spent 28 years in the jungle because I didn't know Japan had lost the war. The foolish *gaijin* will swallow anything."

"Very well. It is but a minor setback. Hiroshima and Nagasaki will be avenged."

"Hiroshima, Nagasaki! *Hai!*"

The silence returned.

Now, her morning had been spoiled, thought Madame Atomos. Should she do some *Sahaja Yoga* before going out? No, it was getting late already.

As she got up, a *shuriken* star whizzed by her face. Madame Atomos plucked it from the air, while diving to avoid two more deadly stars. In a graceful *zhong chui* gesture, she then threw it back at the Si-Fan ninja who had crawled down from the roof onto her balcony. The black-clad warrior collapsed, dead.

Madame Atomos glanced distractedly at the corpse, whom Isadori would get rid of later. Fah Lo Suee did not share in her father's misplaced idealism, but unlike him, she decidedly had no sense of humor, she thought.

She grabbed one of the *shuriken* planted in the wall and walked into a small, adjacent office. Isadori had left some mail for her on her desk. She used the star to slice open the envelopes.

The first was an invitation to a party from Derek Flint. A highly talented man who seemed to know virtually everything, including how to talk to dolphins. He wished to present his latest piano sonata.

Madame Atomos decided to go. Flint was, like herself, a pragmatist–and therefore, not to be trusted–but his sense of style was impeccable. Besides, it would be an opportunity to try that new Paco Rabanne original made up of tiny metal pieces.

Then, there was a letter bearing a familiar design. Madame Atomos sniffed it before opening it. She detected the faint odor of spikenard. It was poisoned of course. She nevertheless opened it. Anyone but she would have been dead within seconds.

Sumuru wished to discuss their respective interests over tea at the Reform Club. I think not, thought Madame Atomos. She needed Sumuru's help like she needed more mutated Teraphosa spider eggs. She would not go. She carefully incinerated the letter. It would not do for Isadori to find it. Good servants were hard to clone.

Having disposed of the day's mail, Madame Atomos dressed and went out.

As she stepped into her Rolls Sedanca de Ville, she noticed the odd couple outside: the dandy with the bowler hat and the umbrella she knew to be deadly, and the seemingly daft-looking girl with the Mary Quant mini-skirt and leather boots dressed straight out of a Carnaby Street shop window.

Mother is sniffing around, she thought. She might have to sell her flat and move. Again.

Soho, 1 p.m.

The Gardener—no one knew his real name—had a small, unremarkable shop off Berwick Street.

The market was still going strong. Madame Atomos stopped at a stall selling fresh eggs. She had more botulism germs in inventory than she knew what to do with. Perhaps... But no, another time.

She walked into the store. It was full of glass jars, amphoras and barrels filled to the brim with roots, exotic seeds and other mixed herbs. The ambient smell was that of compost. The stuff on display was quite harmless, of course, but the Gardener liked to discourage visits. The real goods were not even in the back shop, but in the secret cellars beneath.

The Gardener had promised Madame Atomos a brand new type of Black Lotus, cross-bred with a particularly elusive kind of Blood Orchid found only in Pnom Dhek.

The Gardener, unfortunately, would no longer delight anyone with the fruits of his inventive genius. He was dead, his body wrinkled like an old prune.

Madame Atomos bent over and examined the cadaver. Not that she needed to. She recognized the mark of Alouh T'ho. Madame Atomos was a scientist who had long since stopped believing in the fairy tales of her childhood, but at that instant, she wished all the dire fates the *Oni* could be visited upon the ex-Chinese Empress.

There was nothing more to do here. Either Alouh T'ho had stolen the new Black Lotus for her collection, or she had destroyed it, making sure no one would produce a new one. It was hard to tell which.

In any event, thought Madame Atomos, her plans to plunge Hawaii into madness were now moot.

She sighed. This day was not turning out to be that good after all. But she had had worse.

She derived a modicum of consolation from cleverly avoiding being recognized by Clarissa de Courtney-Scott as the red-haired, murderous nymphomaniac walked into the alley.

Kensington High Street, 4 p.m.

The rejuvenated Madame Atomos loved wandering around Biba's. She loved getting ideas from the great ambiance, buying fab clothes and makeup, and always grabbed something to eat upstairs; it made her feel like she was part of the "in" London scene–even though she wasn't really part of any scene.

The bullet that had earlier crashed onto the special glass that made up the tinted windows of her Rolls had

had her name on it. She knew who had fired it of course. Well, she would deal with Greta Morgan later. What she really needed now was that elusive moment of peace and fun that had eluded her all day.

Unfortunately, a tall, beautiful Eurasian woman came from behind and grabbed her arm.

"What amazing luck," said Tania Orloff. "We must have tea! Come on! I shan't take no for an answer!"

A long, two hours later, Madame Atomos managed to escape from Tania. She had seriously considered poisoning her, but she was working with her uncle on a new breed of deadly butterflies, soon to be tested in Africa; the murder of his favorite niece would cast a pall on the enterprise.

She had also fleetingly considered poisoning herself, rather than continue listening to Tania's long rambling stories about her unrequited love for that French prig; a man who had been responsible for the death of Madame Atomos' protégé, the "Samurai of a Thousand Suns."

Tea with Tania Orloff was enough to drive anyone to suicide.

The City, 8 p.m.

Night had fallen and some remnants of the once-mighty London fog were slowly creeping into the narrow streets of its financial district.

Isadori had returned to tell Madame Atomos that her plan to appropriate the Pink Panther diamond had failed. The Black Lizard had gotten to it before her own force could move in to execute her carefully planned scheme.

Madame Atomos consoled herself with the notion that the stone was cursed. It would serve her rival right.

She was lost in dark thoughts of revenge and failed to see Sinclair emerging from the darkness. The little banker handled all of Madame Atomos' financial assets in Europe. They never met in his office, of course, but in this quiet back alley, after everyone had gone home.

She also failed to see the tall figure, dressed in a ragged coat and a floppy hat, shamble out of the fog.

Two crimson eyes blazed death and struck Sinclair.

At once, the small man, the only one who knew the numbers to all of her secret bank accounts, collapsed in a pile of unattractive charred remains.

Madame Atomos sighed, for the umpteenth time that day.

Two metal plates she had carefully reengineered on her original Paco Rabanne dress produced a deadly burst of disintegrating rays. She only felt a pleasant tingle on her nipples, but the small dacoit who carried the death-ray apparatus harnessed on his shoulders half-vanished, leaving behind a foul-smelling carcass of entrails and blood.

Madame Atomos cursed Miss Ylang-Ylang. The leader of the international cartel known as SMOG had obviously not forgiven her for pilfering some of their secrets after SMOG's failed "Operation Dark Knight" orbital misadventure.

She would deal with SMOG later.

It had been a miserable experience, but she would rebuild, as always.

Now, she had a party to attend.

Ladbroke Grove, 11 p.m.

Madame Atomos arrived suitably late at Flint's party. It was well underway. The band was playing Alkan's *Symphony for Solo Piano Number Four* to waltz-time.

She waved at Catherine Cornelius, avoided Mephista, made small talk with Mrs. Butterworth and danced with Vic St. Val.

All in all, her definition of fun.

Then, it happened.

The outrage. The embarrassment. The crushing blow. The final humiliation in an otherwise abominable and dismal day.

Modesty Blaise entered, Willie Garvin on her arm

She was wearing the very same Paco Rabanne dress as she!

The bitch, thought Madame Atomos.

She stamped her feet and walked out.

The world will pay, she cursed. *Oh, how they will!*

With:

Mme. Atomos, created by André Caroff. *Mme. Hydra*, created by Jim Steranko. *Fah Lo Suee* and *Sumuru*, created by Sax Rohmer. *John Steed*, created by Sydney Newman. *Tara King,* created by Brian Clemens. *Alouh T'Ho*, created by Jean de La Hire. *Clarissa de Courtney-Scott*, created by Peter O'Donnell. *Greta Morgan*, created by Leslie Charteris. *Tania Orloff* and *Miss Ylang-Ylang*, created by Henri Vernes. *The Pink Panther*, created by Blake Edwards & Maurice Richlin. *Midorikawa* a.k.a. *The Black Lizard*, created by Edogawa Rampo. *Sinclair*, created by Dan Brown. *Derek Flint* and *Sakito*, created by Hal Fimberg. *Catherine Cornelius*, created by Michael Moorcock. *Mephista*, created by Maurice Limat. *Mrs. Butterworth*, created by Anthony Skene. *Vic St. Val*, created by G. Morris. *Modesty Blaise* and *Willie Garvin*, created by Peter O'Donnell.

Madame Atomos Timeline
by Jean-Marc Lofficier

1911. Probable birth of Kanoto Yoshimuta in Nagasaki. (She is 50 in 1961 when Yosho Akamatsu conducts his first investigation.)

Until 1930. The Way of the Crane. Friendly relations between the Yoshimuta and Hayashi families. (Kato Hayashi leaves Japan top go and assist the Green Hornet circa 1930.)

1931. (*September*) Beginning of Japanese Imperialism; invasion of Manchuria.

Date Unknown. Kanoto Yoshimuta attends the Nagasaki University and reveals herself to be a very gifted student, especially in physics and biology. She earns several doctorates.

1933. The Red Silk Scarf. Kanoto Yoshimuta meets Harry Dickson.

Date Unknown. Kanoto Yoshimuta marries (likely a colleague of hers) and has at least two children.

1937. (*July*) The Japanese invade China.
The Butterfly Files. Kanoto Yoshimuta and her husband support the war effort and join the Noborito Research Institute, a military laboratory devoted to atomic, bacte-

riological and chemical research; they each rise to a high position.

1938. (*January*) "Rape" of Nanking by the Japanese military.
The Butterfly Files. The Japanese get their hands on Dr. Fu Manchu's notes on his own ABC experiments, which are delivered to the Noborito Research Institute.

1939. (*December*). *Before the War, Five Dragons Roar.* On a ship crossing the Pacific, Kanoto Yoshimuta runs across Charlie Chan.

1941. (*7 December*) Attack on Pearl Harbor. The United States declare war on Japan.

1944. (*October*) *The Butterfly Files.* Beginning of a correspondence between Kanoto Yoshimuta and Shiro Ishii, director of bacteriological research at Unit 731 in Manchuria.

1945. (*May*) *The Butterfly Files.* Kanoto Yoshimuta writes to Shiro Ishii to inform him of her success in various experiments; but this comes too late to shift the course of the war.
(*6 August*) Destruction of Hiroshima by an A-bomb.
(*9 August*) Destruction of Nagasaki by an A-bomb. Kanoto Yoshimuta escapes death thanks to her husband in unknown circumstances; her husband and her children die in the blast.
(*15 August*) Japanese surrender.
(*16-30 August*) *The Atomos Affair.* Alexander Waverly from the OSS helps Kanoto Yoshimuta to leave Nagasaki.

(*30 August*) *The Butterfly Files*. Kanoto Yoshimuta writes to Shiro Ishii to inform him that, thanks to her husband's foresight, she managed to save all of her research, and that the war on the US has just begun. She gathers around her other scientists, Japanese and German, including Professor Aldridge, who will design her future "flying saucers."

(*November*) *Who Made me Such a Woman?* In the ruins of Tokyo, Kanoto Yoshimuta meets Mr. Moto again, and selects her future *nom-de-guerre*.

1946-1950. Kanoto Yoshimuta teaches physics at the Nagasaki University; secretly, she builds her organization and continues her deadly research.

1951. Kanoto Yoshimuta becomes « Madame Atomos ». She resigns from her position at Nagasaki University and leaves the city.

1951-1960. Madame Atomos plans her future campaign against the US. She dispatches teams to build a network of secret bases in America; she builds her stronghold on Atomia Island; she builds the Great Brain computer and her flying citadel.

1960. With the Compliments of Nestor Burma! In Paris, the Atomos organization runs afoul of Nestor Burma.

1961. Madame Atomos attracts for the first time the attention of the Japanese secret police, the Tokkoka. Her base in Sasebo, where she has been testing her new disintegrating ray, is discovered. The Japanese order Yosho Akamatsu to investigate.

1962. The *Mororan* Mystery. Madame Atomos tests her disintegrating ray again. She is now ready to attack the US.

1963. (*February*) *The Sinister Madame Atomos*. Sam Forbes of the FBI discovers the threat of Madame Atomos. He is killed and replaced by Smith Beffort and Dr. Alan Soblen.

Mie Azusa, a music student at the Takarazuka School in Tokyo, is kidnapped by the Atomos organization, transported to Atomia, and operated on in order to becomeMiss Atomos.

(*July*) *The Butterfly Files*. Beginning of William Mulder's investigation on the origins of Madame Atomos.

(*Summer*) *The Most Dreadful Monster*. Madame Atomos kidnaps Bruce Banner.

(*November*) *Madame Atomos' XMas*. Madame Atomos arranges for the assassination of President John F. Kennedy.

1964. (*February*) *Madame Atomos Sows Terror*. Madame Atomos attacks Texas with mutated giant spiders.

(*Spring*). *The Woman in the High Castle*. Madame Atomos becomes aware of a parallel universe in which Japan won WWII.

(*September*) *Madame Atomos Strikes at the Head*. Madame Atomos fakes her own death in San Francisco. Creation of the American Organization of the Friends of Madame Atomos.

(*November*) Lyndon B. Johnson is elected President.

1965. (*February*) *Miss Atomos*. Mie Azusa, aka Miss Atomos, strikes in Florida. Death of the "Boss," head of the FBI anti-Atomos squad; he is replaced by John Edward Evans.

(*July*) *The Butterfly Files*. William Mulder reports on his investigation into the origins of Madame Atomos.

(*September*) *Miss Atomos vs KKK*. Mie Azusa, freed from Madame Atomos' mind control, becomes pregnant with Smith Beffort's child. Madame Atomos returns.

(*9 November*) *The Atomos Affair*. Massive black-out on the East Coast. Madame Atomos invades UNCLE's New York HQ and meets Alexander Waverly again.

1966. (*January*) *The Return of Madame Atomos*. Creation of the Green Dragon force to fight Madame Atomos. Smith and Mie Beffort flee to France.

(April) The End of the Brotherhood of the Sword. Birth of Robert "Bob" Beffort at the American Hospital in Neuilly, outside Paris.

(*May-June*) *The Mistake of Madame Atomos*. The Befforts return to the US. Destruction of Madame Atomos' flying city.

(*July*) Madame Atomos prepares her attack on Rhode Island.

(*August*) *The Way of the Crane*. Madame Atomos meets Kato Hayashi in Hiroshima during the commemorative peace ceremonies.

1967. (*January-February*) *Madame Atomos Prolongs life*. Madame Atomos strikes in Rhode Island, inducing an artificial form of immortality.

(*July*) *The Monsters of Madame Atomos*. Madame Atomos turns the residents of Baltimore into monsters.

(*August*) *Madame Atomos Spits Fire*. Madame Atomos unleashes wild fires in Nevada. Her dematerialization at the end of this adventure will be the cause of her later rejuvenation.

(*November-December*). *The Revenge of Madame Atomos*. Destruction of Atomia Island and most of the Atomos organization. Madame Atomos gains revenge by killing Dr. Soblen and Bob Beffort.

1968. (*February*) *The Evil of Madame Atomos*. Madame Atomos is on the run from Mie in Montana.

(*May*) *The Resurrection of Madame Atomos*. Madame Atomos becomes 20 years younger.

(*June*) *The Seduction of Madame Atomos*. Madame Atomos tries to seduce Akamatsu and use him against the Befforts.

(*September-October*) *The Mark of Madame Atomos*. Destruction of Madame Atomos' latest laboratory in Oakland.

(*November*) Richard M. Nixon is elected President.

(*December*) *The Cold War of Madame Atomos*. Madame Atomos uses an ice ray to kill her victims; she is forced to flee to Mexico and meets Isadori.

1969. (*April*) *The Slaves of Madame Atomos*. Madame Atomos attempts mind control again; John Edward Evans commits suicide.

(*20 July*) *On an Ill Wind...* Neil Armstrong plants Madame Atomos' flag on the Moon.

1972. (*June*) *A Day in the Life of Madame Atomos*. Madame Atomos relaxes in London.

1976. (*January*) *Madame Atomos' Holidays*. Madame Atomos finally rebuilds her organization thanks to the Yellow Shadow's help and Howard Hughes' fortune.

1978. The Spheres of Madame Atomos. Madame Atomos attacks again, using miniaturized, spherical ships.

Bibliography:
Vol. 1: *The Sinister Madame Atomos*
Madame Atomos Sows Terror
Madame Atomos' Xmas (short story by J.-M. Lofficier)
Vol. 2: *Madame Atomos Strikes at the Head*
Miss Atomos
The Butterfly Files (short story by J. Altairac & J.-L. Rivera)
Vol. 3: *Miss Atomos vs. The KKK*
The Return of Madame Atomos
The Atomos Affair (short story by Win Scott Eckert)
Vol. 4: *The Mistake of Madame Atomos*
The End of the Brotherhood of the Sword (short story by J.-M. Lofficier)
Madame Atomos Prolongs Life
The Way of the Crane (short story *by* Matthew Baugh)
Vol. 5: *The Monsters of Madame* Atomos
Madame Atomos Spits Fire
Who Made Me Such A Woman? (short story by G. L. Gick)
Vol. 6: *The Revenge of Madame Atomos*
The Evil of Madame Atomos
The Red Silk Scarf (short story by Michel Stephan)
The Most Dreadful Monster (short story by Matthew Dennion)
Vol. 7: *The Resurrection of Madame Atomos*
The Seduction of Madame Atomos
On an Ill Wind... (short story by François Darnaudet)
Vol. 8: *The Mark of Madame Atomos*
The Woman in the High Castle (short story by Michel Stéphan)
The Cold War of Madame Atomos
Before the War, Five Dragons Roar (short story by Peter Rawlik)
Vol. 9: *The Slaves of Madame Atomos*
Madame Atomos' Holidays (short story by J.-M. Lofficier)

**MADAME ATOMOS
WILL RETURN IN
THE WRATH OF MADAME ATOMOS
BY MICHEL STEPHAN
ADAPTED BY MICHAEL SHREVE**

SF & FANTASY

Adolphe Alhaiza. *Cybele*
Alphonse Allais. *The Adventures of Captain Cap*
Henri Allorge. *The Great Cataclysm*
Guy d'Armen. *Doc Ardan: The City of Gold and Lepers*
G.-J. Arnaud. *The Ice Company*
Charles Asselineau. *The Double Life*
Cyprien Bérard. *The Vampire Lord Ruthwen*
S. Henry Berthoud. *Martyrs of Science*
Aloysius Bertrand. *Gaspard de la Nuit*
Richard Bessière. *The Gardens of the Apocalypse*
Albert Bleunard. *Ever Smaller*
Félix Bodin. *The Novel of the Future*
Louis Boussenard. *Monsieur Synthesis*
Alphonse Brown. *City of Glass; The Conquest of the Air*
Emile Calvet. *In a Thousand Years*
André Caroff. *The Terror of Madame Atomos; Miss Atomos; The Return of Madame Atomos; The Mistake of Madame Atomos; The Monsters of Madame Atomos; The Revenge of Madame Atomos; The Resurrection of Madame Atomos; The Mark of Madame Atomos; The Spheres of Madame Atomos*
Félicien Champsaur. *The Human Arrow; Ouha, King of the Apes; Pharaoh's Wife*
Didier de Chousy. *Ignis*
Jules Clarétie. *Obsession*
Michel Corday. *The Eternal Flame*
Captain Danrit. *Undersea Odyssey*
C. I. Defontenay. *Star (Psi Cassiopeia)*
Charles Derennes. *The People of the Pole*
Georges Dodds (anthologist). *The Missing Link*
Harry Dickson. *The Heir of Dracula*
Jules Dornay. *Lord Ruthven Begins*
Alfred Driou. *The Adventures of a Parisian Aeronaut*
Sâr Dubnotal *vs. Jack the Ripper*
Alexandre Dumas. *The Return of Lord Ruthven*
Renée Dunan. *Baal*
J.-C. Dunyach. *The Night Orchid; The Thieves of Silence*
Henri Duvernois. *The Man Who Found Himself*
Achille Eyraud. *Voyage to Venus*

Henri Falk. *The Age of Lead*
Paul Féval. *Anne of the Isles; Knightshade; Revenants; Vampire City; The Vampire Countess; The Wandering Jew's Daughter*
Paul Féval, *fils. Felifax, the Tiger-Man*
Charles de Fieux. *Lamékis*
Louis Forest. *Someone is Stealing Children in Paris*
Arnould Galopin. *Doctor Omega*; *Doctor Omega and the Shadowmen* (anthology)
Judith Gautier. *Isoline and the Serpent-Flower*
Léon Gozlan. *The Vampire of the Val-de-Grâce*
G.L. Gick. *Harry Dickson and the Werewolf of Rutherford Grange*
Edmond Haraucourt. *Illusions of Immortality*
Nathalie Henneberg. *The Green Gods*
V. Hugo, P. Foucher & P. Meurice. *The Hunchback of Notre-Dame*
Romain d'Huissier. *Hexagon: Dark Matter*
Jules Janin. *The Magnetized Corpse*
Michel Jeury. *Chronolysis*
Gustave Kahn. *The Tale of Gold and Silence*
Gérard Klein. *The Mote in Time's Eye*
Fernand Kolney. *Love in 5000 Years*
Paul Lacroix. *Danse Macabre*
Louis-Guillaume de La Follie. *The Unpretentious Philosopher*
Jean de La Hire. *Enter the Nyctalope; The Nyctalope on Mars; The Nyctalope vs. Lucifer; The Nyctalope Steps In; Night of the Nyctalope; Return of the Nyctalope; The Fiery Wheel*
Etienne-Léon de Lamothe-Langon. *The Virgin Vampire*
André Laurie. *Spiridon*
Gabriel de Lautrec. *The Vengeance of the Oval Portrait*
Alain le Drimeur. *The Future City*
Georges Le Faure & Henri de Graffigny. *The Extraordinary Adventures of a Russian Scientist Across the Solar System* (2 vols.)
Gustave Le Rouge. *The Mysterious Doctor Cornelius* (3 vols.); *The Vampires of Mars; The Dominion of the World* (w/Gustave Guitton) (4 vols.)
Jules Lermina. *Mysteryville; Panic in Paris; To-Ho and the Gold Destroyers; The Secret of Zippelius*
André Lichtenberger. *The Centaurs; The Children of the Crab*
Jean-Marc & Randy Lofficier. *Edgar Allan Poe on Mars; The Katrina Protocol; Pacifica; Robonocchio; Return of the Nyctalope;* (anthologists) *Tales of the Shadowmen 1-10*
Xavier Mauméjean. *The League of Heroes*

Joseph Méry. *The Tower of Destiny*
Hippolyte Mettais. *The Year 5865*
Louise Michel. *The Human Microbes; The New World*
Tony Moilin. *Paris in the Year 2000*
José Moselli. *Illa's End*
John-Antoine Nau. *Enemy Force*
Marie Nizet. *Captain Vampire*
C. Nodier, A. Beraud & Toussaint-Merle. *Frankenstein*
Henri de Parville. *An Inhabitant of the Planet Mars*
Gaston de Pawlowski. *Journey to the Land of the 4th Dimension*
Georges Pellerin. *The World in 2000 Years*
Ernest Pérochon. *The Frenetic People*
Pierre Pelot. *The Child Who Walked on the Sky*
J. Polidori, C. Nodier, E. Scribe. *Lord Ruthven the Vampire*
P.-A. Ponson du Terrail. *The Vampire and the Devil's Son; The Immortal Woman*
Edgar Quinet. *Ahasuerus*
Henri de Régnier. *A Surfeit of Mirrors*
Maurice Renard. *The Blue Peril; Doctor Lerne; The Doctored Man; A Man Among the Microbes; The Master of Light*
Jean Richepin. *The Wing; The Crazy Corner*
Albert Robida. *The Adventures of Saturnin Farandoul; The Clock of the Centuries; Chalet in the Sky; The Electric Life*
J.-H. Rosny Aîné. *Helgvor of the Blue River; The Givreuse Enigma; The Mysterious Force; The Navigators of Space; Vamireh; The World of the Variants; The Young Vampire*
Marcel Rouff. *Journey to the Inverted World*
Han Ryner. *The Superhumans*
Brian Stableford. *The New Faust at the Tragicomique;The Empire of the Necromancers (The Shadow of Frankenstein; Frankenstein and the Vampire Countess; Frankenstein in London); Sherlock Holmes & The Vampires of Eternity; The Stones of Camelot; The Wayward Muse.* (anthologist) *News from the Moon; The Germans on Venus; The Supreme Progress; The World Above the World; Nemoville; Investigations of the Future; The Conqueror of Death*
Jacques Spitz. *The Eye of Purgatory*
Kurt Steiner. *Ortog*
Eugène Thébault. *Radio-Terror*
C.-F. Tiphaigne de La Roche. *Amilec*
Louis Ulbach. *Prince Bonifacio*

Théo Varlet. *The Golden Rock. The Xenobiotic Invasion; The Casta-ways of Eros; Timeslip Troopers* (w/André Blandin); *The Martian Epic* (w/Octave Joncquel)

Paul Vibert. *The Mysterious Fluid*

Villiers de l'Isle-Adam. *The Scaffold; The Vampire Soul*

Philippe Ward. *Artahe*

Philippe Ward & Sylvie Miller. *The Song of Montségur*

MYSTERIES & THRILLERS

M. Allain & P. Souvestre. *The Daughter of Fantômas*

A. Anicet-Bourgeois, Lucien Dabril. *Rocambole*

A. Bernède. *Belphegor*; *Judex* (w/Louis Feuillade); *The Return of Judex* (w/Louis Feuillade); *The Shadow of Judex*

A. Bisson & G. Livet. *Nick Carter vs. Fantômas*

V. Darlay & H. de Gorsse. *Arsène Lupin vs. Sherlock Holmes: The Stage Play*

Séamas Duffy. *Sherlock Holmes in Paris*

Paul Féval. *Gentlemen of the Night; John Devil; The Black Coats ('Salem Street; The Invisible Weapon; The Parisian Jungle; The Companions of the Treasure; Heart of Steel; The Cadet Gang; The Sword-Swallower)*

Emile Gaboriau. *Monsieur Lecoq*

Goron & Emile Gautier. *Spawn of the Penitentiary*

Rick Lai. *Shadows of the Opera: Retribution in Blood; Sisters of the Shadows: The Curse of Cagliostro*

Steve Leadley. *Sherlock Holmes: The Circle of Blood*

Maurice Leblanc. *Arsène Lupin vs. Countess Cagliostro; Arsène Lupin vs. Sherlock Holmes (The Blonde Phantom; The Hollow Nee-dle); The Many Faces of Arsène Lupin*

Gaston Leroux. *Chéri-Bibi; The Phantom of the Opera; Rouletabille & the Mystery of the Yellow Room; Rouletabille at Krupp's*

Richard Marsh. *The Complete Adventures of Judith Lee*

William Patrick Maynard. *The Terror of Fu Manchu; The Destiny of Fu Manchu*

Frank J. Morlock. *Sherlock Holmes: The Grand Horizontals; Sher-lock Holmes vs Jack the Ripper*

Jean Petithuguenin. *The Adventures of Ethel King*

Antonin Reschal. *The Adventures of Miss Boston*

P. de Wattyne & Y. Walter. *Sherlock Holmes vs. Fantômas*

David White. *Fantômas in America*
Pierre Yrondy. *The Adventures of Thérèse Arnaud*

SCREENPLAYS

Mike Baron. *The Iron Triangle*
Emma Bull & Will Shetterly. *Nightspeeder; War for the Oaks*
Gerry Conway & Roy Thomas. *Doc Dynamo*
Steve Englehart. *Majorca*
James Hudnall. *The Devastator*
Jean-Marc & Randy Lofficier. *Royal Flush*
J.-M. & R. Lofficier & Marc Agapit. *Despair*
J.-M. & R. Lofficier & Joël Houssin. *City*
Andrew Paquette. *Peripheral Vision*
Robert L. Robinson, Jr. *Judex*
R. Thomas, J. Hendler & L. Sprague de Camp. *Rivers of Time*

NON-FICTION

Stephen R. Bissette. *Blur 1-5. Green Mountain Cinema 1; Teen Angels*
Win Scott Eckert. *Crossovers* (2 vols.)
Jean-Marc & Randy Lofficier. *Shadowmen* (2 vols.)
Randy Lofficier. *Over Here*

ART BOOKS

Jean-Pierre Normand. *Science Fiction Illustrations*
Raven Okeefe. *Raven's L'il Critters; Rave's Faves*
Randy Lofficier & Raven Okeefe. *If Your Possum Go Daylight...*
Daniele Serra. *Illusions*

HEXAGON COMICS

Franco Frescura & Luciano Bernasconi. *Wampus*
Franco Frescura & Giorgio Trevisan. *CLASH*

L. Bernasconi, J.-M. Lofficier & Juan Roncagliolo Berger. *Phenix*
Claude Legrand, J.-M. Lofficier & L. Bernasconi. *Kabur*
Franco Oneta. *Zembla*
L. Buffolente, Lofficier & J.-J. Dzialowski. *Strangers: Homicron*
Danilo Grossi. *Strangers: Jaydee*
Claude Legrand & Luciano Bernasconi. *Strangers: Starlock*

www.ingramcontent.com/pod-product-compliance
Lightning Source LLC
Chambersburg PA
CBHW030245030726
47493CB00023B/593